FIGHTING DRAGON

DRAGON RISING SERIES, BOOK 3

TRUDI JAYE

WWW.TRUDIJAYEWRITES.COM

Fighting Dragon (Dragon Rising Series, book 3)

Published 20 July 2017 by Star Media Ltd

Copyright © 2017 by Star Media

Cover design: PCTC Design

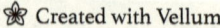 Created with Vellum

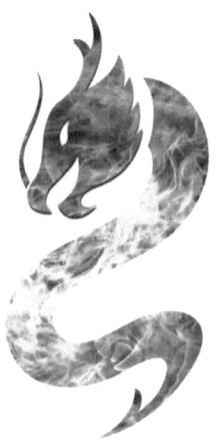

Hi! My name's Trudi Jaye and I've got a secret.

A secret society, that is.

Especially designed for people like you who love reading my books, the Trudi Jaye Secret Society is a place filled with magic and laughter, and most of all... free stories.

Everyone who joins the society is given access to an ancient tome full of the stories, novellas, bonus epilogues, and deleted scenes from all the different Trudi Jaye series.

Called **The Shadow Archives,** you can access it by clicking the link below, and joining the secret society...

Join Trudi Jaye's Secret Society... if you dare!

www.trudijayewrites.com/shadow-archives

Thank you to my readers. You make this all worthwhile. :)

PROLOGUE

THREE DAYS AFTER THE BATTLE AT THE EARTHBOUND COMPOUND

"Come on, Mei. You have to get up." Liling pulls aside the curtains in my room, and bright light streams in.

It hurts my eyes, and I groan, pulling the covers over my head. "Leave me alone," I mutter, unable to bring myself to even talk loudly.

"This has gone on long enough. Your father needs you."

My whole body goes still. My father has been visiting me in my self-imposed prison, asking—begging—me to join him in leading the supernaturals to a life without the spell web. To a life in harmony with the humans. He believes, like Tarsal did, like Jeff did, that the world is a better place without the yoke of the spell web.

The great Damien Walker can't do this without me.

But the thought of moving is too much. Everything is wrong, broken, damaged. And it's my fault.

I blindly led everyone into the enemy's den, believing that we were on the right side, that we were invulnerable.

Assuming that we would come out alive.

Stupid.

Arrogant.

Now he's dead. I'll never see his hazel eyes again, never feel his hands on my skin, hear his soft laugh in my ear. The pain spirals up through my body, twisting and turning like some kind of internal tornado.

"We can't do this without you, Mei," Liling continues. "The world is in chaos. It needs strong leaders like your father." Her voice is earnest, and she believes every word of what she's saying.

"He doesn't need me," I whisper. My whole body is sore. I feel like I'm made of cracked glass. I'm broken. Fractured.

Liling comes over to sit on the bed where I'm hiding. Putting one hand on my arm, she leans in. "He does. We can't do this without you."

He could, but an analytical part of me acknowledges that it would be easier with a dragon. If I stand with him while he delivers the speeches, while he convinces people that we're in the right, then he'll gain something more.

What's that phrase? Ah yes. Borrowed trust.

Except with me it will be borrowed fear. He will look stronger, more powerful with a dragon standing tame at his side.

"You're the reason the spell web is down, Mei. You have to be part of the solution."

Without meaning to, Liling delivers a knife to my heart.

Yes, I'm the reason the spell web is gone.

I'm the reason Tarsal is dead.

I'm the reason... But I can't even say his name in my

head. His face appears in my mind; those hawk-like eyes, his agency-short hair. The rare smile.

A familiar burning hurt rolls into my stomach. I open my mouth to speak, but all that comes out is a keening moan that makes the hairs on my arms stand up.

1

S tretching my wings wide, I let them capture the wind in their leathery membrane, and turn through the dark night sky. The mountain breeze coats my scales and brushes across my face. I let out a small rumble of pleasure.

The night air is cool, but all my body feels is the exhilaration of being in the air again.

Ahead of us the mountains loom, the snow dusting the top of their peaks only just visible in the dark night. The moon is a tiny sliver hiding behind a cloudy sky—the perfect setting for a daring rescue.

Hidden against the rocks, the detention center is almost invisible to the naked eye. It's built from the same kind of stone as the mountains around us, with a huge fortress-like wall out the front, and the main buildings built into the rock behind. If I just had normal human eyes, I probably wouldn't have noticed it.

I don't know how my father—Damien Walker, ex-spy

and leader of the anti-web rebellion—got the coordinates for the detention center. It's in the middle of nowhere, at the end of a narrow dirt road that has cliffs on one side, and a massive gorge on the other. There's only one way in, and one way out—unless you have wings.

It's the perfect place for the human government to shove the "dangerous supers" they've been arresting on spurious charges in the last three months.

Flicking my vision into heat mode, the detention center below glows with varying shades of red, orange, and yellow. There're plenty of people inside the fortress who'll try to stop us.

On my back, Liling clings to my scales, her breathing ragged. She doesn't like it up in the air, and she's only doing it now because it's part of the mission. It turns out that her shifter self is a sea turtle; determined, calm and very much happier in the sea or on dry land. I bank again, veering in closer to land, trying to stay steady.

"Watch out, Mei." Liling's quiet voice interrupts my thoughts.

I blink and my vision returns to normal.

Below us machine guns have appeared along the walls, and the guards are running about like ants in an ant hill. I take a breath, then shoot a wall of fire down toward them, just short of where they are. They scuttle inside like ants who've had their nest disturbed.

Skimming the air, I go lower, aiming another burst of flames at the machine guns. My flames are burning hot, and the weapons redden with heat. The metal melts awkwardly, bending and dripping into strange shapes.

As we swoop down over the wall, I let my powerful back legs hang down, and they crash against the walls of the outside perimeter of the detention center, making stone bricks fly through the internal courtyard. I land near the gate in a flurry of dust and debris, and Liling leaps off my back.

She runs to the gate mechanism inside the guard house, her long dark hair flowing out behind her. I stand behind, keeping her secure.

A footfall makes me twist my neck and glare. Two guards are trying to sneak up on my flank, and I let out a bloodthirsty roar, enjoying the way it echoes around the stone courtyard, bouncing into all the corners.

They scuttle backward, not even attempting to use the guns in their hands. Not that it would do any good. Dragon scales are pretty much impervious to bullets. Taking a breath, I blast fire in their direction and then turn back to the guards assembling on the wall above Liling. Standing on my back legs, I bring myself up to the same height and take another deep breath. They leap out of the way, diving to each side as they try to avoid the fire they think is coming.

Letting out a huffing dragon laugh, I just knock out more of the wall, making it impossible for them to get closer to Liling.

The metal gate swings open slowly; Liling's done it. She steps back out into the open area just as my father, Carrick, and a few of the others in our band of freedom fighters come through the gates. They're all dressed in black, attempting to meld into the darkness around us. Even though Carrick stands head and shoulders above the others, it's my father they're all looking to for orders.

"You all know your tasks. Go to it," says Damien in his best SIG agent voice. At first glance, my father seems very ordinary—medium brown hair, medium brown eyes, medium build—but that's exactly why he's so successful as an agent. He can blend into the background in any situation; hide in plain sight, as the saying goes.

But as soon as you look closer, you can't miss the steel in his eyes, the intelligence in his gaze. Right now, he's focused on the mission, and expects all of us to be just as dedicated.

We still have a shaky relationship, but there's no way I'm going to let him down on a mission. I stake my claim to the front gate, guarding the entrance from anyone going in or out.

The others head inside, and I switch my eyesight to heat vision again. There's a group of guards near the wall and another group further away. It's pretty obvious that they're attempting to plan something, but I can't tell what.

I growl and stomp about, flicking my tail dangerously close to them, and cause one of the groups to break up hastily. The other group is stickier, so I blink back to normal vision and send a blast of flames in their direction. The flames don't quite touch any of them, and they just move further away.

I don't want to move from my position, so I keep an eye on them from a distance. Overhead the sliver of the moon comes out from behind the clouds, and the courtyard is lit with a soft glow. My tail twitches back and forth over the cobblestones, and my scales click gently together with the movement.

Sometimes I wonder why I'm helping my father in this cause. I understand his arguments for why he believes we're better off without the spell web. It was holding the other supers back, stealing our magic and giving a dubious organization like the Earthbound far too much power—Vincent is a prime example of that. My personal desire to keep the spell web in place isn't what's best for the supernatural population as a whole. I get it.

I know all of that on an intellectual level. I can even support my father and his aim of teaching supers to live without the spell web. But it doesn't stop the aching need inside, or keep me from missing the grid; the way I used it in a fight, the way I could wrap it around me as protection, or even just how it could tell me what was hidden around the next corner.

I even miss the anonymity of hiding in plain sight. Having the humans aware of supers is a major pain in the butt.

All in all, it's been a tough transition to living without its protection. The spell web was like a sixth—or is it seventh?—sense to me. I can't help missing it. My tail flicks restlessly from side to side, and I narrowly miss a guard who was trying to sneak up on me again. I growl in his direction and he scuttles away again.

The others are taking too long, and I'm starting to get edgy. I poke my head down toward the entrance in the center, trying to hear what might be happening down in the cells.

I lean closer, stretching out my long neck. I think I can hear my father giving orders—

The sound of many human feet running alerts me seconds before I'm hit on one side with something heavy and solid.

2

My breath's knocked out of me in one big oomph.

Growling, I blink and turn to face my attackers. Beside me, a row of guards holds a large log, an improvised battering ram. Besides a dull ache, I don't think they've harmed my thick hide.

But now I'm pissed.

I let out a roar that shakes the buildings on either side, and then breathe flames over their heads. It hits the wooden side of a building, which bursts into flames.

The guards drop their burden and run back where they came from. I breathe fire over the log, and it disappears into ash in seconds. Then I send a spurt of flames after the soldiers, allowing the fire to lick at their heels as they run into the relative protection of a stone building. That'll teach them to attack a dragon.

The sound of gunshots erupts from inside the main stone structure where everyone else has disappeared. I'm tempted to change from my dragon form back into a human who can actually fit inside the building. As a dragon I'm large and intimidating, but I've been training since I was a kid to survive in any situation in my human shape.

Staying away from the action is like asking a fish to bicycle to work. It just doesn't feel right.

But I didn't bring clothes with me and I'd end up running around buck naked, which just sounds cold and unprotected. I guess I still haven't got this dragon thing figured out.

So I glance around to make sure the guards aren't planning some kind of new attack, and then amble over to the edge of the main building. I grab part of the roof and lift it off, kind of like peeling an orange. I'm careful not to send debris raining down on the people inside, if there are any. Most of the structure actually goes into the mountain behind it, carved into solid rock. It makes for an extremely secure prison, but it's a pain in the butt for me. Once I hit the mountain, all I can do is peer down the halls, trying to see something in the darkness beyond.

The dust from my impromptu roof lifting is everywhere. But then four figures emerge from around a corner in the distance, running down the hallway like they've got a demon after them. Dust swirls around them like it's a dramatic effect in a fashion shoot. Two of the four are instantly recognizable—Liling and Carrick—while the other two are strangers.

They're almost to the section of the building where I've torn off the roof, when a dozen guards erupt around the corner and start firing. I growl and take a breath. I hear Liling yell, "Down, get down," and then aim a burst of flame at the guards, over the heads of Liling's group, who are now flat on the floor.

The guards scatter, and I let loose another burst of burning dragon flames toward them.

Liling and Carrick, plus their new friends, scramble to their feet, sprinting past me and continuing out through the gate. Only two prisoners so far. We were expecting at least ten people. I peel back the roof on another building further along. I feel like I'm cheating at a maze game—looking down from above, instead of taking my chances through the middle. I shrug. We need whatever advantage we can get at this point.

My father turns a corner, another man's arms around his shoulders. Lank brown hair dangles down over the prisoner's face, and his tall frame makes my heart stumble for a second.

Seth.

But then he moves awkwardly, and I realize it's not Seth. The resemblance is only superficial—this man is bulkier, his muscles broader than Seth's long, lean muscles. I try to shake my head to clear it, but the damage is done. Memories rise up, our last battle with Vincent.

Seth dying.

Seth dying.

A wave of nausea hits me and I stumble, crashing into the wall of the nearest building. It crumbles under the weight of my body. I'm gasping for breath, and my heart is racing like it thinks I'm back in that moment when I watched him break apart into a million pieces. I want to raise my head up into the sky and keen the painful mourning song that I haven't been allowed to sing since Tarsal's funeral.

"Mei! A little help?" It's my father's voice, barking orders. Something in his voice brings me back, and I remember my responsibilities. I can't let anyone else die. Not again. A shudder rolls across my body, my scales rubbing together uncomfortably. But I manage to push away the grief, to box it up in a tiny corner of my soul, and focus my attention back on the here and now.

They have guards on their tail, and I step closer, blasting my flames down on their pursuers. All four of the guards stumble to a halt, holding their arms up to protect themselves from the heat. I'm not paying proper attention as I blast out the fire; part of my brain is still trying to keep away the images of Seth dying. But when one of the guards in front of me lights up with burning flames over his body, his guttural cries of pain penetrate my grief and I jerk back.

I've hurt one of the guards. And not just a little bit—he's screaming in agony, and I feel it down every single bone in my body. How could I be so careless? I came on this raid to save people, and my second of grief over Seth has caused a man I don't even know to be hurt. My guilt is like a sour lolly inside my mouth.

But his fellow guards pat him down and put out the flames licking at his body. I loom in the entrance, watching to make sure he's okay, but as soon as the guards realize I'm still standing there two of them start shooting again. Bullets hit my side, bouncing off the scales, and making my skin shudder. It feels like I'm being punched by a dwarf. I growl down the hallway, and they all scramble back again.

"Mei! Come on! Let's go." Again, it's my father's voice that pulls me back to the real world. I turn my head. For a moment, I consider just flying off into the mountains by myself, leaving the people I love behind to let them to fight this battle without me. I'm more of a hinderance than a help when I can't even focus.

Your father needs you, says a voice in my head. It's soft and delicate, with a hint of steel behind it. I feel my connection to the ring that holds my mother's soul go blazing hot. I never take off the delicate gold ring when I'm in human form, and somehow it stays with me when I change. As does my mother's soul.

But even without my mother reminding me, I know I can't leave.

Having a dragon on their side changes things, gives them options they wouldn't otherwise have—like this raid. She's right. My father and his cause do need me.

So I angle back toward them, my large steps eating up the distance between us. Liling climbs on my back, pulling up a man behind her who has a gash on his face and a long cut down his leg. I could carry more, but there isn't the need. I watch as the others run down the steep slopes of the mountain to where the four-wheel-drive vehicles wait for them. They load in the newly rescued supers and speed off, leaving clouds of dust in their wake.

Gun shots erupt from the top of the guard wall, and I turn back. I let off a long stream of fire, burning away at the rocks around me, sending the guards running for cover back inside the stone buildings. I roar, venting my frustration with everything in the world around me, and the sound reverberates through all the buildings, shaking down rocks and stones that were unsteady.

Then I leap into the sky and head home.

3

"W here were all the prisoners?" I ask my father as I stride into the war room back at our headquarters. I'm in human form and ready to debrief.

Damien flicks me a half smile and a wave, but he's deep in discussion with some of the other leaders of his anti-webber group, Supernaturals Against the Web or SAW as they're now being called. The other side is made up of groups called 'pro-webbers', the people who want the spell web put back in place. The phrases popped up in the weeks after our confrontation with Vincent and have stuck around.

The war room is long and narrow, with a large table through the middle, chairs placed haphazardly around it, and several television screens up the front showing the news constantly. It's at the center of our deep mountain hideaway, with the walls, ceiling and floor carved out of stone.

I find it a depressing place to be, because all the news is about how the humans are winning the battle against the supers. How they're putting us away in detention centers and getting us off the streets. They have television programs on how to fight supers, the different kinds, and the ways to ensure each species is dead after they attack a human. As if attacking humans is all we think about.

Most of it's not even true. They're making up new varieties of supernaturals that just don't exist. And the descriptions of how to kill us? It's like there's someone out there trying to come up with the most violent and horrible way to kill someone, just to see if someone will try it on a super.

"We were given incorrect intel," says Roger, a tall watershifter elder. His silver hair flows to his shoulders, and his matching silver eyes seem to see everything.

My father turns a thoughtful gaze to me. "We think they were holding only those they considered the worst of the worst. Of the three supers we found, one is a member of the Boston Brutes and one was a dragon."

A dragon?

My heartbeat kicks up a notch and I frown. I shift uneasily where I'm standing. Is it possible I was so out of focus that I didn't even notice another dragon?

I suddenly register what else he just said. "Dad, the Brutes are dangerous. They don't just want the web gone, they want all of humanity gone. They're as bad as Vincent."

My father nods. "I know. We're just trying to decide what to do with him. I thought I might give Si a call and see if the chameleons will take him."

I glance at the others. Their faces are grave. They know letting out members of the Boston Brutes will only set our cause back. They're the kind of supers who prey on humans for fun.

They're the kind of supers that humans *should* be afraid of.

But asking Si and the chameleons to take him seems unfair. I mean, I understand why—they're set up for it in their hidden forest dungeons. But this problem isn't of their making.

I feel a pang of homesickness, and it's not for a place, but a person. I miss Si. Even though I respect his decision not to join my father's group, I wish he were here.

"What about the dragon?" I ask, attempting to shake off my melancholy.

"We've asked him to join us," says Roger.

I blink and the hairs on the back of my neck prickle uncomfortably. "Just because he's a dragon?"

My father shakes his head. "Of course not. I talked with him and determined his beliefs. He's on our side. Believes the web should stay down and wants to help our cause. It won't hurt to have two dragons."

Frowning slightly, I stare at the five leaders in front of me.

My father and Roger are rock solid, that much I know. Andy and Theresa are old friends of my father's, wolf shifters who believe in the cause. Lucas is a strange-looking man who could be any one of four or five different types of super, and I have no idea which it is. They're our leaders, the ones who have experience and knowledge of their side. So why do I feel like they're jumping in too quickly?

"What do you know about him?" I ask.

My father sighs. "What do we know about anyone who joins us, Mei? I put him through the same vetting process as everyone else, and I'm satisfied. That's all we can do in this kind of situation."

"But he's a *dragon*. That makes it different."

"It makes it *better* for us, because we'll have more fire power behind us when we do our next raid."

"You should be checking him twice as much as the others. He has the power to destroy us all."

Roger slides in my direction in that watery way he has. "Dragons might frighten you, Mei, but they don't frighten the rest of us."

I grimace at his attempt at a joke. "I'm serious."

"He's not joking, Mei," my father says, his expression grim. "You're afraid. You don't use your full powers when we go on raids. It's like you don't trust yourself."

"I don't trust myself?" I blurt, annoyed that I'm having to spell this out. "I'm a dragon. I can't be trusted."

My father shakes his head sadly. "You *can* trust yourself, Mei. You're a strong young woman. Jeff made sure of it."

Mention of Jeff still sets off a little sting somewhere near my heart, and I let out a hiss of breath. I can never be sure with my father, but I think he might have mentioned Jeff just to get me off track. "We need to watch him closely."

Smirking, my father just looks at me.

"You already planned to assign him to me," I say, realization dawning. I walked right into one of his traps. I shake my head. "No, I won't do it." I refuse to be a pawn in his convoluted schemes.

My father shrugs. "As you just said, who else is able to do it? You're in charge of making sure the dragon knows the score around here." His gaze flicks to the door behind us. "And here he is, right on time."

I turn and recognize the man who escaped with my father. He looks much healthier than he did before; his longish dark brown hair has been washed and he's in clean clothes. He's tall and broad, with dark brown eyes that seem almost black in the dim light by the door. He looks dangerous even in human form.

"Hello Damien," he says in a low, gravelly voice, nodding at my father. It irritates me in a way I can't understand.

I don't recognize him, Tarsal murmurs in my head.

The second soul that's stuffed inside my brain doesn't often come up to the surface, but I smile at the sound of his voice. He's been inside me since the day Vincent killed him and he gave me his magic to help destroy the spell web.

Did you know every dragon in the world? I ask.

A long pause. *No. I suppose not.*

My father moves forward, extending his hand to the other dragon. "You look much better."

"I feel much better. Thank you for the rescue." He seems sincere and gives my father a respectful nod.

"We're pleased to help."

His gaze falls on me and his eyebrows descend. "And you're the other dragon?" he says. His shoulders twitch ever so slightly.

"My name is Mei," I say. I don't hold out my hand. I don't want to touch him. "Pleased to meet you."

He gives me the ghost of a smile, a knowing look in his eyes. "I'm not convinced."

I stare up at him for a moment, not sure what to make of his words. Then I shrug. He's right. "Okay, it's annoying to have you here, because I don't know if we can trust you."

"That's more like it," he says approvingly.

My father glances between us, his gaze assessing. "I've assigned Mei to look after you for the next couple of days. Is that going to be a problem?"

I think of Jeff and all the training he's given me over the years. "No problem, Dad."

The dragon looks at my father in surprise. "You're her father?"

Damien shrugs. "Someone has to be."

His dark eyes stare down at me, like he's reassessing something. "And am I right in thinking you're the dragon who killed off the spell web?"

I nod.

"You're young." It's not a question.

For some reason, this statement gets my back up, but I try not to let him see it. "What's your name? I can't keep calling you the dragon," I say.

"Zane."

"What were you doing in that facility, Zane?" I can't help asking the question.

"I was captured, and as soon as they realized I was a dragon, I got dumped into the deepest, darkest hole they could find." His voice has shadows of bitterness through it, but I can't blame him. Even though I really want to.

"How old are you?"

"A lot older than you, little dragon," he drawls.

"Old and senile, then?" I say in a snide tone. Then I crush my lips together and attempt to regain control of my temper. I refuse to fall into the same patterns that got the dragons of old into trouble in the first place. I can feel my father's disapproving gaze on me, without even having to look in his direction.

But honestly, this feeling, this fear of what this dragon might be capable of, makes me want to hit something. My gaze falls on Zane's tall, broad frame looming over me. My eyes narrow.

Or hit *someone*.

But Zane just shakes his head, his dark eyes amused. "I'm old enough to know when it's time to let people get on with things. Come, let's leave the leaders to their business, and you can show me around this place." He gazes around the room like he's memorizing everything.

Perhaps he is. So he can tell our enemies.

I glance meaningfully at my father, but he's nodding like he's the one who suggested it. I don't know what plan he's brewing under all this amiableness, but there's definitely something going on. I sigh. I've also learned that there's no point in trying to figure it all out. My father's brain is like a labyrinth, filled with dead ends and alternate routes.

I gesture at Zane to follow me and then lead the way out into the hallway, stopping only when he's shut the door behind him.

"What would you like to see?" I ask. The corridor's rough rock-hewn walls extend both ways from where we're standing.

"Let's find somewhere to talk. You're clearly annoyed at me for some reason. We need to clear the air."

I frown at him, but lead the way down the hall. Am I really so easy to read? Who is this guy?

Don't trust him. Tarsal's voice is low and irritated.

I stride along the corridor, my thoughts in a jumble.

Watch him, and don't let your guard down. I don't know what he's up to, but it can't be good. Never trust a dragon.

4

———

"Okay, what's this beef you have with me?" His words echo around the small carved-out living room I found nearby. Couches and chairs are scattered about, but it's empty of other people. We're standing in the center of the room, facing each other.

"I don't have a *beef*," I say, but even I can hear the tartness in my voice. I don't sound like someone who's chilled out. I sound like I have a beef.

Zane narrows his eyes at me. "Then what's your problem?"

"Tell me about them," I say abruptly. He's only the third dragon I've ever met. I should be gathering data, not being annoyed. "Dragons, I mean."

"You're talking as if you're not a dragon as well, little one," he says softly.

I shake my head impatiently. "Tell me about the dragons from your time. You were the same as the others? You were hibernating all this time?"

Zane nods. "I was."

"What woke you?" I want to ask him how many dragons

he stole magic from to allow him to hibernate. But if I could forgive Tarsal, I have to let it go with Zane as well. It was three hundred years ago. A different time.

He's frowning at me. His dark hair falls over his cheeks and his lips are a tight line, like he's holding in what he really wants to say. Then he sighs. "I think it was the death of the spell web. The buzzing just...stopped. It was like I could breathe again."

"And are the stories true? Were the dragons killing each other and everyone else?"

Zane takes a step away, and then another, and begins pacing around the small room. He waits so long, I don't think he's going to answer. Then he halts in front of me.

He stares down at me, his expressive brown eyes filled with sadness. "That's what people say about us?" He runs one hand through his long hair. "I guess it's what it would have looked like. Most dragons tended to act first, and think later. But they were the ones who died first." His voice is grim.

My hands clench. They all died, just because they couldn't stop to think first. I'm not going to be like that. I'm not going to allow my dragon nature to take over.

"What else?" I ask grimly.

Zane shrugs, and puts his hands wide. "What do you want to know? I'm an open book."

"I don't know. What are dragons like? What do I need to watch out for? How many other dragons are hidden around the world?"

"You really don't know much, eh, little dragon?" he says.

"Not really," I grind out, wishing I could just punch him in the face and be done with it.

He smirks at my obvious discomfort. "I can sense your

power. It's expanding, will keep expanding for a year or two. You must have only just changed."

"Yes."

"The most important time in a dragon's life, the time when they are most vulnerable, is the change. And you survived that. The rest is plain sailing."

"I only just survived," I mutter.

"The 'how' is no longer important. Only that you did. From now, your powers will expand, and with the spell web gone, you will be even more free."

I don't feel particularly free. If anything I feel more constrained than I ever have been, and that's saying something.

But he's right, I am feeling more powerful. It's not just the two extra dragon souls floating around in my body, both giving me extra magic. My dragon core is expanding, curling out, finding its way.

But it's not a simple matter of more magic. For a long while after the spell web came down, I felt as if I was on a tightrope over the Grand Canyon with no safety net. I was shaky and unsure.

Everything was ten times more difficult.

My sense of the space around me was all wrong—I'd grown so used to seeing the world through the spell web grid that the loss of it made me walk into walls and crash through doors for the first few weeks. It was like losing an arm or a leg, and having to relearn how to find my balance.

I'm finally used to dealing with the world without it.

And I'm even noticing the benefits of not having the spell web constantly stealing a portion of my magic. I'm stronger, I can fly further and faster, and the power pulses through my veins like it's bursting to get out.

Added to the souls hiding inside me, sometimes it feels

like I'm on a magical high, soaring through life, waiting for the moment when all this power lurking in my head can burst out of me. At that thought, a shiver of fear runs along my arms, leaving a trail of goosebumps in its wake. That's my secret fear: there's going to be so much power, I'm not going to be able to control it. I'll end up just like the dragons of old, drunk on power.

"Now tell me how a little thing like you managed to take on the Earthbound and destroy the spell web?" says Zane, looking me up and down.

I narrow my eyes, staring at the large dragon in front of me, trying to figure out if he's serious. My hackles rise, and if I was a cartoon, there'd be steam coming out my ears.

This guy just seems to know what to say to get on my nerves.

Of course he's getting on your nerves. Male dragons are assholes, says Tarsal suddenly.

You're a male dragon, I remind him.

Exactly.

Tarsal's voice is so smug, I have to concentrate on not laughing out loud. Besides, I'm still pissed at Mr. I'm-So-Big-and-Manly.

I open my mouth to launch angrily into a series of very specific—but very impolite—suggestions of where he can shove his question, when I notice his dark eyes are gleaming with amusement.

He's baiting me, purposely trying to annoy me.

I let out my breath in a whoosh of air. "What I don't understand is why all you *ancient* dragons couldn't manage it before," I say sweetly.

"Touché." His mouth momentarily quirks into a half smile. It changes his face, lightening it, and making him bearable—for about a second.

I'm struggling with what to say next when Liling comes around the corner and enters the room in a rush. "Mei, come with me. I think you'll want to see this."

"What is it?" I ask.

Liling looks unusually flushed, her eyes anxious. "Vincent is holding a press conference on television. He's apparently got some big announcement. They're running it on all the networks."

"Really?" In the months since I destroyed the spell web, Vincent has been keeping a low profile. We know he's been building alliances, and he's been influencing the humans against supers.

I'm almost 100 percent certain that the detention centers were his idea. But this is the first time he's ever held a press conference. Apprehension slides up my spine as smoothly as a snake through grass. "What's he up to?"

Liling doesn't answer, just grabs my arm, and forces me into the corridor.

5

I follow Liling at a run, her longer strides eating up the ground faster than I can match.

We reach the war room just as the cameras flick to an image of Vincent walking up to a podium. Voiceovers announce excitedly that the Earthbound leader will be revealing a breakthrough in the ongoing war against the supernaturals.

There's a muttering through the room at the mention of a war—from our perspective, there doesn't need to be any conflict at all. But fear has done a great job of whipping humans into a frenzy.

"Thank you all for coming today," Vincent is saying. His face looks more haggard than I remember, and his hair has gone completely white. His blue eyes stare straight into the camera like he can see me directly, and I shiver.

I still have nightmares about my last confrontation with him, where he's looming over me like a scary cartoon figure, laughing maniacally, long spindly fingers stretched out in my direction.

If I'm honest, I'm terrified of him.

"I have an announcement that I believe the world's populations will be very pleased to hear." Vincent pauses for effect, and I can almost feel audiences the world over leaning forward.

"Since the destruction of the spell web by the notorious dragon-shifter criminal, Mei Walker, we have experienced a period of sustained violence and brutality like never before in our history."

"Only because the humans keep attacking us," I mutter, stung by his description of me.

"We have been studying the old texts from my Earth-bound ancestors and have rediscovered much that was lost to us."

I'm trembling now, remembering the machine that immobilized Tarsal. This is starting to sound like my worst nightmare.

I give myself a small pinch on my arm, just in case. It hurts, especially given the goose bumps that are still running along my skin. I rub my hands up and down over my arms, trying to warm myself up, but the chill is coming from somewhere deep inside me. My father moves into place just behind where I'm standing, but he doesn't actually put out a hand to touch me. It's comforting nonetheless.

Onscreen, Vincent gives a small half smile. "Most importantly, we have discovered a way to reinstate the spell web layer that kept the supernaturals in line before it was so maliciously destroyed. We know how we can put these horrific creatures back under the powerful control that kept us safe for three hundred years."

He pauses, and the area in front of him flares with voices as the waiting journalists fire questions at him. He holds up his hands, indicating he has something more to say. His face is serious, but I can see him trying to hide his God-awful smirk from the world.

"Not only that, we know how to make it stronger. We have found a way to extract even more supernatural magic, so they will be weaker and never be able to harm humans again."

This time, the room around me erupts, and many of the supers who are part of my father's resistance stand and start gesticulating at the television. Most supers are just getting used to living without the spell web and have adjusted to the extra magic flowing around our bodies.

But Vincent isn't finished.

He pauses as the journalists again bombard him with questions, their voices raised like dogs baying to be fed. Then he gestures for silence. "I can take us back to the safety of the spell web, where we will control the supernatural abominations so they can't give in to their baser natures.

"I can save the world. But there's a problem we must work together to solve. We need a certain kind of magic. A type of power like no other."

Again, Vincent pauses for effect.

But I know what's coming. Vincent is nothing if not predictable. "He wants a dragon," I whisper. Beside me, Zane glances in my direction, his eyebrows lifted.

Up on the screen, Vincent's eyes again turn toward the television camera, and it's like he's staring straight at me. The urge to take a step backward is overwhelming, but I manage to hold my place. "I need a dragon. A live dragon, who will provide me with the magic we need to protect the world.

"I can save us all, but we must capture one of the beasts to do it."

Zane is staring at me, his dark eyes unreadable. But I know what he's thinking. He's on the number one most wanted list, just like me. Maybe he's thinking it's *because* of me. Neither one of us is going to be safe until this is over. Maybe not even then.

The journalists erupt again, and Vincent points to a woman down the front.

"Vincent, how do you plan to capture a dragon?" she asks, her voice heavy with anticipated drama.

He pretends to consider the question. "I have machines that can immobilize a dragon. I have fought and killed dragons in my lifetime, so I do not anticipate a problem—if we all work together, that is."

One dragon, more like.

"What makes you think everyone will work together on this?" asks another journalist.

"We have a common enemy. We have all suffered at the hands of the supernaturals, especially the dragons. Returning to the spell web is the only way to guarantee that we can control them. Otherwise we have no hope."

"How much stronger do you plan to make it?"

"We will take 50 percent of their magic. That will leave them weak enough to control. They will no longer be a problem for ordinary humans."

I gasp, unable to control my reaction. I'm only just getting used to being without the spell web, I admit that. I even secretly wish I hadn't destroyed it. But I don't want a situation where it's taking half my magic. Would I still be able to change into a dragon? To fly? I think the answer will be no.

"Why didn't you kill that crazy old man when you had the chance?" Zane mutters in my ear. He breath makes the hairs on my neck rise up.

I frown at him. "Because I was too busy destroying the spell web," I mutter. *And trying not to let Vincent break me into a million pieces like he did Seth.*

Up on the screen, Vincent calls for silence again. "It's only through co-operation that we can return our lives to the safety and peace of mind that we knew under the spell web. I've been working with other groups—including non-humans—to make this happen. There are groups of supernaturals who understand that we need to ensure our world is secure again."

The feed switches, and it's an icy landscape. There's a reporter standing outside, next to a brick building, all bundled up in a massive jacket and hat. Snow falls gently around her.

"I'm pleased to bring you this special report," she says with a faint European accent. "I have with me a representative from the largest supernatural pro-webber faction here in Europe, the United Supernatural League." She turns to the man standing just next to her, and the camera widens out to include them both.

The man has an eye patch over his left eye and an angry red scar running down the same cheek. He looks haggard and his hair hangs in a scruffy cut around his head. If I met him in a dark alley, I'd be scared.

But then he turns to look directly into the camera and his one good eye stares out at me.

I could never forget his hazel eyes.

Seth.

Somehow, Seth is alive.

6
———

My legs give out from under me, and I would've collapsed to the ground, except Zane snatches me up just in time.

He places me carefully in a nearby chair then steps back as Liling and my father crowd around.

"It can't be him," says Damien, shaking his head. "We saw him die. He was smashed into a thousand pieces."

My eyes widen at his description, and I swallow hard, trying to keep the visions of Seth's death out of my head.

He immediately realizes what he's just said and winces, his eyes cutting over to mine. "I'm sorry. I didn't mean—"

"It looks like him, right?" I nod to where Seth's still talking to the journalist. "I'm not going crazy?"

"It seems to be Seth." He hesitates. "I think."

I stare at the screen, greedily taking in every bit of light and shadow over Seth's face. I should probably be taking in every word he's saying, but I can't concentrate on more than the familiar lines of his face and the ragged scar across his cheek. What happened? How did he survive?

He's a phoenix. I know that. But being frozen and then

shattered into a million pieces had seemed too much, even for his breed. Everyone has some kind of limit, right?

Apparently not.

I gaze at Seth's face, drinking it in like an alcoholic at a rehab clinic. I don't notice the murmuring around the room at first, but eventually I tune in to my surroundings again.

"I can't believe he's talking like that," says Liling.

I frown and look back up to the television. Seth is still speaking.

"We don't accept that supernaturals are the only problem in this equation, but we do believe that returning to the spell web is the only solution. We're prepared to work with forward thinkers like Vincent.

"We all know dragons are pests, dumb brutes too focused on their own selfish needs to do anything that would benefit the rest of us." He gestures behind him to a fire-marked building. "Just look at the damage done to this fine city only last week by a recently re-emerged dragon. The only way to stop them is to forcibly control them.

"If the only way to restart the spell web is to have a dragon, then the USL will be working with the Earthbound and others to make sure that happens."

My hand goes over my mouth and I feel lightheaded. I don't understand.

It's Seth's voice. It might have a little more gravel, possibly from the same event that took his eye and gave him the scar, but the intonations, the way he speaks is the same. But he's talking about capturing and torturing a dragon, someone just like me.

The female journalist asks him about the detention centers for supers that have been springing up in the US and Europe, and he shakes his head. "They're complete bullshit, and just another example of why we need the spell web back in place. Humans don't get supernaturals; they're afraid of us. We're prepared to give up some of our powers to make them understand that we're not the threat here."

"But you've just admitted that dragons *are* a threat," says the reporter.

"Dragons are a blight on all our lives, both supernaturals and humans," Seth says. There is a slight sneer on his face as he says the word "humans", but I only notice because I'm watching him so closely. "We need a tool, a strategy to keep both races working together. So, frankly, we're prepared to give up a dragon, yeah."

Zane moves forward. "Who is this jerk?" he asks Roger.

Roger glances back at me and then speaks softly into Zane's ear.

Liling grasps my hand in a tight grip. "We'll figure it out," she says softly.

I nod, but I have too many thoughts spinning inside my head to really understand what's going on. How can Seth still be alive? And why is he talking like this about dragons? Why is he prepared to work with Vincent, the very man who killed him, to put in place a spell web that will steal half our powers? None of it makes sense, and I shake my head in an effort to clear it.

It doesn't work.

"What's he doing?" I whisper to Liling, with a mixture of hope and fear. Has Vincent somehow brainwashed him? Was his death a slight of hand I didn't notice at the time?

I try to remember what happened when we fought Vincent in the spell web chamber, and it comes out blurry. But I'm certain that Seth died that night.

The only explanation is that it's because he's a phoenix, a creature reborn out of the ashes. I just don't know enough about how that might happen. He was shattered into a million tiny pieces. Surely Seth's body was too broken up for that kind of rebirth?

And yet... here he is.

His face is still showing up huge on the screen, and not once does he smile. He looks haggard and a little mean, like he's had a tough life. Nothing like the squeaky-clean SIG agent who turned up to 'babysit' me all those months ago.

What's happened to him? What is it that's changed him?

The reporter finishes up the piece, and the camera goes fully to her face. She wraps up and the screen goes back to Vincent, who starts fielding questions about dragons and how one might be caught.

"We had one in captivity here in the US, but yet again, the dissident Mei Walker has destroyed our efforts to return peace and order to our community. Last night she and her group of anti-webber terrorists from SAW attacked one of our detention centers and helped dozens of hardened supernatural criminals to escape."

"Son of a bitch," says Zane. "They were going to fry me." He turns to me and grins, this time genuinely grateful. "Thanks, little dragon. That was a close one."

I nod, because that's all I can think of to do, but my brain is still stuck back on Seth. What I really want to do is talk to Seth.

If it really is Seth.

Maybe he's got a twin brother. A look-alike cousin. Or it's his *doppelganger*—don't we all have one? Maybe he's a clone made from pieces of Seth's DNA? Could Vincent have created a second-Seth, just to piss me off? To get me off balance and uncertain?

I try to think through all the logical reasons Seth could have been standing there in that European city, talking about dragons as if he didn't care a single jot about any one of us.

As if he didn't care about *me*.

I stare up at the television screen where Vincent is still laying out his plans to capture a dragon. His barely suppressed smirk is because he knows I'm watching and he's managed to pull one over on me.

He's turned Seth, my partner in crime, into my biggest enemy.

7

I press the rewind button to the beginning of the interview and watch it again.

It's dark in the war room, everyone else has gone to bed.

But I can't go anywhere. I can't leave this strange version of Seth, who seems so beautifully familiar and so disturbingly different at the same time. It unsettles me, and a strange humming vibration roams my body.

The door opens behind me, but I don't turn. I know who it is already—my sense of smell picked him out before he came through the door.

"So you really know him? That idiot spouting nonsense?" says Zane from the entrance.

I scowl, wanting to deny that Seth would ever spout nonsense. But I keep my mouth shut. I'm not a liar.

"What's your story? How'd you end up on the other side of this fight?" He seems genuinely curious, and in the darkness he's much less annoying. Perhaps it's because I can't see his face as easily, so his cynical expression is less obvious to me.

I think about it for a moment. "I don't actually know how it happened. We fought alongside each other right up until I destroyed the spell web. Until today, I thought he was dead." Tears well at the memory, but I remind myself that it's not true anymore. Seth is alive. Or perhaps his long-lost twin-cousin-clone is alive. I don't know. I shake my head, too wrecked to make sense of it.

"He's on the wrong side now," says Zane, nodding to where Seth is silently mouthing the words I can't bear to hear again.

"Everyone is entitled to an opinion. This has been hard on all the species." I absently repeat the sentiment my father has been giving since he launched the revolution.

"No need to be diplomatic in front of me," says Zane drily. "I'm a dragon too, remember?"

"How do you see it?"

"We're enemy number one. I woke from hibernation two months ago into a world gone mad. Dragons all but extinct, supers not much better, and humans ruling the world." His voice makes it clear what he thinks about humans. "In my time, dragons ruled. We told the others what was going to happen, and they did it." His voice is matter of fact, but it still makes me shiver.

"What made you decide to go into hibernation?" The only other dragons I know who hid were either completely mad or a dangerously sly enemy. Tarsal had emerged as a friend before he died, but he'd almost killed me before he changed sides.

He shrugged. "I was injured. My clan made the decision for me." Again his smooth, expressive voice lets me know exactly what he thinks about that.

"Your clan?" I say, surprised. I've never heard that kind of term used. Did that mean he didn't steal another dragon's magic?

"My family." He hesitates. "They're all dead now. Killed by the Earthbound." His voice carries a desolate tone.

"My mother was killed by them too," I say. "Tell me about your clan. None of the other dragons I've met talked about living in a group."

He lets out a breath. "Not all dragons could live in groups. Many were loners, but many more weren't. My clan lived in a cave system together, everyone working together, including our various supernatural partners and children."

I lean forward in my chair, trying to imagine this life, so different from what I've been told before. "Did you have a wife and children?"

"Thankfully no. This has been hard enough as it is."

I nod again. It was difficult losing Seth. I glance up at the screen, still flashing images into the darkness. Even if he's actually alive again now.

It switches back to Vincent, and I press rewind again. One more time, I tell myself. Just one more time, and I'll be done.

Seth's new gravelly voice flows into the room, and Zane comes to stand beside me, gazing up into Seth's face. The light flashes over Zane's skin, making him look strange, full of edges and angles.

"The USL has the rights and the safety of supernaturals as its primary focus," Seth is saying. "We believe that a new spell web is the best way to protect the supernatural community from the kind of chaos and harm that has been brought about by the destruction of the old one."

"What about the hundreds of humans who have been hurt or killed by supernaturals since the spell web was lifted? What do you say to their families?" asks the reporter.

"What do you say to the families of the innocent super-naturals who have been lynched or stoned, or simply mobbed by humans since the spell web lifted?" Seth returns. "The supernatural community is afraid to go out, to leave their homes. We've lived with humans peacefully for centuries. It's the humans who have changed the nature of our world, not the supernaturals."

"So you deny that supernaturals feed off humans?"

Seth pauses for a moment, choosing his words carefully. "I deny that supernaturals are the problem. Like any other race, there are good people and bad. But since the humans found out about us, the violence against supernaturals has exploded. We believe a return to the spell web would ease the concerns that humans have."

Zane shakes his head. "Is there a reason no one is mentioning that the humans will forget about the supernat-urals as soon as the spell web goes up again?" he says.

I shrug. "I think there's a chance they don't know, not officially. Vincent's obviously not telling them, and the supernaturals who are pro-web aren't going to tell them they'll go back to wandering around among us and not know about it."

"Not exactly what the humans want to hear," he murmurs.

"No."

"So why don't we let them know?" asks Zane.

"I don't think they'd trust a couple of dragons," I say wryly.

"Your father then?"

"We've been blacklisted by the humans. Mostly because Vincent has been vigilant about telling everyone that I was the one who destroyed the web. They all think I'm a crimi-nal, and my father's name has suffered as a consequence."

We hadn't realized what it would be like when I first started helping him. "Damien is still convinced that my staying and helping SAW is more helpful than me leaving." I shrug.

"You did ruin things as far as some people are concerned," says Zane with a grin.

"I had no choice. It was the only way to stop Vincent." I snap out the words, feeling defensive after the night I've had.

Zane holds up his hands, palm up. "I'm against the spell web. I'm happy you brought it down. It was a yoke around our necks."

"Sorry," I mutter, annoyed at myself. I look back at the screen. "Someone will realize soon enough how it works. How else do they explain the fact that they didn't know about us before?"

"People will believe what they want to believe. Take this Vincent guy. Why does he think dragons are so evil? What proof does he have?"

"Pictures on the walls of the Earthbound compound?" I say. I've never really thought about it before. "He mentioned some old books, too."

Zane shakes his head. "He's such a weak supernatural that he's practically human, but he's got just enough magic in him to make him dangerous."

"Where does he get his magic, if he's so weak?" It's been a question that's hummed in the back of my mind for a long time.

"As soon as the spell web went up, the Earthbound had access to that magic. They used it to become stronger. Before that, they were the weaker supernaturals, jealous of the strong supers like us." Zane shrugs.

I pause, thinking. "He was using the spell web to give extra power to his guards as well." I was able to use that against him just before he captured me and Seth the first time.

"That's new. See, he's been learning. Figuring things out. He's dangerous."

"He's a smart guy." I think back to my meetings with Vincent. "He wants more magic. He's after mine, has been for years."

"Maybe. But he also seems like the kind of guy who wants control, and sees magic as a way to do that." Zane's dark eyes stare down at me like he's trying to tell me something with his eyes.

I'm not in the mood for games. "Just tell me what you're trying to say with that look," I say impatiently.

He raises his eyebrows and then grins appreciatively. "You're not like any other dragon I've ever met."

"Well, I'm younger," I say, smirking up at him.

"You don't play by the rules. I'm not even convinced you *know* the rules. I like that."

"Rules are for wimps," I say with a hint of a smile.

"In my day, dragons mostly kept to themselves. Even clans like mine, we all needed our space sometimes."

I shrug. "I've always had other people around me, just no dragons. I didn't even know I was a dragon until I started to turn."

His eyes bug out, and I can see I've shocked him. "You didn't...? But how?"

I look up to the screen where Seth is still talking to the reporter, his words on mute, but his familiar face scowling into the camera. "They didn't know how to tell before I turned; and they thought it was likely I wasn't a dragon. They didn't want to get my hopes up, I guess. Or scare me."

I keep watching Seth, and something crystallizes in my head. "Seth didn't care whether I was a dragon or not."

Zane snorts. "He didn't understand what it means to be a dragon. We're different to everyone else. Stronger, smarter. We can do more. It's just the way it is. People are scared of that."

"They're scared of the damage that dragons can't seem to help causing," I say, unable to keep the resentment out of my voice.

Zane shrugs. "Sometimes that's just the way it is."

I shake my head. "That's not acceptable. Even if we are smarter and stronger, that's a reason to take *more* care, not less. Dragons have been careless for too long. We've made the mess we're lying in, and we have to figure out a way to get out of it that doesn't involve killing thousands of innocent people."

8

"We have to stop Vincent." Roger is pacing up and down the war room, so agitated that his hair flows like water around his head. "If he gets enough people together, he'll do it. He'll put up this new spell web, three times as strong as it used to be, and we'll be powerless again."

"But how do we beat him?" says Teresa, her wolfish eyes narrowed. "He's got the attention of the media, he's saying the kind of things the humans want to hear, and he's even convinced supernatural groups that his way is the only way to be safe."

"Our arguments are just as persuasive," says my father. He glances at me. "We just have to use our assets more wisely."

I nod in agreement. "We need to start doing what Vincent has been doing. Making alliances with the other supernatural groups. We need to prove that Vincent is a bad ally, and the spell web isn't the answer."

"And just how are we going to do that?" asks Roger. He gestures at me. "You're taking the blame for every bad part of this new existence we're in, and they're pissed." He runs a hand through his silvery water-hair, and I feel tiny splashes of water on my face. "That affects us as well."

It's the first time Roger has ever directed his anger at me. I can't help feeling hurt, even though he's right. Instead of helping my father, I'm becoming a liability.

Your father needs you.

The ring on my finger glows hot for a moment, and I clench my fist. My father's staring at Roger, his face strangely bland. It's the most annoyed I've ever seen him. For the first time, I wonder if I've been misinterpreting what my mother is saying to me. What does my father actually need me for? Maybe it's not the help I thought she meant.

I shake my head. I can't worry about it right now. Vincent has put a massive target on me, and if we don't do something fast, it'll affect everything my father's group are trying to do. I take a ragged breath. "Vincent isn't the only one with a voice. It's time to coerce them, to turn this around and show them the choice I made was actually the best one for everyone."

My father turns his full attention to me. It's the first time I've said those words out loud. "Do you really believe that it's the best decision?"

I nod slowly, thinking it through. "I didn't want to destroy the spell web. I loved it, I used it in my everyday life, and I couldn't imagine not having it in my life. But now... I can do other things. I can be more than I was before. I can see that the spell web was a crutch and that I can do more and be more without it." I take a big breath. "And all we have to do is convince everyone else that it's the best thing for them, too."

Roger shakes his head. "We'll never convince the humans of that, and they outnumber us three to one."

"If the humans go back under the spell web, they'll forget all about the supernaturals," I say slowly. "Is that what they really want? To have the very people they fear invisible to them again?"

"What other benefits are there for the humans?" asks Zane. "If we can explain them clearly, we might stand a chance."

We all stop, and I wrack my brains for a good answer. "They can work with us, instead of being oblivious? They can harness the power of supernaturals to make their lives better? They won't be living in a nightmare world, blind to the potential dangers? There are opportunities for the humans as well as supers."

"What kind of opportunities?" asks Roger curiously.

I raise my eyebrows, confused he's even asking me the question. Has he really never thought it through? "Think of what the supernatural community could achieve if we weren't in hiding all the time. Just the heat from my dragon flame alone could have huge potential for various industries. There are potential benefits to humans through working with every single race of supernatural."

"And how do we calm their fears about attacks and deaths?"

"We create the supernatural and human police force to protect everyone that Dad's always talking about. Similar to the SIG, but out in the open. People are punished in a clear and legal way, instead of by shadowy organizations that no one is allowed to know about."

"That could work," says Zane. "We just need to tell people about it."

My father nods, glancing between me, Liling, and Zane. "We need to use the people at our disposal more wisely. We've been focused on the wrong aspect of this whole situation. We need to send representatives to the various groups to talk about what they want out of this whole situation."

"I want to visit the USL," I blurt out. Seth's group. I try to keep my expression calm and not show any of the nervousness that's causing butterflies to dance in my stomach. My father and the other leaders stare at me.

"I don't think..." starts my father, glancing at Roger and Theresa.

"Perhaps it would be better..." says Theresa. She clears her throat. "Seth's death upset you. We wouldn't want you to go back to those days."

I shake my head. I tossed and turned all night, dreaming of Seth and the moment when his body smashed into a million pieces. It was like it was happening all over again, and I woke sweaty and crying at five o'clock this morning determined to do something. "I'm going to convince them they should join us instead of Vincent."

"What makes you so sure that's a good idea, Mei?" asks Zane. "He hates dragons. Maybe Liling should go to Seth, and you and I try some of the other supernatural groups that aren't quite so closely aligned to Vincent?"

He's probably right. I'm a dragon, a prize for most of the population out there, and more so for Seth's group. They've stated on international television that they're going to hunt a dragon for Vincent so he can put the spell web back in place.

But I'm determined. "I know Seth. I can convince him that we're better off without the spell web. I know I can."

Liling smiles at Zane. "That leaves some of the other groups for us, then."

My father nods at both of them. "You two would make a good team. Liling's charm can soften Zane's hard dragon edges." Both Liling and Zane frown at my father, but neither says a word in protest. I just grin, pleased to have my way.

"Where are you going?" I ask my father.

"I'm thinking that Roger and I should talk to the water and the mountain people. We did start some discussions a month or so ago. They've been vocal about putting the web back in place. They feel the most vulnerable. Maybe we can convince them otherwise."

I think of Carrick and his grandfather and nod. The Mountain supers are angry with me, even though Carrick has explained a million times that it's not my fault.

But perhaps it is. I did the deed; I made the decision.

I'm not afraid to admit it, or accept the consequences of my actions. However... "Carrick says they're still pretty angry with me. I know my presence there won't help."

Damien nods. "I actually think you visiting Seth is the best decision. You have the best chance of changing his mind."

"But will she be safe on her own? Shouldn't someone be with her?" Liling looks at me with such concern, I can't be mad at what amounts to a lack of belief in my ability to take care of myself.

"I can go with her if you like," says Zane, a little too quickly.

I frown at him. I don't want him hanging around. He's unpredictable. What if he does something that makes Seth even more angry with us? "You're already going with Liling. I can handle myself."

Damien nods, and I let out a relieved breath, until I realize he's nodding toward Zane. "Zane and Mei can go together to Europe. It's a long trip, perhaps better suited to two dragons. Liling can go with Theresa to visit the human anti-webbers to see if there's any common ground. Roger, if you go with Andy to the water people, then I can take Carrick with me to the Mountain supers."

Everyone nods like it's a done deal. "But, but... I don't need a bodyguard. Zane could be useful elsewhere."

Damien shakes his head. "They're a dangerous group we don't have much intel on. If they try anything, you'll need the backup of another dragon to get you out of there."

I open my mouth to fight some more, but my father holds up his hand. "I'm against you going out into the world at all, Mei. You've got a bigger target on your head that most. Don't make me give in to my instincts and keep you here where you're safe."

I zip up my mouth immediately. No way am I going to be stuck here in our mountain hideaway while everyone else goes out.

"Then it's settled." He turns to several of the other supernaturals in the war room and starts assigning them groups to contact as well. I glare at Zane, but he just grins at me, his expression anything but contrite.

"The meetup Damien arranged is at the cafe across the road," says Zane. "Why are we here?" He pulls the collar of his black winter coat up around his neck.

We're sitting at a table outside a tiny coffee house in Prague, huddled over steaming cups of hot coffee, the only customers braving the chilly weather.

I glance at him through my dark glasses, trying to figure out if he's just pretending to be thick. "It could be a trap. We need to assess the area, gain some intel on who we're meeting. I'm not going in there until I'm sure about our contact."

Zane is lounging back on his chair, his expression skeptical. "It wasn't even someone from the group. It was a friend of a friend."

"Even more reason." I shake my head and go back to watching the cafe across the road.

He's a loose cannon. I don't know why you're trusting him.

Tarsal's voice makes me jerk in surprise. It's been a while since he last made his presence felt.

I like to leave you be, he says gruffly.

Thanks for the thought, I say. *But I can handle him. You were a loose cannon too, if you recall.*

It didn't exactly turn out well for me.

I shrug, forgetting I'm essentially talking to myself. *It's too late now. He's here, and I have to deal with him.*

A blast of air catches my neck and I shiver. I'm bundled up against the cold in a warm winter jacket, and I'm using a woolen hat and large sunglasses to hide my features.

Zane hasn't bothered with a disguise, but his face hasn't been thrown up all over the world's media channels like mine has. I'm enemy number one as far as the general human populace is concerned.

At the cafe, I see a young man arrive. He's tall and skinny, like he hasn't had a good meal in a while. His jeans and dark shirt are rumpled, as if he just pulled them off the floor of his apartment.

He stands at the entrance, hesitates, then goes to sit at the prescribed table and places a book in front of him.

Harry Potter.

He's our guy.

"Right. Let's go say hello," says Zane, standing up.

I pull him back into his chair. "We're not going anywhere until we've had a chance to watch him. Make him a little nervous."

"And what will that achieve?"

"If he's got people backing him up, he'll start giving off nervous glances. He won't be able to help it."

"And you know this because...?"

I only just manage to stop myself from rolling my eyes. Zane has obviously decided that I'm a nice little innocent dragon raised outside of the comfort of the clan who doesn't have a clue.

He hasn't seen me in action and has no idea how I've been trained. I'm not about to brag. "Just trust me."

He leans back in his seat and crosses his arms over his muscled chest. "You've got five minutes to do whatever it is you think you're doing, and then we're going in. I can't be bothered playing your games."

"Don't you dare give me ultimatums," I hiss back at him. "I'm not playing games. I'm trying to save our lives. If you're too thick to understand that, then you can go over there on your own and see how well you do."

My anger works where my ambivalence didn't. He shuts up, but gives me a narrowed look for the next ten minutes while I watch our meeting point and our mark.

"Satisfied?" he asks a little while later.

"He's got someone watching him," I say quietly. "They're sitting at the same cafe at another table. The older balding guy." I nod my head toward the cafe.

Zane looks where I indicate. After a moment, he nods his head. "Smells like a snake."

"Yeah. They can be particularly difficult," I say.

We sit in silence for another few minutes, watching as our young guy gets increasingly agitated.

"Can you tell what the boy is?" asks Zane.

I shake my head. "I think he might be human. I can't smell a thing on him."

Zane shakes his head. "He's not human. But he's been scrubbed clean. Almost like he's hiding something."

I raise my eyebrows at him.

"I didn't notice it at first," he says begrudgingly.

I turn back to the young guy and narrow my focus to him, concentrating on everything I can see in front of me. My senses take over and my intuition kicks in, just like Si always taught me.

The scents from the cafe street are all around me, the noises of people chatting, of plates clattering and glasses clinking.

But underneath it all, there's a heart beating. Thump, thump, thump. Thump, thump, thump. Thump, thump, thump.

"He's something big. He's got a triple heart beat." I can't believe I missed it.

"Dragon?"

I shake my head. "No. But something close. They've sent him in to capture us. It's not the bald backup that we've got to worry about. It's him, our contact."

We sit and watch the young guy in silence.

Zane leans forward, his brow furrowed, and puts his clasped hands on the table. "He's nervous. Like they're forcing him to do it somehow. What are they doing to him, that he's doing it anyway?"

"I don't know. But I think we should find out."

"What kind of supernatural can take on two dragons?"

"Dad didn't say it would be two dragons. He didn't mention who would be meeting them. I wanted to take Seth by surprise."

"So they've sent in someone who can beat another supernatural, but possibly not two dragons?" says Zane.

"What would that be?" I wonder out loud, staring at the crumpled young man.

Zane stared back down at the young guy sitting glumly by himself. "I think I know."

"What then?"

"Chimera."

The way he says it sends a tiny shiver down my spine, but I refuse to let him see it. "What on earth is that?"

"A creature that holds several inside it. When he shifts, it will probably be a lion or a tiger, mixed with other creatures to give it extra supernatural strength and agility. Usually it has the tail of a poisonous snake, and often a large goat with fierce horns coming out its back."

"That doesn't sound too bad," I mutter. "Not against two dragons."

Zane looks at me like I'm crazy. "They've got the power of three animals behind them instead of just one."

"Why send him? And not entirely on his own terms?"

Zane shook his head. "I don't know any more than you. Perhaps they wanted the kudos of catching a member of the infamous Mei Walker anti-webber group?"

I make a face at him and his sarcasm, but keep watching the young man closely. He's nervous, and it definitely seems like he's being forced to meet with us. He doesn't know who he's meeting precisely, but he knows it's going to be another super and someone he's going to have to fight. And then it happens. He glances my way, and our eyes meet for a moment. Even behind my glasses, I know he's seen me. But he doesn't stop, doesn't flinch or call out. He's made us, but he's not giving us away.

What the hell is going on here?

I see his nose twitch. He's a cat. They have super strong sense of smell, don't they? Maybe he knows we're dragons and doesn't want to mess with us? Or perhaps he's giving us a chance to get away before we're captured, like they're planning.

Whatever is happening, I don't like it. Not a bit.

But I can't leave this guy here in the control of these people either. He should be free to do what he wants.

I stand up. "Come on, we're going in."

Zane stays seated. "But we've established that it's a trap. What's the point of all this if you're going to go in anyway?"

I hesitate for a moment. "You stay here. Come save me when it all goes to shit."

He frowns and then stands. "How about we do it the other way around? You're too recognizable. If I go, it'll be better."

"Are you sure?" I say, narrowing my gaze and looking up into his face.

"You better come in when you're needed, or I'll be pissed," he says. There's a note in his voice that makes me think he's just saying that to play along. He doesn't think he'll need me, and he doesn't think I'll be any help.

Part of me is annoyed and wants to tell him to go to hell and that I'll go.

But he's right, it's better not to show our full strength straight away.

And I almost *want* him to get into trouble, so I can go in and rescue him.

He's an arrogant bastard. He kind of deserves it.

10

Z ane walks casually over to the cafe, then meanders toward the table with the young chimera. The guy has been watching him surreptitiously since he started down the alleyway, so he's not surprised when Zane pulls out the seat and sits next to him.

They talk for a little while, neither giving too much away, and I consider moving a little further forward so I can hear what they're saying.

"You're not going anywhere but with me," says a voice behind me. It's gravelly and hard, but I know who it is immediately.

Seth.

I turn slowly, trying not to make any sudden moves. I drink in his face greedily, but it's not enough. "Seth," I whisper.

"How do you know my name?" he says, anger in every line of his face.

"Who did this to you?" I ask, not properly registering his question. I reach up one hand, meaning to touch his face where the scar extends down his cheek.

He bats my hand away with one of his before I get close. I almost expect electricity or something equally shocking when his hand touches mine, but he just feels like hard edges.

"Don't touch me," he says harshly.

"Seth. It's me, Mei," I say stupidly.

But his expression never wavers. There's no spark of recognition or even anything to show he's hiding the fact he knows me. It's as if we're meeting for the first time.

"I know who you are," he says, as if he can read my thoughts. "You're the one who's going to return the spell web you stole from us," he says. And then he presses a button on his cell phone.

Red light and a terrible screaming noise erupt inside my head, and I can't do anything other than hold my hands to my ears. It doesn't help; the screaming is still running through my head—it's some kind of magical device.

Vincent has his machines, the ones designed to destroy a dragon, and now other supers are designing them too.

It's my last rational thought before I collapse to the ground.

11

Consciousness slowly fills my brain, and immediately I wish it hadn't. A painful pounding, like a mallet on steroids is being used inside my head, is making it hard to think. I try to lift one hand, and discover my is body locked in place.

I open my eyes and look down. I'm on a metal table with my hands and legs locked into metal casings. I lay my head back on the table and close my eyes with a groan.

Then I remember I'm not alone. Where's Zane?

My eyes jerk open, and I look around the room, trying to find him. But I'm the only one in a white-walled prison, not unlike where the SIG kept me all those months ago. I push at the bindings on my arms and legs, but even with my enhanced strength, I can't move them.

Someone has thought this through. It's been planned and prepared for. But I don't know if it was planned for me specifically, or just a dragon shifter in general.

The thought that it might be specifically for me sends me into a panic, and I push and pull frantically at the metal loops holding my hands in place. I'm bleeding by the time I admit defeat.

It feels so similar to my capture by the SIG, that when the door finally opens, I'm surprised it's not the director standing in the doorway.

Instead, it's Seth, looking harsh in the bright white light of the prison.

"Seth," I whisper.

He doesn't reply, just walks over and stands next to the bed, looking down at me.

"You don't remember me at all?" I say.

"No," he says. His single eye drinks my face in like he's memorizing what I look like. It's unnerving rather than special.

"What are you doing?" I ask.

"I'm memorizing the face of the woman who destroyed my life," he replies, his voice like flint.

"What?" I'm dumbfounded. "What the hell are you talking about?"

"The woman who took away our protection, the woman who opened supernaturals everywhere up to violence and harm."

"Ha. You're not paying attention. Supernaturals don't need help. We're twice as powerful as the humans. We can protect ourselves."

His remaining eye flashes an angry brown. He points to his patch. "Does this look like nothing to you? This is the work of those harmless humans you're talking about."

"How did it happen?" I ask softly.

For a moment, I think he's going to tell me, but then he snaps his mouth shut and scowls down at me. "Keep your mouth closed. I'm just here to determine that you are indeed Mei Walker before I call Vincent and tell him we've got you."

His words hurt, but I can't let that hinder me. "You're really okay with Vincent making the spell web stronger? Taking half your magic for who-knows-what kind of activities on his part?" I ask.

He shrugs, his eye glittering darkly. "It's the price we have to pay for your betrayal. I would prefer if it wasn't that way, but we have no choice but to accept it." The bright light makes shadows on the planes of his face, making him seem brutal and distant.

He's nothing like the Seth I once knew.

"There's always a choice. You don't have to go in with a man like Vincent. He's not a good person." I pull my head off the metal table, trying to force him to believe me.

"I think you're confusing his deeds with yours. He's not the one who pulled down the spell web in a fit of pique," Seth sneers at me.

"Do you not remember anything at all? Have you really forgotten everything?" I say, little pieces of my heart breaking all over again. I fight uselessly against the bindings over my hands. If I could only be closer to him, touch him, maybe he'd listen.

"I know enough to know you're the cause of all our problems." He watches me with disdain in his single eye. There's no softness there, nothing that hints of indecision. He moves away from me, like he's about to leave.

I'm breathing hard, but I can't give up. "Vincent *killed* you. He was going to kill us all. Destroying the spell web was the only way I could stop him. He doesn't care about anything or anyone except regaining the power he lost that day."

"He said you'd twist the facts."

"I'm not twisting the facts. He killed you right in front of me." A sob breaks free. "I went through months of hell because I thought you were dead."

"I don't believe you. I'm still here, aren't I?"

"You're a phoenix. You must have risen again. I didn't know..." I trail off, seeing the disbelief in his eyes.

"I thought you knew it all? Why *didn't* you know? If you really were my friend, where were you when I resurfaced?" A red flush heats up his cheeks, and his anger breaks through his icy contempt.

"I thought you were *dead*. I came here as soon as I realized you were still alive." I'm desperate for him to believe me, but he clearly doesn't.

"So you could finish me off?" he sneers.

"What happened to you, Seth? What's made you so bitter and angry? You never used to be like this." A hollow pit opens up inside me. This is worse than Seth being dead. He's here, so close to me, but completely off limits. He hates me. My eyes feel swollen, and I struggle to breathe normally.

"You don't know me. You don't know what I'm like."

"I do know you. You were there for me when I needed you. You're loyal, and strong and...loving." I say the words quickly, trying to convince him. Wishing he would believe me.

He leans in closer, and I see a facial tick next to his good eye. "Stop talking."

I try to keep quiet, but it's like asking a rooster not to crow. "I know you," I whisper.

"You don't know anything about me," he grinds out.

"And you know *me*, Seth. I don't know what's happened to make you forget, but you used to be my friend." I hesitate. "More than friends."

"Perhaps you shouldn't have destroyed the spell web, then?" Seth glares at me, his scar turning a blotchy red.

"It's your fault the spell web went down," I snap. "Once Vincent killed you, I realized he would do anything to kill us all. Destroying the spell web was the only way to prevent him from taking over the world."

"Don't you think that's a little melodramatic? Vincent just wants to protect people."

I can't help the unladylike snort that comes out. "You're kidding, right? Vincent is only out for one thing. He wants power, plain and simple. He likes to think he's helping—but he's just addicted to the power of having the spell web at his disposal."

"He can't use the spell web."

"Of course he can," I almost shout. "For a start, he used the magic of the spell web to enhance his guards, and make himself stronger. He used it to secretly punish or kill any supernaturals he felt were dangerous. No court or jury needed. He's struggling without it."

Seth frowns, like this is new information to him. "You don't know what you're talking about," he says, but he sounds less certain.

I shrug—or as much as I can shrug, tied up like I am. "Check it out. Ask some people about him. Don't trust me." I hesitate, but can't help adding, "I'm right, though."

"It doesn't matter. Supers still need the protection of the spell web to survive."

"Do you know why Vincent was chasing me? Why he captured me?" I pause, waiting for his answer. He just frowns deeper.

"The old spell web was dying. Supernaturals aren't as strong anymore, and they aren't reproducing as much. The supernatural population has halved in the three centuries since the Earthbound put the spell web in place."

"What's your point?"

"The spell web was slowly killing off the supernatural population."

Seth shakes his head. "It's nothing to do with the spell web. Just a natural change in population." He's on firmer ground now; he's lost the almost-indecision he had only moments ago.

I let out a frustrated breath. "Whatever the reason, the spell web was dying. Vincent needed a dragon to boost the magic required to keep the spell web in place. He thought he could take my magic and stay in control of a dwindling population of supers."

"If that's true, you're only proving our point. There are fewer supernaturals, so we need greater protection. And Vincent hasn't been shy about saying he needs a dragon to put the spell web back in place."

"I'm trying to make you understand that the spell web isn't good for supernaturals. It steals our powers and lowers our populations. It's driving us to extinction."

"You've got an overactive imagination."

I shake my head. "I've met Vincent more often than you. I know what he's like. Why do you think he hasn't told the humans they won't be able to see the supernaturals? Because he knows that's the last thing they'd want. He's keeping that juicy bit of information to himself on purpose." I glare at Seth. "As are you and your group, I might add."

Seth glowers at me. "We're not responsible for the humans. We just want to protect supers."

I let out a ragged breath and drag in more air. "I didn't want the spell web to come down. It was a last resort on my part, a desperate move. But my reasons for keeping it were selfish. I was worried that I needed it to help *me*, to protect *me*. But it turns out I can do that for myself. I don't need a secret organization stealing my magic so they can keep their own power."

"*You* might be fine, but most supers are weaker than dragons. We need the spell web to protect the majority of supers," says Seth stubbornly. "It's the only way."

"If protection is really the problem, then why don't supers get together and create something? Why do we have to rely on Vincent? Are we really that stupid?"

Seth shakes his head, but I can see I've put some questions in his head. "Supers could never pull together like that. We need Vincent and his spell web. End of story."

"You don't really believe that. Haven't you and your group managed to band together?"

"You need to stop talking. I'm leaving now, and I'm going to instruct the guards to not let you talk. You're dangerous." He glares at me, his single eye darkened to the color of molasses.

"I'm just telling the truth," I whisper.

"Tell it to Vincent. He'll be here tomorrow to pick you up."

12

————

For a long time after Seth leaves, I struggle against the metal bonds that hold me against the table.

Scrapes and scratches from the friction, then blood from the now-open wounds appears on my wrists and ankles.

Eventually I give up. I'm strong, but not strong enough.

I can't think about Seth, or the gaping hole that's inside me.

External pain and blood is better than thinking about the fact that Seth has completely forgotten me.

Closing my eyes, I force myself back to the mission. I need to figure out where they're keeping Zane. He might not be my favorite person in the world, but I don't want him hurt.

I think back to the situation at the cafe. It was almost embarrassingly easy for them to catch us. Although, being honest, as soon as I recognized Seth, I didn't fight back. I wanted to be taken back to their headquarters to speak to their leaders. I just didn't realize they'd lock me away and refuse to speak to me.

I hope Zane is faring better.

The door opens again, but this time it's just one of the guards. He sidles in like he's expecting me to leap up from the table and attack. Placing the food try nearby, he starts to back out again.

"How am I supposed to eat the food?" I ask in exasperation.

He glances from the tray to me. "I was told not to speak to you," he says.

"You're going to have to feed it to me," I say. I try to look sad and meek. "I'm so hungry."

"They said I shouldn't get close."

"Why not? What do they think I'm going to do?"

"Hurt people."

I open my eyes wide, going for the harmless and innocent look. "I would never hurt people." My small size helps when I'm trying to get people to overlook me.

He stares at me for a moment and then inches forward. He takes one of the sandwiches on the plate and holds it out with his arm straight, holding it out to my hand, not my mouth. Idiot.

"Perhaps you could hold it to my mouth?" I say sweetly, trying to suppress the edge in my voice.

He inches closer again, and I open my mouth. I'm actually hungry and could do with something to eat. I can smell the peanut butter from here.

I lean forward, and am just about to take a bite when the rancid scent of something underneath the peanut butter hits my nose. An unpleasant, bitter flavor makes my nostrils flare and my mouth snarl.

I lean backward. "You're trying to poison me?" I ask the hapless guard. I can feel the flames showing in my eyes, and my angry dragon tries to break out. I'd been attempting to stay calm and not get into a confrontation. I want to discuss things rationally.

But they're not playing fair.

They're trying to kill me.

The guard looks down at the sandwich and drops it like it might burn him. "I didn't... It wasn't...." he says before he runs out of the room.

I growl in his general direction, but my brain has kicked in. The fire has gone out in my eyes and I'm thinking though what just happened. It doesn't actually make any sense, because they need a dragon to start up the web again. They've called in Vincent. What would killing me gain?

I don't know. It seems personal. Like someone is trying to get rid of me not for the betterment of the community but because they hate me.

It's hard to know who that might be—other than Seth.

My heart clenches inside my chest. Surely Seth wouldn't try to kill me?

Then I think of the look in his eyes, and I'm not so certain.

I look up to the door and finally notice what the stupid guard has done. He's left the door open in his haste to leave.

I push against the metal bonds in my human form, straining to break out. It's too good an opportunity to miss. I'm not having any luck convincing Seth, and there's no way I'll be able to finish any conversations if I've been handed over to Vincent.

I glance at the sandwich on the floor nearby. Or killed.

Something heavy settles inside my stomach and I accept that Seth doesn't remember me. What we had is lost. Gone forever. The hope that surged to life inside me when I saw Seth on television has now completely died.

I pull on the metal bindings. There's one way that might

work. I could turn into a dragon and break the metal during the transformation.

There's no guarantee it will work—it could be made of some kind of special metal, some alloy I'm not prepared for. My large dragon limbs could be cut off in the process of going from tiny human to full-size dragon.

Surely they'd be expecting me to try it at some point? It seems too easy, until I think back to the sandwich. Perhaps it wasn't poison? What if it was a dragon-sized sedative? Maybe they had figured it out and were trying to disable me again? That actually makes more sense than someone trying to kill me.

But still, shifting into my dragon form could be the worst thing I could do. I'm here to offer a deal, to talk to the leaders. Going all dragon on them seems the opposite of what I should be doing. And if Vincent prepared them for dealing with dragons and this metal is something special that I won't be able to break... well, I can't stop mid-transformation, so it wouldn't be a pretty sight.

Gory images spin through my head, of my dragon paws being cut off by some unbreakable metal, my legs bound and unable to move.

But in the end, there's no choice.

This is too good an opportunity. I'm not going to let myself end up in Vincent's control again. I shudder as I remember the machine that immobilized both Tarsal and myself.

That's not going to happen again.

I look down at my favorite pair of jeans. Once I go dragon, my clothes will be ripped off me. If I want to go human again, I'm going to have to find new clothes, or just be prepared to run about naked.

I grimace. Now I'm just wasting time.

I close my eyes and prepare for the change. It's better these days, much easier than when I was first learning to be a dragon.

I managed to pick up a few tricks from Tarsal before he was killed, and I've talked to the mountain supers—the ones who will actually talk to me, that is. Many of them think I'm worse than a demon because I disturbed their peace when I destroyed the spell web. They'd rather talk to a rock than me.

I growl under my breath and remind myself to concentrate. Turning my focus inward, I think about my dragon form, gold and blood-red, all sharp lines and hard edges.

A killing machine, with large teeth, long claws, and a fiery ferocity that's always close to the surface. A stretching sensation runs over my whole body, and my limbs go stiff. I'm stretching, expanding, moving. It's still painful, but it's not the unbearable lightning-based pain of my first transformation. It's more like I'm being stretched too far, my whole body expanding beyond what nature intended.

One second I'm twisting and groaning and wishing it would hurry up, and then I'm not. I'm a full-sized dragon in a tiny room, the metal brackets that had held me in place lying broken on the floor. I huff out a satisfied dragon breath, smoke and heat hitting the floor next to me.

I take a step toward the door and stop. There's a major flaw in my plan. The ceiling is against my ridge of scales at the top, and the metal table has been pushed to one side of the room to fit me inside.

The door might be unlocked, but it's far too small for a dragon.

I swear under my breath.

For someone who was trained from an early age to think on her feet, I'm being remarkably stupid today. I'm going to have to change back to human. I let out a breath and roll my eyes. I'm not even twenty-four hours into my latest assignment, and I'm already captured and naked.

Jeff taught me better than this.

Although to be fair, Jeff actually focused most of my teaching on escape and survival. I know how to get out of situations quickly, to avoid coming up against players with more strength, and the best moves to disable my opponents in the fastest possible timeframe. Approaching people, forming alliances, trusting other people—this is all foreign to me.

I rifle around for a moment, looking for new clothes to replace the ripped ones lying at my feet. But it's a small, almost bare room. There are no other clothes for me to wear. If I return to human, I'll have to run about naked.

I run the scenarios in my head.

Either I stay a dragon, and push my way through the wall, not bothering to hide the fact that I'm escaping. I would have to find Zane really fast, get him out of his chains, and then find the way out, all the while fighting off the attacks from our would-be kidnappers. I don't think I could convince Zane not to kill anyone who was shooting at us, which means there would be a strong chance that Seth could get hurt.

The other option would be for me to turn back into a human and run about naked through an enemy fortress with hundreds of men around, trying to find Zane and preferably some clothes. It has the bonus of being more secretive and faster, with a lower chance of being found... but I'm naked.

The temptation to go out there in dragon form, to wreck a bit of havoc on the supers who have given up is strong. I'm pretty sure neither Zane or I would get hurt—at least not fatally. But I don't want to be responsible for any more supers dying. They hate me enough as it is. I'm sick of the burden on my shoulders, and I don't intend to add to it if I can help it.

Zane hasn't exactly shown himself to be concerned for anyone other than dragons. And even then, it's fairly limited. He's willing to put up with supers, but he's also likely to be pissed that they kidnapped us during what was supposed to be a friendly meeting. I don't think he's going to be feeling charitable, wherever he is.

A thought occurs to me—why hasn't Zane gone all dragon on them already? There are only two answers: he's either still unconscious...or he's dead. The thought speeds up my transformation into human form. If there's a chance that moving faster will save Zane, I have to take it.

Seconds later, I sneak up to the door. I take a deep breath and peek outside. It's a long hallway, and my cell is right down the end, the last door. There's no one else around. The cold air raises goose bumps all along my skin, and I glance back wistfully at my destroyed jeans.

Then I harden my resolve and take a step into the hallway.

Immediately red lights start flashing and a siren wails.

13

I run down the hall, pushing at the doors along the side wall as I go.

The first one is unlocked, as is the second. When I push them open, no one is inside.

The third door is locked, and I push against it with my shoulder. A couple of good hits and it smashes open.

Inside is Zane, lying on the same kind of metal table as me, with his ankles and wrists also held in place by thick metal clasps. But Zane is also attached to a pic line and has drugs being pumped into him.

For a second, I'm insulted. They obviously think Zane is the bigger threat of the two of us. But then I notice a partially empty plate, with the crusts of a sandwich toppled over each other.

The dumbass ate the sandwiches.

How did he not smell the toxic fumes? Leaning over to sniff the sandwich, I concede the smell is slightly less on these ones. Perhaps they simply gave him a smaller dose. Or maybe he was really hungry?

Whatever the case, this is a huge problem. I can't carry

him in human form. He's much bigger than me, and a dragon to boot.

But with the sirens screaming, it doesn't matter anyway. The quiet escape I'd been hoping for isn't going to happen.

Closing my eyes, I complete the change again in record time, and then bend down to Zane. Using my dragon strength, I pull the metal apart and grasp him in my front paws. Then I smash my way through the wall, using my tail and my powerful back legs.

The hallway is marginally bigger, and I manage to get down it without breaking too much of the wall. My dragon self growls at my human self as I try to do as little damage as possible. The dragon part of me just wants to destroy everything it can find. It wants revenge for the indignity of being captured.

Zane groans in my arms, and it reminds me I don't have time to mess around. I need to focus on our primary goal: getting out of this place before Vincent arrives with his big bag of death-to-dragon toys.

I swing my body round a corner at the end of the corridor, and come up against a hastily erected barrier. Large guns rest over the top of the wood and metal is piled high in front of me. I whip back behind the corner and look back down the hall. I don't think I can get past all that without getting a bullet stuck in Zane's puny human form. I need another way out.

Stepping back, I bash my way into the nearest room, a storage cupboard of some kind, and then push through the wall of that room on the other side. This one is some kind of meeting room. It leads to another room, and then another.

Eventually I smash through a wall that ends up in a large dining hall, with amazing smells wafting from a commercial kitchen. Surprised diners lift their heads and stare at me. No one moves for a second, and then I'm off at a run toward the other side of the room and the large exit doors.

Gunshots ring out, but I flatten down my dragon scales and the bullets slide off. I hold Zane to my chest, trying to protect him as best I can.

I run awkwardly across the shiny linoleum floor, skidding and sliding when my clawed feet don't quite find purchase. I'm almost to the door when Seth pops up in front of me, waving his hands.

He's yelling something, but I can't quite hear it in the middle of the other noise around me.

I slow down and lean my neck in to see what he's saying. Maybe he's realized I'm right. Perhaps he just wants to talk some more. Whatever it is, I'm willing to give him a second chance. Maybe he'll get everyone else to lay down their weapons and talk. I glance around, but everyone else is running like they're ants at a picnic, unable to decide which way to go first.

I skid to a halt in front of Seth and lower my head.

He reaches up, and I think he's going to touch my dragon skin, like he used to. It's only seconds before he touches me that I realize what he's got in his hands. An amped-up Taser running to a large battery pack at one side.

I jerk backward, my long dragon neck able to move in ways that a human couldn't manage. The Taser skims my scales, but it's enough to send electric shocks through my whole body. Even Zane groans in my arms.

I growl and wish I could yell at Seth in a voice he could understand. What's he doing? We came here prepared to work together, to find a solution to the problem, and all they've done is attack. I breathe flames at Seth's feet, making him stumble backward and drop the Taser.

I turn my head to assess the situation behind me, and am immediately glad I did. There's a group gathering ropes, like they think they're going to throw them over me and hold me steady. What am I, a fucking giant from one of those kids' stories? Don't they realize I have flames at my disposal?

My fury is rising to the surface now. Seth isn't going to suddenly change his mind and these people see me as nothing more than a means to an end. They don't care that I'm a person, too. All they see is their own fear.

Taking a breath, I push out a massive line of flames, burning the ground at their feet to prove my point. Most of them drop their ropes and fall over themselves to get away from me. I snarl, showing off my dragon teeth, satisfied with their response.

Turning back to Seth, I let out smoke through my nostrils, letting the haze hang around him. He just stares up at me, his eyes focused on mine. I don't know what he sees, but I don't care. I lift one lip, sneering at him and his pathetic attempts at capture. I breathe a single line of fire, hitting the small battery attached to his amped-up Taser. It bursts into flame and sparks fly.

I take another step toward Seth, daring him to come at me again. But he holds his hands up, palms out, and moves to one side. He even gestures for me to exit via the main door.

I've only taken one step when I hear a familiar sound outside. The rotors of a helicopter. Vincent's favorite form of transportation.

Helicopters. Vincent is here. Get out! Get out now! Tarsal's voice shouts inside my head. I can feel him sitting at the edge of my consciousness, nervy and anxious for me to escape this place.

They've not been trying to capture us, they've been trying to slow down our escape until Vincent could get here with his proper dragon-fighting gear.

I roar with anger. My chest hurts, and an irrational sense of betrayal sits in the pit of my stomach. Seth lied to me.

I search the room, trying to decide where to make our escape. Seth stands to one side, his smile mocking. He knows as well as I do what this means, and he's happy about it.

Blast him. He deserves it, says Tarsal again rising to the surface.

A rage fills me, so quick and deadly, I almost send a burst of dragon flame over Seth, just like Tarsal is suggesting. Unfortunately, Seth's a phoenix, so it probably wouldn't do anything to him.

Then again, it might.

But it's not revenge enough. I want to make him suffer for daring to send me back to Vincent when he knows just what the Earthbound have done to me before.

The one person I thought would care for me forever has just orchestrated my capture by the only man in the world that I truly fear.

Red fills my vision, and I growl, a pitch so low and menacing that I feel rather than see the other supers around us turn and run.

I reach out with one hand and grab Seth. It's so unexpected and quick, I manage to grab him in one go. I tuck Zane under one arm, holding him tight, and clutch at Seth with the other. He's struggling like there's no tomorrow—and perhaps for him it might be true. I don't know what I intend doing with him, but my sense of betrayal is strong.

I turn and scramble back the way I came, pushing people and furniture out of my way. I don't know precisely where I'm going, but I know that I can't stay here with Seth trying to bite his way free from my impervious dragon hands, and Zane still unconscious.

I push my way through the building, causing destruction at every turn. The only thing I know is that I have to get away from Vincent.

14

Zane starts to move restlessly as I run back through the building, smashing and crashing everything I see. Seth has stopped struggling—perhaps he saw how little effect he was having. It makes me wonder why he doesn't just turn into a phoenix and fight me, if he's so set on escaping. I remember his phoenix form vividly, all fiery and magnificent.

But for whatever reason he stays in human form, his body stiff and tense in my dragon claws as I trample through walls and push aside furniture.

A red-colored haze covers my vision. I'm mad at Seth for not remembering me, and mad at myself for assuming I'd be able to talk him out of whatever he's doing. He doesn't even seem like the same person. Is that what happens when a phoenix dies? They lose everything of who they were and start all over again?

I'm so focused on being annoyed, I almost miss a potential escape route. It's only when something flickers in the sky outside that it catches my eye. A large skylight is set into the ceiling up ahead, brightening the long hallway.

I skid to a halt, and stare up through the glass. The skylight might just allow me to break through the ceiling and roof, out into the open. As soon as I'm outside, I can spread my wings and fly, and I'm pretty sure I can outmaneuver a helicopter—even if I'm not faster than one.

Clutching my two human-shaped captives to my chest, I pull out my wings to full size. Using the talons on the corner tip, I crash my way through the ceiling around the skylight, ducking my head as glass, plaster, Gib, and other building materials shower down over us.

I push higher and higher, until I break through to the outside. Wintry sunlight makes my eyes contract, but I keep moving, pushing at the crumbling architecture with my claws until there's a hole big enough for me to climb through. With a triumphant growl, I burst out into the open.

Helicopter on your flank. Tarsal is playing guardian angel today.

I turn as a helicopter appears beside my head, its rotors spinning madly like a giant-sized hummingbird. The little figures inside are all focused on me, several guns pointed straight at me. I snarl and react instinctively—a jet of dragon flames roars toward the helicopter, burning away its rotors.

The small vehicle plummets to the ground, and I don't wait to see the results. I'm off, flying hard and high, away from this place.

Away from Vincent.

I'm still clutching Zane in one hand and Seth in the other.

Zane is barely moving, but Seth has started punching and kicking again like a maniac. He obviously wasn't expecting me to get away. To be honest, I'm beginning to regret the impulse to snatch him.

I don't know what I'm going to do with Seth, but for now, it's enough that I'm getting out of here. I keep checking behind me, but no other helicopters launch into the sky.

Was Vincent on that helicopter? Did I just kill him? My heart is still beating fast, and my senses are on overload. It feels like I can hear every bird squawk, and every murmur of conversation from the ground below.

Colors are brighter, stinging my eyes. I have to take deep breaths, trying to match my inhalations with the beating of my wings to calm myself down.

I check behind me again.

There's still no helicopter buzzing behind me. No other flying contraptions about to storm down on me. I let out a relieved breath.

The city soon gives way to countryside. My massive wings beat rhythmically, and I use the air currents to keep me going when I need a rest. The cloudy winter sky hides my shape from the humans below—I'm grateful not to have to figure out a way to stay hidden.

I don't know how long it is before I slow my furious pace. My wings are heavy, and I'm panting like I've just run the dragon equivalent of a marathon. I'm reluctant to slow down, but I know I have to, if I'm going to avoid falling out of the sky.

I soar just below the clouds, my wings out wide, still coasting on air currents. I'm flying over rolling countryside, green fields and big leafy trees.

Thank you, I say to Tarsal, but he's gone, back into the nether-regions of my subconscious.

My heart has calmed down, and I can finally breathe a little easier. In the distance, I spot a higher section of land, cliffs on one side and a grassy patch on the other. I soar in, landing softly, my wings outstretched.

I open one paw and place Zane onto the ground. Seth I hold onto—I'm pretty sure he'll run as soon as I let him go. He's been biting and kicking me the whole way here.

Once upon a time, he touched me gently, reverently, like he was awed by my dragon skin. Now he's glaring at me like I'm a demon in disguise.

Ignoring Seth for the moment, I gently poke at Zane. He groaned a couple of times through our ride, so I know he's not dead. At least not yet. I can't even ask Seth what they gave him, and I'm not changing in front of both of them without something to put on to cover my nakedness.

Zane rolls over slightly and then pushes himself to sit up. He holds his head in his hands, leaning over like it's difficult to stay upright.

Son of a bitch, what did they do to me? he asks quietly inside my head.

I shake my head, relieved to have him awake. *I have no idea. All I know is that I smelled something bad in the sandwiches, so I didn't eat them.*

He glances up at me. *You saying you've got a better nose than me?*

I smirk. *The evidence speaks for itself.*

He shakes his head and then glances to where I'm holding Seth. *Oh shit. Tell me you didn't kidnap a representative of the group we're trying to woo.*

They kidnapped us! They didn't want to be wooed.

Your father is going to kill us.

I snort out a puff of smoke. *Like he could.*

And I thought I was a troublemaker. He clears his throat and speaks to Seth. "If you want her to put you down, you're going to have to apologize for kidnapping us. She's pretty pissed at you."

What are you doing?

Zane winks at me. *Just helping out the cause.*

What cause? What are you talking about?

Get the guy to apologize, and you're halfway to getting back together with him.

I let out a huff of breath. *I don't think it's going to be that easy. He's basically declared that I'm enemy number one and need to be destroyed. That's a pretty big problem for the relationship.*

Zane snorts, but manages to keep in actual laughter.

Seth starts struggling again. "I'm not going to apologize. She's the one who destroyed the spell web."

Zane shakes his head. "Why does it mean so much to you? You're a phoenix, from what I hear. You're more powerful than most supers put together. Nothing can stop you."

Seth sneers. "Do I look like nothing can stop me?" He gestures at his eye patch and scar.

"What happened?" asks Zane curiously.

I hold my breath, waiting to hear if he'll tell Zane.

Seth pauses so long, I don't think he's going to answer. But then he does.

"I was born in the center of a volcano in Iceland. When I emerged from the lava, I was weak and innocent. I didn't know anything about myself or who I was other than my name and that I was a phoenix. As weak and useless as a baby.

"I was set upon by group of humans who had recently found out about supernaturals. I didn't know how to use my powers, and I couldn't defend myself. There were too many of them, and they didn't hold back. I would have died if it wasn't for the supers who rescued me." His face looks gaunt, as if even now he can feel the pain.

"People from USL?" asked Zane softly.

"Yes. They risked their lives to rescue me and then helped me heal. Without them, I would be dead. I owe them everything." He glances up at me as he says it, and I know he's speaking for my benefit too.

And now I know what happened, I'm not surprised by his stance. The spell web coming down directly caused his wounds. But... *he wasn't born in the volcano—he was reborn there. And the reason he was so weak was because Vincent had recently broken him into a million tiny pieces. Vincent is not a good man.*

It's at this moment that I remember something. *You can understand our head talk, can't you?* I say, turning my head to stare at Seth.

Seth hesitates, then nods. *Yes.*

It had been such a new skill for Seth that I forgot he could even do it. I frantically try to remember if I've said anything I might regret to Zane while we've been here.

What did you give Zane to knock him out? Will he be okay?

Seth frowned. *Nothing. We didn't knock him out.*

I roll my dragon eyes and point to Zane. *Does he look like he's 100 percent?*

Seth looks over at Zane and his eyes narrow as if he's assessing him.

"I'm a lot meaner usually," says Zane, lifting his hand to wave weakly.

"I don't know what a dragon looks like normally, so I couldn't tell you."

The only reason I'm not like that is because I smelled the toxin in my food and didn't eat it.

"Then how come he didn't...?" Seth nods toward Zane, who scowls at both of us.

I huff out a laugh at Zane's expression.

"I was hungry and I ate. I wasn't expecting you to drug me," says Zane.

"We didn't drug you," insists Seth.

Someone in your organization did. Perhaps you're not as well informed as you think you are. I glance over at Zane and remember my initial instinct. *They could have been trying to kill us.*

Zane shakes his head. "That makes no sense, Mei. Why do that when they want the spell web back up? They need us alive."

I think about it for a moment. *Maybe it was just aimed at me? I think maybe someone has a grudge against me they couldn't control. They cared more about getting revenge for some perceived slight than the group's stated aim of reinstating the spell web.*

"There's no point trying to make up stories," says Seth. "I know who my friends are."

It's painful to watch Seth's reactions. He doesn't believe me and isn't listening to what I'm saying. Once upon a time, he vowed to never leave me, to always be by my side.

If I could cry in my dragon form, I think this version of Seth could make me do it. *I used to be your friend. More than your friend.*

He glares at me, his single eye sparkling with hazel-colored dislike. "Not anymore," he says coldly.

15

"What are we going to do with him?" asks Zane, gesturing at Seth.

Let him go. I shouldn't have taken him in the first place. My whole body feels cold and numb. Seth really doesn't know who I am. He remembers nothing. His coldness chills me to the bone.

Seth looks at me in surprise.

What? Did you think I was going to eat you for dinner? My hurt makes me sarcastic.

"I wasn't sure," he says warily. He looks small and pale and somewhat beaten by life, and my heart lurches.

What happened to the Seth I knew? He was strong and loyal, and he fought to stay with me. When he turned into a phoenix, he glowed. His whole body was covered in flames and he was beautiful.

Do you change into a phoenix often? I ask.

Seth shakes his head. "No. It's too dangerous. I'd just make myself a target for the humans."

What, never? But... I can't even begin to understand how he could suppress his phoenix nature like that.

"But what?" he says. "You can't imagine showing that kind of restraint? I know it's foreign to you, but some of us take a little care when and where we change."

"When was the last time you changed into a phoenix?" asks Zane.

Seth shrugs. "When I fought the humans. I tried to turn, but it didn't work."

"It must have been too early," says Zane, like he actually knows what he's talking about.

So you've never...? Not since before your death? I can't keep the shock out of my voice. He was so beautiful as a phoenix, so calm and relaxed. It was a part of him, and he's suppressing it, denying it. *Surely the others have encouraged you?*

He shakes his head. "Our group isn't about hedonistic pursuit of whatever takes our fancy. We support what's best for everyone as a whole."

"Even if that's not really what's best?" says Zane angrily.

"You think the way the world works now is best?" asks Seth angrily.

Of course not. But there are things we could do to change it, to make it better. Make a place where we all can live, a place where despots like Vincent don't get to steal our magic for their own purposes.

"Like what?" Seth says, sarcasm heavy in his voice.

Like a police force for supernaturals. Agreements between the major players. Any number of ideas that are better than the simplistic notion of putting the spell web back in place.

"The spell web protected us like nothing else does. It kept us safe from the humans."

What makes you so sure? You don't remember anything from before.

"I know."

No you don't. You don't even know how to be a phoenix. How could you know anything? My hurt is so strong, I'm lobbing wounding words at him, trying to hurt him back.

Flames appear in Seth's eyes, and for the first time, I see something more in him. Something like the old Seth.

"I know how to be a phoenix. Just because I don't lose control like you do, doesn't mean I don't know anything."

At least I know how to embrace my true self, the being that is a part of me. You're just living a shell of a life, pretending to be human and wishing for the Earthbound to protect you.

"I'm not pretending to be human. That's the last thing I'd pretend to be." He spat the words out like they were poison.

Then why don't you turn? Why don't you let your phoenix go?

The flames in his eyes burn hot now, and all of a sudden, tiny flames ignite over his body. "Don't tell me what to do."

You were amazing as a phoenix. The most beautiful thing I've ever seen. Now you're a pathetic shell, a pretend-human, talking to the humans on human television. Making deals with terrible people like Vincent, because you're too afraid of your real self to take a chance.

My scales are humming I'm so angry, and I've lost all sense of what I'm saying. He's hurt me with his indifference, and I want to make him feel something in return. Tendrils of smoke escape my nostrils.

Flames leap over Seth's body, matching the flames in his eyes. I don't think he's even aware it's happening. He's standing in front of me, blazing angry, hands clenched, and the fire finally coming out from inside him. If his rage weren't directed at me, it would be perfect.

"You don't know anything about me."

Is it the people you're with? Have they told you to dampen down your magic? Who are they really, that they want you to hide who you are?

"No one is asking me to *hide* who I am. It's just safer that way. We all know and understand that." He starts to pace in front of us, like a caged animal trying to get away from its owners.

Is anyone else as powerful as you? Is anyone else forced to hide from their true self? I didn't stop to get a handle on the magic around me when I was there. *They're trying to cage you. They're scared of how powerful you are.*

"You don't know anything about them! Stop talking like you know them!" His body shifts with the flames, the lines of his human body becoming blurred. I blink, and my dragon vision goes to heat sensitive. All I can see in front of me is the blazing ball of heat that is Seth. I blink again, unable to see anything else but the bright white light that burns off him.

Then why are they telling you that you shouldn't change? And why are you complying? There's no need for you to fear them.

With an inhuman howl, Seth hurls his hands into the air, and giant wings made of air and fire appear out from his back. He's morphing into his phoenix form right in front of us, his skin bursting with flames. He screeches as it's happening, and I wonder if it's the same painful feeling it is for me to turn into a dragon, or if he's just angry.

It occurs to me that he'll be more likely to fight me as a phoenix; he's certainly angry enough to attack. I take a small step back, trying to prepare.

But then I notice a pile of clothes to my left. Zane has transformed next to me into an enormous black and golden dragon, even as Seth becomes a blazing phoenix.

The power around us is almost a physical presence as the two men morph into their supernatural forms.

In front of us, flames burn high around Seth's phoenix form. His golden-red body is sleek and muscular, his head held proud. It's the most beautiful thing I've seen. My heart beats double time in my chest, and I wonder if he feels anything for me. In his human form, I know he thinks I'm the enemy.

But does his phoenix recognize me?

Seth? Can you hear me?

He turns his head so that his hazel phoenix eyes are staring straight at me. The scar is missing in his phoenix form.

He doesn't say a word.

My heart beats faster. I know he remembers something. But what?

There's a long moment where he just stares at me through the flames.

Zane roars into the silence, his dragon form stamping at the ground in front of him. He's challenging Seth, power to power.

I don't know who would win that fight.

Probably Zane; he's a powerful, old, and wily dragon and would win against an untried phoenix who's been refusing to change.

Seth rears up on his hind legs, screeching back at Zane, his wings turning up the dirt around us, creating a dusty fog as a backdrop to his flames. Then suddenly, on a massive whoosh of air, he leaps into the sky. He takes several powerful beats of his enormous wings, and he's gone, up into the clouds.

Zane and I watch him fly until he's a dot in the sky.

That was unexpected, murmurs Zane.

He remembered something.

Yeah, but what? asks Zane. *Did we just unleash something we shouldn't have?*

I shake my head. I don't know. But then I grin, unable to stop my appreciation for the power and strength I saw in Seth as he leaped into the sky.

16

"I can't believe you kidnapped him. They're telling the world you're unpredictable and dangerous. You just made everything worse!" My father paces around the war room, waving his hands around like it's going to change something.

"They kidnapped us first. They tried to hand us over to Vincent. I was acting on instinct." I'm feeling sulky, not because he's wrong, but because I took what should have been a simple mission and made everything more complicated.

But I'm not going to give up. I saw the look in Seth's eyes before he took off. He loved being a phoenix. If I can convince him that giving up his magic so Vincent can have more power is wrong, then maybe he'll be able to convince the rest of his group. "Let me go back. I'll get Seth alone, talk to him."

Damien shakes his head. "You're not going anywhere. You've done enough damage."

"If I can prove that the supposed *most-wanted criminal* is actually not that bad, surely that's going to change some minds? That's what we need to make this happen, right? We need as many people as possible to change their minds about us."

But I can tell from the stony expression on my father's face that he's not going to change his mind. Not for a while at least. We haven't known each other for long, but I already recognize his stubborn look.

Jeff used to have a similar expression.

That doesn't mean I'm going to give up. It just means he's not going to know about it.

"And don't think you can get away with doing anything behind my back. I'm assigning Liling to shadow you."

I want to groan like a teenager and mutter how unfair it all is, but I manage to widen my eyes and look innocent. Liling might hamper my plans a little bit, but I'm still pretty sure I can wrap her around my little finger. "It'll be nice to spend some time with her," is all I say.

"Now go and get some rest. You look like death warmed up."

I frown at his unflattering assessment, but I haven't slept in a while, and I do feel pretty crappy. Maybe he's right. "Fine. Talk later." If nothing else, I can use the time to plan what I'm going to do next.

He seems surprised at my easy acceptance of his decree, and I try not to look suspicious as I leave the room.

We've been getting to know each other better in the last three months, but my father still doesn't really know who I am. If it had been Jeff, he would have known something was up and never have let me leave the room on my own.

But then Jeff would also have had more faith in my abilities, mainly because he was the one who shaped them.

The thought of Jeff hurts, and I try to think of something

more cheerful. Seth's return from the dead is the first thing that pops into my head, but that's also bittersweet.

He's not dead, killed by Vincent in our last battle. But he's not mine anymore; he's no longer vowing to be with me until the end of time.

Are there any women who've caught his eye in his new group? Has he been flirting with someone other than me? The thought sends little icicles down my spine. He doesn't remember anything that happened between us. Doesn't know that we made promises to each other. As far as he's concerned he's free to act on any feelings for another woman.

I'm so engrossed in feeling sorry for myself that I turn the corner in the corridor and run smack into Zane. He smiles as soon as he sees me and holds out his hands to make sure I don't fall over.

As if I'd fall over.

"Were you coming to thank me for saving you?" I ask sweetly.

He opens his mouth to deny it, then shakes his head. "I didn't thank you, did I? You're right, I would have died in there without you." His dark eyes sparkle with something other than gratitude, and at first I don't understand.

"No problem. Any time."

He watches me closely for a moment. "Dragons don't always get along," he says.

Tarsal snorts inside my head. *That's an understatement.*

I nod, trying not to make it obvious I have another dragon inside my head.

"But you and I have developed a bond."

I frown, not sure what he's talking about.

"You're a refreshing dragon to be around. I enjoy your spark."

Tarsal laughs. *I didn't see that coming,* he says.

Finally it clicks. I stare at Zane. He's tall and handsome, dark brown hair and flashing eyes that express what he's feeling. Part of me flutters at the thought that he wants to be more than friends. "You *like* me?"

He smiles, far too experienced to be so lame. "I enjoy your company and would like to spend more time with you." He gives an elegant little flourish with his hand that reminds me he's probably several hundred years old.

I take a breath, then another, trying to decide what I think about the possibility. Would Tarsal be inside my head if I kissed Zane?

Ew.

"You don't have to answer right away. You can think about it," he says into the silence of my indecision. His voice is smooth like melted chocolate when he wants it to be.

A shiver runs along my spine and I blink. "I don't think I have time for anything other than friends right now." My heart is beating a little too fast, and I look away from Zane, down the hallway.

You're scared, says Tarsal. He sounds surprised.

Zane's smile doesn't even slip, like he was expecting my answer. Maybe he was. "Friends, then. I have your back, you have mine."

Good decision, Mei. He's got shifty eyes. Tarsal's voice in my head is making this whole situation worse. I try to keep my expression neutral.

"Sure," I say, nodding. "Right now, I'm going to catch up on all the sleep we lost on that last mission."

He bows, another old-fashioned movement that's so graceful it seems natural. I manage to restrain the urge to curtsy, and stride off down the hall.

You need to stay out of my head during conversations like that, I say to Tarsal.

I don't always have control over it, he replies. He sounds like he's laughing.

How the hell am I ever going to have any privacy ever again? Even if I'd wanted to say yes to Zane, I couldn't have. Scowling, I arrive at the security of my bedroom not long after.

Except it's not empty. Liling is waiting for me inside.

"Damien sent me to tell you I'm your guardian angel for the next couple of weeks," she says with a smile.

"I don't think he used those exact words, did he?"

She smiles, the expression lighting up her whole face. "It's how I choose to take his words. And we're not going to be bored. We've got hours of planning ahead of us."

I frown. "Planning for what?"

"We need to convince others that our vision for the future is one that will make us all happier. We must get to work immediately."

I sigh, but nod. "I'm happy to help however I can." And I am, truly I am. It's just that paperwork isn't my forte. I'm a dragon after all. I should be shooting out flames and scaring people.

A knock at the door of my room interrupts my thoughts. "Come in."

Zane pokes his head around the door. "You might want to turn on the television. Your boyfriend is on again."

I frown at him but use the remote to turn on the tiny television in the corner of my room. Instead of Seth, as I was expecting, it's Vincent. "...we have captured a dragon, although he's not as strong as he once was. He will be useful for testing, but we need a younger, stronger dragon to spark the necessary magic." He points to another journalist in the room with him.

"How did you capture the dragon?"

Vincent gestures to someone off camera. "Our associate Seth was able to provide us with the coordinates of this particular beast. We used our specialized machinery to neutralize his powers and knock him unconscious. It was an easy task from there to load him onto a boat and bring him here."

Images flick up on the screen, and I see the icy waters of northern Russia. "Sergei! It's Sergei." I turn to Liling. "That means he remembers. Something must have happened when he turned into a phoenix. He remembered."

"Unfortunately for that other dragon, he remembered where he was hiding and gave that information to Vincent," says Zane.

I wave a hand at Zane. "Sergei tried to kill Seth a couple of times. He's not exactly fond of him."

"But still, giving him up to Vincent is pretty bad," ventures Liling. Her expression is concerned.

I don't like to admit it, but Liling is right. The old Seth would never have given him up to Vincent. Sergei had gone insane after years of living next to a nuclear testing ground. He didn't deserve to be captured by Vincent and used for "tests."

"We have to rescue Sergei," I say.

Liling is unsurprised, but Zane can't help a small exclamation. "What?"

"We can't let Vincent run God-knows-what tests on Sergei. He's mad as a hatter, but he doesn't deserve that."

"You're grounded. We're doing paperwork," says Liling. She gives a half smile, even as she says the words.

"More importantly, it's a useless mission, saving some

crazy dragon who won't thank us for it. What would we do with him once we had him here? How would we contain an *insane* dragon?" Zane is speaking like he's already one of the crew, and he's only been here a few days.

I shake my head. "I don't know the answers to those questions. I just know we can't let Vincent get away with this." I stare at his face on the screen.

"What if it derails the peace process? We can't go around attacking people if we want to prove to them that we're serious about all this."

"Why is *Vincent* allowed to harm an innocent person? How is that fair?"

"Because he's not a dragon. You are."

"So are you. This should concern you, the fact they captured one of ours so easily."

Zane lets out a big breath. "Of course it concerns me. Quite frankly, I'm terrified. Especially if we go in there and they use the same kind of weapons against us."

I shake my head. "This is a quiet raid; so small a party they won't know we're in there until we're gone. Liling knows the layout of the buildings. We can all fly in together, and between us, two dragons should be able to carry even an unconscious dragon."

I hesitate, looking at the television screen again. "Besides, I don't think Vincent is actually at his compound at the moment. That press conference, it looks like it's in a city."

Liling stares at the screen, trying to confirm what I'm suggesting. "I think you might be right," she says slowly, as if she's thinking it through. "He'd never let anyone from the media into the compound. He's away from home."

Suddenly, my idea seems a lot more doable. I grin at Zane. "You coming?"

Zane stares at Liling in disbelief. "You're on board with this?"

She smiles and nods. "Being friends with Mei isn't for the fainthearted."

He shrugs. "Then I'm in. When are we going to do it?"

"How about right now?"

17

It's late at night, and I still haven't had that nap I was planning. We're flying low over the countryside on an errand we haven't mentioned to my father, who is already angry at me for the last botched mission.

What could go wrong?

I'm troubled by Seth's involvement in this. Has he changed so much that he doesn't mind giving up innocent— or at least crazy—dragons, as long as it suits his cause? Did the Seth I thought I knew even exist? How could he now be so different?

To be fair, Sergei did try to kill Seth when we first arrived, and they didn't exactly hit it off. But does that give Vincent the right to torture him?

We're almost there, I say to Zane. With the night sky creating a backdrop, he's all but invisible.

He's even managed to hide his golden scales under his black ones. It's a trick I'd like to learn. My gold and red scales are more obvious, even in the night sky.

Liling is on my back, clinging to the ridges and keeping low. She's still not comfortable flying on my back, but she's determined to stay with me like she promised my dad. She's also got a bag on her back with a change of clothes for myself and Zane. Liling is dressed in black, and our spare clothes are too.

The plan is to get in and out fast. With only three of us, we should be able to maintain the element of surprise. We're prepared for a secret mission. I just hope it goes the way we want it to. If we stay out of the way, no one will ever know we were there. At least until we're gone.

It will be fine. No one will get hurt.

I repeat the words in my head like a mantra.

Down below is the arid landscape that surrounds Vincent's stronghold. I turn into the wind, using the air currents to get the right angle, and then head downward. Behind me the shadow that is Zane follows.

We fly in low and land inside the wall, then transform into our human shapes before hurriedly getting dressed.

"This way," whispers Liling, and we follow her to the outside of a building around the back.

"You're up," says Zane, gesturing to the lock. Again, I give thanks to Jeff for providing me with a well rounded education, as I pull out my lock pick kit and open the door.

So far, we haven't seen any guards.

Inside it's still exactly the same. The floor is tiled and the walls are made of stucco, kind of like a Spanish hacienda, or at least what I imagine one might look like. It's not scary at all. Except I get goose bumps along my arms, my heart starts to stutter, and my vision goes a little blurry. I feel like Vincent is about to storm around a corner any minute. I've never been so scared as I was the first time I was here and he tried to prove I was a dragon by drowning me and then burning me alive.

This is one of your worse ideas. Tarsal's voice in my head makes me jump, I'm so nervy. *Maybe even your worst ever.*

Shut up. You're not helping. I don't have time to be nice to Tarsal right now.

Don't you remember what he did to us?

Of course I do! Clenching my fists, I try to ignore the terrifying memories that his words bring back. The pain of the noise from machine, the way it held us both helpless. Tarsal dying.

Why are you back here? This is the last place you should be.

They have Sergei. I have to save him.

There's silence for a while, and then Tarsal speaks again, this time so quiet I almost can't hear him. *All they have to do is serve someone up to be rescued and you come running. You're too predictable, Mei.*

It stings worse than if he'd kept yelling at me. *I can't let him hurt an innocent dragon. It's my fault Sergei is here, and it's my responsibility to get him out.*

The words spur me into action. Swallowing hard, I force myself to push away the memories and focus on what we're doing. I'm here for a reason, and I won't let anyone distract me.

Liling leads the way down the corridor, her long black hair tucked into a bun at the base of her neck. I follow her, trying to be as naturally graceful as she is. Years of elite gymnastics training have made her supple and strong, not to mention elegant. It's only because of my martial arts training that I can even come close to comparing to her. Dad likes to get her doing fitness training with the younger recruits, just to freak them out.

I feel a pang in my chest when I think about my father. He's going to be pissed at me over this mission. But I can't leave Sergei here with Vincent, and I'm not willing to give them the opportunity to object by telling them what I'm doing.

We come to a corner and Liling peers around. She jumps straight back and flattens herself against the wall. Zane and I do the same. The sound of footsteps becomes obvious. I should have noticed earlier, but I was too self-absorbed. I give myself a mental shake.

The guard passes by without even a glance in our direction, and I thank our lucky stars for incompetent staff. But from now on, all my senses are focused on keeping us alive.

Beside me, Zane seems less concerned about our close encounter. Si would say he's too used to being the biggest predator in the room. He doesn't notice the small things, because the small things have never been a threat before.

Once the guard has turned down another corridor, we continue down the hallway he just came from. Liling leads us to a set of stairs, and we head down into the bowels of the building. We're concentrating on quiet and stealth over speed, and it seems a long time before we make it to the bottom. My legs burn and my breath rasps in and out. I've been neglecting my fitness if this is what I've come to.

Si would never have let me get so unfit in the old days. I grin. At least I know I'm in the right mode of thinking when Si's voice starts reminding me of my training inside my head.

We enter a dim hallway, and even this part of the building is familiar. I've been here too, in my first visit to the Earthbound compound. My body starts to shake again. But I refuse to let Vincent and my memories overwhelm me, so I grit my teeth and keep going, forcing the reaction down inside me. The trembling subsides, and I keep following Liling.

We're looking for a particular room, one that will keep a dragon immobile.

The thought scares me, given what I know about Vincent and the machines he's been able to resurrect from the Earthbound arsenal. I've had firsthand experience with how effective they are. I can only hope that having Liling here will help us if it comes to that. As a sea turtle shifter she has her own supernatural powers—mostly to do with protection and strength—which, added to her natural grace and poise, makes her a formidable enemy.

Not to mention the fact that I spent the first twenty years of my life not being a dragon and learning how to take care of myself in my human form. I shouldn't be afraid.

I'm not afraid.

I'm not afraid.

I keep repeating the words under my breath until Zane growls and I realize he can hear every word.

I put my lips together and manage to hold it in. *I'm not afraid.*

"Up here," says Liling, pointing.

I can feel a buzzing vibration coming from that direction; it's either Sergei, or my reaction to some kind of dragon contraption they're going to use to capture us.

One or the other.

"What are we going to do with him once we have him?" asks Zane.

"I don't know," I say truthfully. He's as crazy as a loon, but I can't leave him here for "testing."

I won't.

Zane sighs and shakes his head. "I knew you were trouble as soon as I saw you."

I can't help grinning at his fake fear. He's totally enjoying this.

"Sergei is a little... nuts," I say. "So we might have issues with him. I'm just hoping they've got him drugged or something." It's a big hope.

We get closer and closer to the buzzing, and I shake my head to try and dislodge the sensation of my bones shaking. We turn a final corner and come face to face with three large guards, all dressed in the familiar Earthbound uniform, their muscles bulging out the arms of the sleeves. They were expecting us as little as we were expecting them, which was dumb on both our parts.

My face flushes as I realize how stupid we were to think the room would be unguarded. But that's all the reflection I allow myself.

I step in front of Liling and throw a quick punch at the first guard's stomach and then knock his feet out from under him before he can even think about what's happening.

He lands with a thump onto the ground, winded. Leaving him for Liling or Zane, I move on to the next guard, blocking the punch he throws my way. His second attempt is a wide hit, and I duck, sneering at him as I move. "Is that all you learned in guard school?" I say, before landing a punch to the kidneys and then slamming a knee into his groin.

It's not pretty, but it's effective. He crouches over in front of me and gasps for breath. I swing my arms wide and land the side of my fists precisely on his ears at the same time. He falls to the ground, unconscious.

I turn to find the last guard fighting with Zane, who seems to be enjoying toying with him. "Come on, we don't have time for that," I growl.

Zane glances at me, amusement on his face, and then slams a meaty fist into the guard's face. Blood spurts from his nose and he lets out a strangled cry. Zane punches him in the stomach and he goes down, still holding his hands to his nose.

Liling has found handcuffs and keys on the first guard, and she's already put the first guard's hands behind his back and immobilized him. I step in to get the second guard cuffed.

The third resists the efforts to tie his hands behind his back. "My noz iz brokin'," he says through the blood.

"Do his legs, and let's get on with it," says Zane briskly, grabbing the last set of handcuffs off Liling. He slams the cuffs into place around the ankles of the guard. They barely fit, but he gets them on. The guard glares at us but doesn't make a move to stop him. I notice a set of keys on his belt and put my hand out to grab them. He swipes at me, and I react instinctively, snapping the side of my hand into his jugular. His eyes roll back in his head, and he flops backward on the ground.

I grab the keys and look up to see Zane staring at me.

"What?" I ask.

"Remind me never to piss you off," he murmurs.

We step around the three guards and carry on down the hallway. The buzzing intensifies, and I glance at Zane to see if he feels it too.

"It's because he's not controlling his magic. He's like a broken livewire, sending out chaotic signals to everything around him," says Zane through gritted teeth. He seems more affected by it than I am. It was the same with Tarsal— he reacted faster to Vincent's machines than I did. I'm not sure why, only that they're both much older and probably more powerful than I am.

Although I do have Tarsal's soul inside me now and my mother's ring on my finger. Perhaps it's because *I'm* stronger?

Whatever it is, I can see Zane is struggling to hold onto his concentration. We need to get in and out of here fast.

"Liling, you might have to take charge in there," I whisper, nodding my head to the door ahead of us. "I don't know what kind of weaponry they're going to have, but it's likely to be aimed at dragons." Liling's sea turtle form is all about protection. If anyone is going to be okay against their machines, it's her.

Liling nods at me and sets her mouth in a determined line. She steps forward and turns the handle on the door. It's locked, but I pull out the keys I took from the third guard and hand them to her.

As I wait next to her, my whole body is tensed and ready to react, my attention focused on whatever is on the other side of that door.

18

The door opens and Liling peers inside. When nothing happens immediately, I move in behind her and scan the room. It's a cavernous space. The walls are metal, and there are no windows. I look around for the large silver and blue dragon I met in Russia all those months ago.

Instead there's a pale man lying on a single bed at the side of the room. He's asleep, but it isn't a gentle sleep. He twitches and turns on the bed, making the sheets twist up around him.

"You better wake him up, Mei," whispers Zane.

"I'll do it," says Liling, glancing back at me.

"Zane's right," I say reluctantly. "He knows me. I'll wake him."

I move cautiously over to the bed, trying to figure out if Sergei really is asleep, or if he's been drugged. I'm not even sure this is the same dragon I met in Russia. He's definitely a dragon, there's no way to hide that. He has silver-blond hair and pale skin that seems almost translucent. He *could* be Sergei.

But then again, he could also be someone completely different.

He's still tossing and turning, and a low moaning emerges from his narrow lips. A shiver scuttles down my spine. What have they done to him?

It doesn't matter if it's Sergei or not. He's still a dragon being tortured by Vincent, and I won't stand for it. Reaching out with one hand, I place it on the arm of the man in front of me.

His eyes snap open. He reaches out, lightning fast, and grabs my wrist. "Gotcha," he says, glee in every line of his face. His grip is painful on my arm.

For one dreadful second, I think he's working with Vincent and this has all been an elaborate plot to capture me. But then I see the swirling lights in his eyes and realize he's not all there. The dragon in front of me couldn't be part of any kind of plot, because he couldn't keep it straight.

"Come on, Sergei, it's me, Mei. We met in Russia, remember? We need to get out of here." I use his grip on my wrist to pull him up and then out of the bed. He's not letting go, but he's not resisting my movement either. Luckily, he's dressed in a shirt and pants—I don't think I could get through dressing a crazy dragon.

He leaps up and starts making a squealing sound, like a baby pig being chased around a paddock. He runs around the room, leaping about as if he's trying out for the high jump team. I glance helplessly back at Liling and Zane. How the hell are we going to get him out of here?

Zane strides over. "Dragon," he says, one word with a depth of meaning. His eyes swirl with a dark magic I've never seen before.

Sergei stills. He turns and stares. "Who are you?" he whispers, his eyes locked onto Zane's.

"My name is Zane. You need to come with us."

Sergei watches Zane with wary eyes, but he calms down and walks to the door, waiting until the older dragon joins him there. His movements are slow, the opposite of the frenetic dance he was doing only moments before.

Frowning toward Zane and his dragon-whispering powers, I follow Sergei toward the exit. Liling brings up the rear.

Just as we're about to leave the room, Sergei bounces himself through the doorframe and yells, "Fooled you!" at the top of his voice. He runs down the hallway ahead of us, flinging his arms around as if he's trying to fly. Perhaps he is.

It would be funny if we weren't underneath Vincent's stronghold, with the potential to be caught at any moment.

The only thing that keeps me steady is the knowledge that Vincent isn't here. "Come on," I say, chasing after Sergei. Hopefully we can catch him before we run into anyone else down here. I take a running leap over the three guards who are still lying prone on the floor and hear Zane's footsteps behind me.

Sergei is fast, but he's not trying to outrun us, not really. He's off in his own world. I see him stop a couple of times and close his eyes as if he's concentrating, his hands clenched at his sides. At first I don't understand what he's doing and I slow down. And then it hits me. He's trying to transform back into his dragon self. In a tiny hallway at the bottom of a large complex that we need to sneak out of quietly.

"Hurry up! We need to get to him!" I whisper fiercely and take off again.

Zane swears under his breath, but runs after me. We catch up to Sergei before he finds the stairway up to the higher floors. I grab his arm, but Sergei slips out of my grip without much effort. He's wiry, rather than strong, but he also seems to be very good at evading capture. He stops again a little way off from me.

"How did they capture you?" I ask, trying to get him to stay in one place.

He shakes his head twice. "Wouldn't have gotten me. That stupid phoenix was looking in the wrong cave. But then they pulled out one of their machines. It turned me back into this weakling skin." He gestured down with disdain at his human body.

"How long has it been since you were in your human skin?" asks Zane.

"I'm in my skin now, aren't I?"

"But before that?"

"Not since I woke up from all the explosions. Heal faster in dragon form. Humans weak."

"Explosions?" asks Zane with raised eyebrows.

I shake my head. "We can talk about it later. Right now we need to get out of here. Sergei, listen to me. We're here to help you escape from the Earthbound. The bad men. You need to be quiet and you need to come with us."

Sergei shakes his head. "We can't escape. He said so. He's got the machine that keeps us human."

The fear rises through my stomach into my chest. "Was he expecting us to come and free you?"

"Oh no. No, no. Not that. He didn't think you'd care about me, not Sergei." Sergei shakes his head. "But he wants you. He has plans for you."

The words chill my blood. Vincent terrifies me as no one else does. He's tried to steal my magic on more than one occasion. And he has access to machines that can negate all the power of a dragon. The last time I saw him, he neutralized me and Tarsal with the flick of a switch.

And now he wants to do it again.

"Come on, let's go," says Liling as she races up behind us. "They will have heard all that noise. This is the least quiet stealth mission I've ever been on."

Sergei shakes his head. "I'm not going with you. He's gonna come after Mei. She's dangerous to be around."

"Sergei, just come with us while we escape from here. You can go wherever you like once we're safely back at our base." I'm begging, but I can't help it. Liling is right, we need to leave right now.

"It's not a request," says Zane, menace in his eyes.

Sergei backs away from him, but quietens down and meekly follows Liling up the stairs. We're about halfway up when the first set of guards emerges just ahead of us, guns at the ready.

I rush forward, pushing Liling out of the way. As Si always said, guns make people lazy.

The first of the guards is out for the count before he even sees me coming. I grab his gun, but instead of using its bullets, I use it as a club and whack the next guard on the back of his head in just the right spot. He collapses to the ground, half covering the first guard.

There are two more of them, and they both try to retreat through the door when they see what I've done with their buddies. One guy makes it back, just barely, but I manage to grab the front of the shirt of the other guard and pull him toward me. I use a hefty elbow strike to the side of his head to set his ears ringing and then follow it up with a knee to the stomach. He tries to grab me, but I'm too fast and step back, using a solid elbow to his back and then a none-too-gentle shove down the stairs. He tumbles, coming to a stop on the next landing down.

"I don't know why I ever thought you were harmless," says Zane.

I roll my eyes. "A girl's gotta know how to protect herself," I say sweetly.

I push Sergei up ahead of me, and he runs on, his eyes twitching. "He hates you, and I see why. You're too wily. You fight dirty. I can see why he doesn't like that," he mutters.

He's getting on my nerves with his talk of Vincent. "Just concentrate on putting one foot in front of the other, Sergei, and everything will work out fine."

"Unlikely. This is all bad."

"Shut up," says Zane sharply.

I jump at the force in his voice, but I can't help agreeing with the sentiment. I don't need Sergei feeding into my already large fear of Vincent.

We're silent for the next few flights of stairs, but we all know the next attack could come at any time.

They know we're here, and they're not going to give up easily.

19

My ears are pricked for the sound of running shoes or footsteps other than our own.

We're at the top of the stairwell, and I don't know what lies outside. Vincent's men could have anything there—one hundred guards or no guards. Just one machine or several machines. I literally have no clue what to expect, and my nerves are completely shot. Beside me, Sergei is humming some indecipherable tune. This rescue mission no longer seems like such a good idea.

"I'll open the door and check. Then we run. As fast as we can," says Zane.

I swallow and nod. My breath sticks in my throat as Zane opens the door, but he glances back at us and nods. "Come on. Coast is clear."

Frowning, I motion for Sergei to follow Zane and then make Liling go next. I take up the position at the back of our group. The hallway is indeed clear, and I don't understand it.

Something is wrong, and I'm worried we're going to find out what very soon. I peer around us like someone is going to leap out from behind the potted plants. It's a weird feeling to be so jittery.

My lips tighten and I force myself to chill the hell out.

Vincent has managed to get inside my head, and I'm sick of it. This kind of jumpy vigilance can be just as dangerous as not being sufficiently alert. I roll my shoulders and concentrate on what we're doing. Up ahead, Sergei is muttering to himself, and Zane is carefully retracing our footsteps from earlier.

"Wait." Liling holds up a hand. "I think we should go out another way," she says.

"Why?" whispers Zane.

She gestures out a high window up ahead. "They're waiting for us out there. I'm sure of it."

She's a powerful supernatural and a very smart operator, but she shouldn't be able to tell stuff like that ahead of a dragon. "What are you talking about?"

"I can feel them. Outside, amassing like they're ants in their hive. Can't you feel it?"

I shake my head, and the other two stare at her like I am. Dragons have the superior senses. We should all feel what she's feeling if it's real. I head over to the window, set high in the wall. "Give me a lift up?" I gesture to Zane, the strongest of us.

He pushes me up and I peer around the edge of the window. The breath stops in my throat as I look out over the grassy lawn. It's covered with guards, all dressed in the same black uniform. "She's right." Then I spot them. Not just Vincent's guards, but others, from different organizations. "They're here. They're *all* fucking here."

Zane lets me down. "Who are here?"

"Other leaders. Pro-webbers." I hesitate. "Seth."

"And they're all outside waiting for us?"

I nod.

"This was all a plot to capture us?" Zane's voice is hard.

I hope not. I glance at Sergei, but he's inspecting a nearby potted plant. "They couldn't know I would feel responsible for Sergei. Seth wouldn't know that. Unless he remembers more than he's letting on."

My heart skips a beat. He remembered where to find Sergei in the first place. He could have remembered other things. Seth had always seen inside me, known more about me than anyone else.

Had he known I'd come for Sergei? Had he set me up? For a moment, it feels like I'm suffocating and a buzzing fills my head. It's so much like the machine that disabled Tarsal and me last time, I start shaking.

Zane grabs me and shakes my arms. "Mei! Sort your shit out."

It's his hands on my arms that force me out of my downward spiral, more than his words. He's right. And looking at Zane and Sergei, neither of them is being affected the same way.

"They have a machine that can disable dragons. We need to get rid of it, destroy it before we can go out there."

Liling steps forward. "Find me a gun big enough, and I can shoot it out."

"We need to get to the roof. Higher ground."

"Won't they expect that?" asks Zane.

"They're all out on the sodding lawn. I don't know if there's anyone on the roof, but if there are, it will be fewer than the numbers out there." I gesture through the window that we're still standing under.

Zane shakes his head grimly. "They should expect us to leave from the roof. We're dragons."

"But they're not used to dragons. I've always come

through the doors whenever I've been here before. Most other supers don't fly. I'm hoping they've not thought it through properly."

"And if they have?"

"We'll cross that bridge when we come to it." I don't know how we've ended up in this position. Why are they all out there? There are too many missing pieces to this puzzle, I can't begin to figure it out.

Liling leads us back the way we came, taking us down another hallway and into a stairwell. It's empty, but now it feels eerily so. I should have realized earlier that we hadn't met up with enough opposition. Of course there would be more people guarding Sergei.

They know we're here, have known the entire time we've been inside. They've gathered outside, waiting to catch us like tadpoles in a net. We run up the stairs, and I try not to think of all the possibilities for why they've emptied the building. I just concentrate on putting one foot in front of the other, on getting ourselves to where we have to go.

We're almost at the top when I hear a strange noise. A rhythmic banging that seems to echo around the building. I glance up at Liling, but she shakes her head.

"I don't know what it is," she says. "But we need to get out of here. Something bad is happening."

We double our efforts and reach the door to the roof not long after.

"They're closing it up," says Zane suddenly from behind me.

"What?"

"It's a lockdown. Those banging noises. They're closing up the building. Open that damn door."

Liling reaches out to turn the handle just as metal shutters come down over the window next to us. I surge forward with all my speed and strength and push open the door, propelling Liling and Sergei ahead of me. We fall into the daylight of the rooftop, and I scrape the skin off my elbows as we land clumsily on the concrete.

Behind us the metal door slams shut over the doorway. I turn.

Zane's not behind us. He's inside, behind the metal barrier.

I glance up. An array of almost a dozen guards are standing there, holding machine guns directed at us.

20

I let out a breath. I've been in situations with worse odds and survived.

"Who's in charge?" I ask politely.

"Shut up. Prisoners are not allowed to speak," says a mean-looking guy to one side.

"Are we allowed to untangle ourselves?" I ask, not without a hint of snark.

"You will all move slowly and carefully into a sitting position."

I move like he asks, not because it's an order, but because it will be easier to take them out if I'm in an upright position. "Everyone okay?" I whisper as we move.

Liling nods, and Sergei looks at me with his swirling eyes. He seems less twitchy now that we're out in the open.

"Don't change until I tell you to," I whisper to him.

He blinks and nods slowly, but I don't trust him to follow my orders.

"What now?" I ask the guard closest to me. I'm not entirely certain the mean-looking dude is actually in charge.

"No talking! Just sit still."

I notice that several of the guards seem to have sweat dripping down the side of their faces, and they're looking nervously around them. I grin. They're freaking terrified of this mission.

"I could burn you all to a crisp," I say conversationally.

The guy closest to me flinches.

"Not for long, dragon. You'll regret ever turning up here soon enough."

I twist my head back to the mean-looking dude who spoke. "Oh, so there's a time limit? Then I better act fast, huh?"

"As soon as the machine arrives, you're toast."

In that moment, I change. It's faster than it's ever been; I don't linger in the moment or assess how the magic works. I just turn, concentrating on eliminating the threat as fast as possible.

Beside me I feel Sergei doing the same, except his change is far more painful, electrical sparks giving off unpleasant fumes and making my scales shudder.

But I can't concentrate on Sergei. For the moment, I have other things to focus on. Keeping us all alive for one. The guards closest to me have backed up, and none of them are firing. They must have been told not to—Vincent wants us alive. At least me alive. I glance back at Liling, but she's okay. She's not turned, but her change is faster and easier than mine.

I send a hot burst of flame toward the feet of the guards, and they all back up. My inability to speak to humans when I'm in dragon form continues to frustrate me. I want to ask them how to open the door to get Zane out. I want to make sure he's okay.

Instead I breathe fire at the guards, singeing the hair on their hands and head. They continue to back up.

Someone yells, "Fire!" and several of them start shooting at us. I let out a roar and stand up to my full height. The bullets bounce off my scales, and I snarl, showing off my large dragon teeth. I leap forward, and my dragon self just wants to push these attackers off the roof. Quick and simple, no further bother.

I manage to stop myself and simply push them all into a corner of the roof.

Behind me, I hear Liling's voice. "Throw your weapons over the side of the roof, or she'll make you jump. They're no use against a dragon anyway." I give a toothy snarl, pleased that Liling is still in human form and able to speak for me.

Several of the guards drop their machine guns over the edge with no hesitation. Mean-looking dude is one of the reluctant ones. I send a burst of flames his way and he hurries to comply.

"You're not going to get away with this, dragon. Your time will come," he says.

"Just do what you're told," says Liling. "Get down on your knees and put your hands behind your heads."

They all reluctantly comply. I'm pretty sure they're going to be in trouble with Vincent for letting us do this. Although I can't understand why they came so ill-prepared to this fight. The thought chills me. Maybe they didn't. Maybe this is some kind of diversion?

Looking around, I spot Sergei crouched near one edge of the building. *You okay?*

He nods, rather than answering. Nearby, Liling picks up a machine gun and hefts it to the side of the building. She looks through the sight, checking for the machine that disables dragons.

Behind me, I hear thumping coming from inside the building. Zane. *Can you watch the guards for me? I need to get Zane out of there,* I say to Sergei.

I stride back over to the door and scratch at the metal, but it doesn't bend or even mark. I breathe fire over it, and when the smoke clears, there's nothing to show that I've even attacked it at all. Behind me, I hear the sound of a machine gun being fired. I turn to see Liling firing at something below. Fingers crossed it's the machine.

I'm about to start clawing at the door again when the roof of the building starts to buckle and bend behind the door. Rocks fall over the edge, and an explosive crash rents the air.

Black dragon scales emerge from the wreckage as Zane pushes his way through the roof. He lifts his wings up and out, and with one great burst, joins us on the rooftop.

His dragon eyes are sparking with anger, and I'm sure he's been attacking that door on the other side the same way I have.

You okay? I ask hesitantly. He looks anything but.

I'm fine. But we need to get the hell out of here. They were pumping some kind of gas into the building. I'm lucky we don't need to breathe as much as humans.

Let's go. We've got what we came for.

Behind me, I hear a dragon roar and the whooshing sound of dragon flames. I crane my neck around, hoping it's not what I think it is.

Sergei is standing on his hind legs, his beautiful dragon form blowing a blast of flames toward the guards. But unlike my flames that fell short of the men, Sergei's dragon flames go right to the center of the group, burning them instantly into ashes.

No, Sergei! Stop!

They were trying to attack. Sergei's voice is filled with such glee that I find his assertion hard to believe.

Zane shakes his head at me. *You're too attached to the humans. He's only doing what's necessary to protect us all. What would we do with them? They would attack us as soon as we took our eyes off them. Why shouldn't we do the same?*

It's not necessary to kill them all! They're only doing their jobs.

They chose to work for someone like Vincent. They know his morals and what he stands for.

But... I look over to where the ashes of all ten men are now drifting over the edge of the building and into the air. *It didn't have to be that way.*

It is always that way between dragons and humans. It has always been and will always be. Zane's voice is a knife that strikes deep into my heart.

Nothing I ever do will change the fact that I'm a dragon. The same as these two men beside me. Destructive and violent, unable to curb their tendencies toward death and destruction.

Liling stands to one side, watching Sergei impassively. I let out a small noise, and she turns her gaze toward me.

"I destroyed the machine," she says quietly. "We can go." Her face reflects what I'm feeling. But there's no room for regret, not until we're safely out of here.

I gesture with my nose that she should get onto my back. She nods, and moments later is sitting astride the ridges, ready to leap into the air with me. I can't look at Sergei; his brilliant white shape is beautiful in the way that broken glass is beautiful—sharp and painful to anyone who touches it.

Zane leaps into the sky ahead of us. Sergei motions for me to go next, and I have my hind legs flexed and ready to leap when a bird screeches overhead. Looking up, I see a firebird swooping in toward me.

Seth.

He lands just inches from me, his flaming body magnificent in the afternoon sun. I stand my ground, unwilling to give him anything. Liling is on my back, and I'm putting her in danger by remaining like this, but I can't help myself.

What are you doing here? he asks.

What do you care?

His eyes glow red. *You're making a big mistake. Vincent was happy to have Sergei. Now you're just pissing him off.*

Were you expecting us? Did you plan this? The words tumble out, unbidden.

He screeches and unfurls his wings wide. *Vincent planned a summit for his allies. Finding you here was a bonus for him.* He screeches again. *I can't believe you came for the crazy dragon.*

The old Seth would have known I would come. *It's not okay for him to experiment on dragons. Get that through your thick skull.*

Seth's fiery body burns brighter for a moment. *Better him than you.*

Better no one at all. I poke my face directly in front of his. *When did it become okay in your books to attack innocent people?* Even as I say the words, my eyes flick to the ashes of the guards. I know what Seth's going to say before he says it.

Did those guards deserve to die?

I can't argue that point. I wish Sergei hadn't killed those men. It makes it harder to think of him as the innocent party.

Sergei doesn't think like everyone else. And they had him

trapped here. *It doesn't make it right to kill those people, but it's not like they didn't provoke him.*

Well, now you've provoked Vincent. And me.

Seth rears up onto his back legs, his wings stretching out. Flames blaze from his whole body, and for a moment I'm transfixed.

And then dragon fire hits him from above and I scream.

21

J ust above Seth, Zane and Sergei have positioned themselves on either side of him. They're blasting enough dragon fire to kill an entire army.

Hurry, Mei. With your added flames, we can destroy him. Zane speaks directly into my head.

Stop! Stop it now!

No matter that Seth is now my enemy, that he would be happy to see me dead, I can't let them kill him. Especially not while I'm standing here watching. I leap forward, pushing out with my magic, desperate to protect him from the heat of the flames. I shove him to one side, a move that was obviously so unexpected, he tumbles easily to the ground. He growls up at me, and I immediately understand my intervention doesn't matter. Seth's body is absorbing the flames like it's water and he's a sponge.

He laughs and turns around to taunt them. *I'm a firebird, you idiot dragons. Did you think I would crumble under your flames?*

My relief is immense. And then I remember Liling on my back. I turn to make sure she's okay—and discover there's some kind of shield around both of us, a glowing layer of protection that's keeping her away from the flames. She's barely holding on to my back, but the heat of the flames didn't even singe her. I let out my breath in a whoosh of relief and the magic around us dies down. I know where it came from; I can feel the extra souls inside me, pushing out their magic.

Thank you, I whisper for their benefit only. Tarsal is still protecting me, even though he thinks I'm nuts for being here. Given what's just happened, he's probably right.

Get out of there. Now.

Tarsal's voice is urgent, and without thinking about it too much, I back away from Seth and leap into the sky.

Tarsal's right. We have to get away from here as fast as we can. Away from Seth who doesn't love me anymore. Away from Vincent who wants to steal my magic. Away from these people who think I did the worst thing in the world when I broke the spell web and stopped Vincent from killing us all.

I'm up high in the air when I notice Zane and Sergei haven't followed. I turn and look back, beating my wings against the air currents to stay in one place. Below me I see flashes of fire—Zane and Sergei are flaming the compound and all the soldiers within it.

I roar with rage. This isn't how it was supposed to go. We're supposed to be finding a way to work together to find a solution where dragons and humans can live together. Killing everyone in sight isn't a solution.

My wings beat hard, and I streak back down to where Zane and Sergei are shooting flames at any movement they see.

Stop it! Stop it! I scream at them, hopefully making the

words echo around in their thick sculls. *This isn't our mission. They aren't the ones making the decisions!*

Leave now if you can't handle it. Zane's voice is heavy with scorn.

You're sabotaging our whole plan. This will be on the nine o'clock news, two dragons firebombing innocent civilians.

But they're not innocent and they're not civilians.

It won't matter! That's how it will be portrayed. They'll probably say I was behind it all, as well. This doesn't help us. You're only making it worse.

Sergei seems to be arrested by my impassioned pleas, but Zane ignores me.

I'll tell my father you disobeyed a direct order.

You're forgetting this whole mission is against a direct order.

He'll be pissed off that you're destroying our chances like this.

Zane shakes his head and turns his long neck in my direction. *He knows about it. He and the whole council approved this raid and this firebombing. They wanted to send a message to the pro-webber factions that we mean business and we're not going to stand by if they capture dragons.*

I'm trying to take in this information when a flash of silver way down below catches my eyes. My dragon eyesight is better than my human sight, and what I see chills me to the bone. *They've got another machine. Like the one that disabled Tarsal. We need to get out of here now! Before they turn it on.*

I fly higher, my fear overcoming any further attempts to save either Zane or Sergei, or even the guards down below. My wings beat up and down, and I don't look back.

I don't know if Zane and Sergei are following, but I have Liling on my back, and I'm not going to risk her life as well as my own.

So much for my rescue attempt. All I managed to do was

get more people killed. Watching as Zane and Sergei flamed the humans has given me an insight into what it was like three hundred years ago. Perhaps the spell web really *is* necessary? Dragons like Zane and Sergei can't be trusted to do the right thing.

I'm used to the absence of the spell web now. I still miss the extra senses it gave me, but I agree with my father's assertion that the Earthbound shouldn't be allowed to take the magic of supernaturals and do whatever they like with it. I had even been thinking there might have been a chance that we could work with the humans and come to some kind of arrangement.

But watching the two dragons burn the people in the compound makes me think twice. Knowing my father sanctioned it only makes it worse.

It makes me doubt everything he's been saying, all his lofty ideals, everything he believes. What makes my father believe that it's okay to do this?

And why are the dragons doing it with so little hesitation?

Zane and Sergei catch up to me in no time at all, and I hope that means they didn't waste any more time trying to flame the rest of Vincent's guards. The shape of the Earthbound machine is burned into my memory, as well as the acidic taste it left in my mouth last time it was used on me.

And Tarsal. I mustn't forget Tarsal.

Exactly, he says in my head, right on cue.

I glance over to where Sergei is flying alongside me. Was Sergei worth all this? Should I really have convinced the others to come with me?

But I shake my head. It's about more than Sergei as a person, or his dubious moral compass. It's about what's right and wrong, how people should be treated, even if they *are* dragons. No one deserves to be a test subject for someone like Vincent.

Even if they're a little hazy with their own set of principles.

Almost two hours later, we're nearing our home base in the mountains. I'm exhausted; from the painful thoughts whirling around inside my head, but also the confrontation and then flying all the way home again.

I wish I could go back in time, and tell myself not to go. At least it would ease the heartache currently burning a hole inside my chest. I turn in slow circles down toward the mountain landing site. It's a huge outcrop of rocks that leads to a shelter where we can change back to our human shapes before heading down into the bowels of the rocky hillside. This place is an old Mountain super stronghold, long since abandoned for nicer digs.

Carrick found it for us, before just as quickly disappearing back to his people. I wish he was here right now. I feel the sting of homesickness for Si and Jeff, even for Carrick—people I trust, who wouldn't start acting like homicidal maniacs the minute they don't get their way.

The main difference between the two people I'm with right now and the people who raised me?

They're not dragons.

I want to believe I can claim my own destiny; that I don't have to follow the violent, instinctual habits of a species. But being around other dragons has made me think that one day, that's just what I'm going to do. For all my morals and particular beliefs, one day the fact that I'm a dragon will overwhelm me and it will no longer be about me, Mei Walker.

It will be about me, a dragon.

I land and put out my leg so Liling can climb down. I

want to get away before Zane and Sergei arrive. The transition to human form hits me hard, and the pain twists through me before my body comes back into place. I grab the T-shirt and jeans I left there earlier and move toward the door.

"How did it go?" asks a voice from the shadows. I jump, my heart leaping into my throat.

My father.

"Did you really give him permission? To burn them all?" The words are out of my mouth before I can think about it.

My father looks at me, his eyes shadowed. "We had to show the world we mean business. We need to show leadership and strength."

"By killing innocent victims?"

"They're not innocent. They work for Vincent. They understand what he does."

"It wasn't just Vincent's people. There were other groups there. And you don't know those people. They have families, kids, just like you do. That's no way to start a dialogue, to create a world we can live in peacefully." The words spill out of me, like a tap that won't turn off.

"We can't just hide here and wait for him to find us, Mei. We have to take action." He runs an impatient hand through his short hair, and for the first time I notice his blood shot eyes and the stubble on my father's usually clean-cut chin. My suave and charismatic father looks like the strain of leadership is getting to him.

It doesn't matter. I'm not going to let him get away with killing innocent people. "You're all talk. You don't really mean any of the words you spout so easily," I snarl at him. I'm so angry, it feels like I'm about to change back into my dragon form.

"I mean everything I say. And the time has come for us

to stand up for what we believe in. We can't try to be friends to everyone anymore. We have to pick our side and stick with it."

"What's our side?"

"Everyone who believes, like us, that the spell web was crippling the supernatural world."

"What about the people who don't believe that?"

My father's eyes flicker, and he hesitates. Then he shrugs. "They might just get caught in the crossfire."

22

"Am I being naive like he says?" I ask Liling. We're in the training room, boxing gloves on, trying to spar. I'm too agitated to concentrate, and Liling, who normally takes a pummeling from me, is actually getting some decent punches in.

"Probably."

I lower my guard, and she lands a punch to the side of my face. We're wearing gloves, but it still hurts.

"I thought you were good at this?" she says with a grin. I think she's getting me back for the rough journey I took her on at Vincent's compound. She's still a little singed around the edges.

But maybe not. Maybe she's just getting almost as good as Jeff at getting under my skin.

I raise my hands again and force myself to concentrate. It's been a day since we returned from our raid. Sergei is still with us, but he's causing enough trouble that the leaders of the group are giving me sideways glares.

I would feel guilty, except that they approved Zane's plan

with the proviso he destroy as much of the compound—
including the people—as he could.

It's not even the deaths of Vincent's guards that I'm most
upset about. Or even how this whole situation has the
potential to set our cause back. It's that Zane went behind
my back and schemed with the others without telling me.
Like I'm a kid they can't trust.

To be fair, I *did* go on the raid without telling the SAW
leaders. That's probably not in my favor. But Zane could
have told me that he'd gone to them. He kept it secret from
me and that pisses me off.

I growl under my breath, and kick out with my left leg. I
land a sidekick and then a stomach punch on Liling. She's
tougher now than when I first met her—mainly because I've
been using her as a sparring partner ever since we arrived at
the mountain hideaway.

She's used to getting hit, and even manages to get in a
few good ones when I'm not paying attention.

Like now.

She lands a punch to the side of my face and then a
second punch to my stomach as I try to deal with the
ringing in my brain. The look of triumph on her face—
mixed with a little bit of trepidation—makes it worth the
pain.

I'm dancing around, trying to buy myself recovery time,
when the door to the gym opens and a pale wisp of a man
enters.

Sergei.

He's twitchy and nervous, glancing around the room as
if he's expecting someone to leap out at him any minute. I
glance at Liling, but she's already moving toward him. I'm
not going to forgive him so easily.

"Hey Sergei," she says softly.

Trust Liling to want to talk to the crazy dragon. She probably thinks she can fix him, too.

"You were fighting? I heard you," he says.

Liling nods. "We were practicing. For when we fight someone for real."

"There's no point practicing. They're going to get us all." He says it with certainty and in the kind of voice a fortune teller might use.

It sends goose bumps along my arms, even though I don't believe him. I frown and try to shake them off.

"What makes you so sure?" I say. As soon as the words are out of my mouth, I wish I hadn't spoken. It gives credibility to his statement, like I'm actually considering it.

Sergei moves forward carefully. Most of the spaces in our stronghold won't fit full-size dragons, so he has to stay in human form. He's still getting used to it. "They won last time, and there were many more dragons to fight back then. Now we are so few. And most of us are old and scared, like me." Sergei shrugs. "We can't win."

"It's not just the dragons fighting against them this time."

"No one but a dragon can fix this," he replies, his eyes steady on my face.

"What do you mean?"

"Vincent needs a dragon to restart the spell web. He's found the instructions."

"And?"

"He spent a bit of time with me, running tests." A twitch appears below Sergei's left eye. "He talked as he worked."

Liling makes a choking noise. The subtext is clear: Vincent chatted as he tortured Sergei.

I try to ignore what he's not saying and concentrate on his words. "What about?" My heart beats faster in my chest.

I don't want to hear what he's going to say. It's going to be bad.

Sergei swings his arm wide, almost knocking himself off balance. "Everything. What he wants to achieve. Why he's doing what he's doing." He pauses, visibly swallowing. "How he's going to make it happen."

It's like fireworks going off in my head. "He told you his plans?"

Sergei shrugs. "He didn't think I would survive very long, and it didn't seem likely that anyone would bother to rescue me."

"But you survived," says Liling softly. "You *were* rescued."

He glances at her, his eyes swirling. "He didn't take into account my heritage, or my time on the island."

"You're stronger than he realized," says Liling, nodding.

Sergei shakes his head. "I'm not strong. It's driven me crazy, I know that."

Strangely, Sergei seems the sanest I've ever known him to be. "You need to tell us everything," I say.

"The only thing I need to tell you is that he's going to win. He's going to beat us all."

I shake my head, frustrated by his pessimistic attitude. "There's always a way. Who'd have thought I could get to twenty years of age without knowing I was a dragon? Who'd have thought we could rescue you?"

Sergei glances my way, a sly look on his face. "You and the firebird don't see eye to eye any more."

"Vincent killed him."

"Ah, he moved on to his next life? That explains it."

"What?"

"It's a tough process, restarting a life. They lose their memories, at least at first."

I go completely still. "He could get his memories back?"

"Over time. He knew where to find me. He was the one who told Vincent."

For the first time, hope crawls into my heart. "So he might remember about me. About us?"

Sergei shrugs. "He'll remember eventually, but he's already been through much in this new life. It might never go back to how it was."

"But it could." I glance at Liling.

"Perhaps," she says.

I shake my head to clear it, reminding myself that I have more important things to worry about. "I'm more concerned about why you think Vincent is going to win."

"The machines," says Sergei simply.

"Did he test them on you?" I still wake in the night with nightmares about the machine he used on Tarsal and me.

Sergei nods. "He wanted to test them. He said you'd destroyed his other one." Sergei stares at me as if he's trying to understand me. "He hates you. He thinks he's going to be able to use you to restart the web, but he hates you so badly, I think he's more likely to just kill you."

I blink. My feelings toward Vincent are equally strong. But it's fear I feel when I think of him. The thought of being in his power again is more than I can bear. "Why does he hate me so much?"

Liling raises an eyebrow. "You really have to ask that question?"

"He started it. He killed Tarsal and Seth. I was just reacting."

"As if that matters."

Sergei takes a step toward the seats in the corner of the gym. He trips over his own feet, and it's only a quick move from Liling that saves him from falling flat on his face.

"Thank you. This form is unnatural to me now. It feels like my mind has been put into the wrong body," he says.

"You can change back, if you want. There's space in the higher chambers," says Liling.

Sergei shakes his head. "It's good for me to stay like this. I can feel my mind settling down the longer I'm in this body."

"So we need to change back to human to stay..." I struggle for a word that doesn't imply he's crazy.

"Sane?" He looks at me, his eyes showing his pain. "Yes, it helps keep the equilibrium. Most dragons prefer their dragon form, but changing back into our human form is important. Except during hibernation. Dragon is the only form to use for hibernation."

"What's Vincent planning, Sergei?" says Liling, interrupting the question I was going to ask about hibernation.

Sergei takes a seat and gestures for us to join him. "He's going to restart the spell web with not one, but two dragons. He's going to steal their magic. He plans to make them into shadow dragons."

A chill forms along my skin. I remember what a shadow dragon is, Tarsal talked about it. He also tried to turn me *into* a shadow dragon by stealing my magic so he could go back into hibernation.

"What's a shadow dragon?" asks Liling, oblivious to my reaction.

"Dragons who've had their magic stolen from them," says Sergei in a whisper. "They remember being dragons, the feeling of flight, but they cannot change from their human form. In the same way that it's wrong to stay in dragon form too long, it's also bad to stay in human form. So they all eventually go crazy."

"Why are you so certain he's going to win?"

"His machines," says Sergei simply. "And now that he's tested them on me..."

"He knows how they all work," I say.

Sergei nods. "Every single one of them worked. Without fail. We have no defenses against that kind of thing."

"What happens if he uses the magic of two dragons to restart the spell web?"

"He's found an ancient spell, something in one of his oldest books. He knows how to change the spell web from its original form. Not only is he going to make it more powerful, so half of our magic is being stolen from us, he's also going to make it so that humans can see supernaturals. There will be no hiding this time around."

"But... that's the only reason groups like Seth's are working with him," I say, stunned.

"That's why he's not telling anyone, especially the supers who are supporting him."

It occurs to me to wonder why he told Sergei. Is this some kind of elaborate trick? But I look into Sergei's face and know he's telling the truth, at least as he understands it.

"We have to tell the other supernatural groups," says Liling. "No one would support him if they knew what he's doing."

I nod, and we both stand. "Thanks, Sergei. You might have just turned the tide on this thing."

He shrugs. "I doubt it."

23

"I'm going to visit the Boston Brutes with Zane. I need you to take Liling to see the Mountain supers." My father stands at the door, putting on his coat. Zane has already gone to change into his dragon form. He's staying out of my way; he knows how pissed I am at him.

"You're not seriously trying to get the Brutes onside?" I say, incredulous.

He shrugs. "The more people we can get against Vincent the better."

"The Mountain supers hate me." It used to be that the dragons and the Mountain supers were intimately connected. They kept the dragons' secrets and looked after their young. But in the three hundred years since the disappearance of the dragons, the Mountain supers have had to fend for themselves, and they've ended up relying on the invisibility of the spell web to survive. And I'm the one who took it from them.

"That's why you're not doing any of the talking, and if you can manage to stay outside without offending them, do it."

"They're supposed to love me," I mutter.

"They'll get over it eventually," he says. "But for now, stay out of the way."

I try to bury the resentment that's boiling in my chest, but it's hard. My father is pretending nothing has happened, that his orders against Vincent's compound don't mean anything. "I'm a glorified donkey," I say.

"Just keep out of trouble," he says as he strides out the door.

When I find Liling, she's in her room, packing a few items into her travel bag.

"How long are we staying?" I ask, eyeing the clothes she's packing.

"This is just in case," she says, blushing. "Nevan might be there. He said we could stay at his house when we visit."

Carrick and his brother Nevan visited our stronghold just after Seth's... fake death. Liling and Nevan hit it off and have been writing and calling each other ever since.

"I'm not staying in a love nest built for two," I say, making a face at her.

"You could stay at Carrick's place."

I make a face. "They all hate me. You remember that, right?"

"Not Carrick. And Nevan says they'll get over it once they realize they can live without the spell web."

"Mountain supernaturals seem to hold a grudge." I'm thinking of the old Mountain super I took with me to Tarsal's burial. Carrick and Nevan's grandfather. He didn't seem the forgiving and forgetting type.

"Once they learn what Vincent is doing, they won't support him anymore."

I nod, but I'm not convinced. The Mountain supers don't

do things fast. I doubt they'll suddenly change their mind about me. Or the spell web.

It doesn't take Liling long to finish her packing, and I begrudgingly add a couple of items to her bag, so I'm prepared to stay as well.

I've got a pretty thick skin, both literally as a dragon and figuratively because of the training Jeff and Si drummed into me. But the idea of heading into an environment where everyone hates me makes me cranky. Should I wait outside in my dragon form? Or change into my human form so I appear less threatening? Should I be guarding Liling? Or is my presence there just going to make her job harder?

My thoughts rattle around in my head, and I still haven't figured out what I should do when I land on the rocky outcrop next to a lesser-known entrance to the main Mountain super stronghold.

Guards stand to attention at the door, their long poles crossed and their swords at their sides. Their eyes are hard, and they stare at me like I've come to steal their children.

"We're expected," says Liling, smiling as she climbs down off my back. "Please inform Elder Rasmussen that we're here." Her tone is perfect, and she's radiating calm and serenity. "Change to human form, Mei," she whispers under her breath.

I glance around and see an area nearby suited to that very purpose, hidden behind rocks so I don't have to be naked in front of the guards. I grab the bag and put one strap between my teeth before hopping through the air to the changing room.

When I come back, wearing the black pants and T-shirt Liling was carrying for me, nothing has changed.

"They're making us wait?" I say to Liling, loud enough for the guards to hear.

She glares at me. "The elders are busy people."

"They're expecting us. My father contacted them. They're just playing games."

Liling decides the best way to shut me down is to not reply, so she turns her back on me and smiles at the guards.

We're there for another thirty minutes before someone opens the door.

It's the smallest Mountain super I've ever seen. As a race, they're generally massive. Carrick is a good example. His broad shoulders and muscled chest are matched by long, thick legs like tree trunks that could carry a dragon. Probably.

This guy in front of us doesn't look like he could carry a notebook, let alone anything heavier. "Welcome to Bedrock, our stronghold," he says with a nod of his head. "Please follow me."

"I think we're being insulted," I whisper to Liling.

"Just keep quiet. Your tongue is going to get us into trouble."

"I'm not saying anything you're not thinking," I say grimly.

She glares at me.

We follow the tiny Mountain super along corridors dug out of rock. I feel a vibration, a humming sound coming from the walls themselves. It's the first time I've been inside a working Mountain super stronghold. I can see why they love it so much.

Our guide keeps darting ahead, like he's trying to lose us in the maze of corridors, but we stay behind him without problem.

"Elder Rasmussen is behind this door," he says with a bow as we come to a large set of double doors made out of enormous slabs of wood crossed with iron. It looks like the kind of door that's been there a very long time.

"Thank you for showing us the way," says Liling with a sweet smile.

The little man glances to one side then the other, as if he's embarrassed. "It's nothing," he says, before scampering off.

We turn to look at the door. "Is this a knocking type situation?" I ask. "Or do we just push it open?"

Liling smiles over at me, showing her perfect teeth in genuine amusement. "I have no idea."

I move forward, sniffing at the door, trying to figure out how it opens. My sense of smell in human form isn't as strong, so I'm not sure why I'm bothering. Except that you never know.

"I'm going to knock," says Liling, lifting one hand.

Just as she's about to bring her knuckles down on the hard wood, the doors start shifting inward. A gap in the middle slowly emerges, and we stand in front of it, waiting to see what it reveals.

The room is a cavern, with high ceilings and a large empty space through the middle. It's filled with Mountain supers along the sides, near the walls. At the far end, a raised dais holds a large chair and an even larger Mountain super is sitting in it.

Two guards directly on the other side of the door glare at us. One indicates that we should move forward.

I glance at Liling, and we both move at the same time, our steps matching. We walk slowly and precisely through the middle of the room toward the dais at the end.

As we pass, conversations on either side of the room stop, until everyone is staring at us. It's not a friendly or even simply an interested gaze. I can feel the animosity in this room like a living, breathing presence.

My hands clench and I wish I brought more weapons with me. In fact, any weapon would do. I glance around. There are probably a hundred or more Mountain supers in this room with us. I don't think I can take them all on, if it comes to that.

Where are Carrick and Nevan?

There are no windows or other exits around the room, and my arms start to itch. This whole thing is beginning to feel like a really bad idea.

"Calm down," Liling whispers to me. "You're so agitated, you're practically glowing."

"Can't you feel the anger in this room?"

Liling touches my arm. "They've let us in here, which means we'll have the chance to talk, to try and convince them about Vincent. This kind of thing takes time," she says.

I nod, trying to convince myself I believe what she's saying.

By the time we get to Elder Rasmussen, the entire room is silent. I'm itching to leap back into the middle of the room and change to dragon. Nothing about this situation feels right.

I really hope Liling knows what she's doing.

The elder remains seated, and I know from Carrick that this is another insult. His large arms rest along the arms of the chair, and he's got at least three visible knives on his person. They could be ceremonial... but I don't think so.

His eyes are dark, and his face craggy, like most of his people. His lips are tightly compressed, but I think I can see a sneer trying to escape from his stern expression.

"You dare to come here, dragon? To our innermost sanctum?"

His words are directed at me, pure venom in every syllable. I look at Liling. She's right, I'm not the diplomat.

"We come to you with important information. Damien asked you to see us personally, because he felt we needed to discuss it with you," she says.

"When we agreed to speak to someone from Damien Walker's group, we did not expect him to insult us by sending *her*."

"Mei wants peace as much as we all do."

Rasmussen pushes himself to his feet in a rush. "You say she wants peace, but her actions show otherwise."

A new figure emerges from the shadows. "The elder's youngest daughter was... murdered... by humans recently," he says, his strange, gravelly voice filling the otherwise silent room. He's dressed in black from head to toe. Even his hair is black, and his eyes seem to reflect the deepest darkest black hole.

"I'm sorry for your loss," I say. Every alarm bell in my head is ringing. I don't know who this new guy is, but he's not here for peace talks.

He's not here to talk about cooperation between our two groups or to figure out the best way to move on in peace.

He doesn't care that Vincent is planning to screw us all over.

"You should be sorry. Because it has been decided that her death should be laid directly at your door." He pauses and stares directly down at me, his black eyes swirling with magic. "You are hereby sentenced to death."

Before I can even think or move, the man in black raises his hand. There's something silver clenched in his fist. I vaguely realize it's a gun.

Everything happens so fast, I can't think, I can't act. Something is wrong with me. My usual reflexes have been blocked. The man in black is holding me in one place using some kind of magic.

But Liling doesn't have that problem. Just as the explosive retort of the gun goes off, she leaps in front of me, protecting me. I see her determined expression, and her eyes meet mine as the bullet hits her body.

"No!" I yell, trying to stop her. My body is stuck, motionless.

As I watch, Liling collapses to the floor in front of me, blood already covering her chest and the floor around us.

24

"No! No, Liling!" Whatever was holding me lets go, and I scramble to the floor next to Liling, gathering her against me. I try to stem the blood, but there's too much.

"Mei," she whispers. She's not dead. Thank goodness. I can still undo this.

I ignore everything else going on around me. There's fighting and yelling, but I don't care about any of it.

The only person I can see is Liling. Her beautiful face, her lips fighting for breath.

I try to use healing magic, but I can't get it to work. No matter how hard I push my magic, I can't access it. I can't feel Tarsal or my mother's soul, even though the ring is in its usual place on my finger. There's definitely something wrong with me, some kind of magic that's preventing me from helping her. Tears drip down my face.

I'm not going to let this happen. "It's going to be okay, Liling. I'll get you out of here. I'll get you home."

She shakes her head, her eyes glazing over. "No, Mei. I can feel... Promise me..."

I lean in closer. "Promise what?"

"Make my death worth something... Do something important."

I want to shake her and hug her at the same time. "You shouldn't have done that. You're the one with the goodness, the morals. You should have let him shoot me," I whisper.

Liling closes her eyes. "I love you, Mei," she murmurs. Her breath goes out... and doesn't come back in again.

"No! Liling, hold on. I'll find someone," I say, glancing around me for the first time.

It's chaos.

The cavernous room is filled with fighting Mountain supers. Weapons clash, shouts ring out through the struggling mass of bodies. I search for someone I know, but even Elder Rasmussen and his man in black have disappeared.

"Come with me, Mei," says a hard voice behind me.

Carrick. He's standing right in front of me, blocking me from the overwhelming mass of people.

"Oh thank God. Carrick, we have to find a healer. Someone who can help Liling." My words are scrambled, and I can barely see him through the tears. But I know he'll make everything better.

He glances down at Liling and doesn't say a word. He just gently pulls her out of my arms and into his. "Come with me, Mei," he says again.

I follow his massive form without hesitation. He'll find a way to save Liling. He has to. That's the kind of thing Carrick's good at. He leads a path through the fighting, and they part for him, almost like they can't help it. For the first time, I wonder where Carrick sits in the Mountain super hierarchy. I've never seen him here, only in places outside. Right now, he's sort of glowing.

But then I catch a glimpse of Liling's dark hair against

his shoulder and I forget everything except the fact that the sister of my heart just stopped breathing in front of me, because of a bullet meant for me. "Hurry Carrick. We have to find someone who can help her." If anyone were going to have the kind of magic that might save Liling, it would be the Mountain supers.

Carrick doesn't say anything, doesn't look back, just keeps us moving through the chaos. As soon as we get to the edge of the room, Carrick breaks into a run. "Keep up with me, Mei."

I'm glad of the chance to run, and stay just behind him as his long legs pound down the hallways. I'm lost within a couple of minutes, but Carrick never falters.

I'm gasping for breath by the time we stop in front of a small door. Carrick knocks, and an old Mountain supernatural answers. He's stooped and wrinkled, more like a giant prune than a person.

"I need you to look at this woman, healer," says Carrick.

He hesitates for a moment, glances at me standing in the hall, but the expression on Carrick's face doesn't brook no for an answer. The old man opens the door wider, and Carrick strides in. I follow closely behind, hoping he'll forget about my presence. Carrick lays Liling down on a table in the middle of the room.

The old man leans over Liling. He pries open her eyes and sniffs at the blood that covers her chest. "She's dead."

A gaping hole opens in my chest. My heart thumps erratically as I try to ignore the blunt words. She can't be dead. "Use your magic, old one," I say urgently. "Bring her back!" My own magic stutters in my chest, like something that's been short-circuited.

The old healer looks at me for the first time, and his eyes narrow. He turns back to Carrick as if he can't bear looking at me. I try to swallow down the sobs that are pushing their way up my throat. He's refusing to help her because of me.

"Can you do anything for her?" asks Carrick.

The old man shakes his head. "Too long since she died. Too much blood lost."

"No!" The word bursts forth from my body. "You can save her. You *have* to save her." I reach out to the old man, planning to force him to use his magic, but Carrick steps in between us. His usually serene face is grim as he catches my arms and holds me close, preventing me from moving.

I'm not thinking, just feeling. I strain to access the magic that's usually at my core, and again I'm stopped by some kind of strange feeling of emptiness. I hiccup and sob on the same breath, and feel a wildness pushing its way up my body. "There's something... Carrick. I can't use my magic. I can't heal her. Why can't I use my magic?" I gaze up at him with a tearstained face, needing him to fix this. He knows how much Liling means to me.

"Mei, we have to leave this place," says Carrick as if I hadn't spoken. "They're hunting for you, even now. I can't hold them off for long."

I nod quickly, rubbing the tears from my face. "There will be someone back at the stronghold who can help," I say.

Carrick shakes his head, his eyes pools of sadness. "Mei, she's gone. There's nothing we can do for her now. Nothing but take her back with us and bury her among friends."

I shake my head. "No. No." I won't let her die for me. Not like all the others.

Carrick picks up Liling's limp form in his arms and pushes me first out the door. "Thank you, old one," he says over his shoulder. Then he urges me into a run. "We don't have much time."

He again leads me down a series of corridors that I

would never have found my way through on my own. I'm running for everything I'm worth. If we can just get Liling home quickly, someone will be able to help her.

We exit out onto a ledge in the middle of the mountains, and for a moment, I consider leaping off. The vision of my small human body toppling down toward the earth is replaced by my dragon body soaring up into the sky.

I glance at Liling, her body draped over Carrick's arms. I take a running leap off the edge of the cliffside, Carrick's shout all that I hear, aside from the rushing in my ears.

The wind is my only companion, and after a second of momentum, I'm falling. Down, down into the mountain valley far below me. My scream is full of fear, sorrow, and frustration.

I want to live and I want to die at the same time.

You need to choose life, Mei... My mother's voice appears from deep within, jolting me out of my haze. Resentment rises up, bitter on my tongue.

Where were you when Liling was dying? Why didn't you help then? I ask her.

Choose life, she says again.

The rocks race toward me, faster than my brain can comprehend. My dragon magic doesn't immediately kick in, and panic overrides everything else. My magic was short-circuited. I couldn't heal Liling or even move at one point while we were inside. What made me think my ability to transform into a dragon wouldn't be affected?

For a second, the wildness inside me is glad. It's willing and eager for my deserved end, howling at the wind as it assaults my body on its downward spiral toward the rocks below.

No, Mei! You need to live. Choose life. My mother's voice urges me again, the soft tone somehow managing to draw me away from the desperate wildness that's pervading my soul. It fills me with the desire to live, to feel the warmth of the sun on my body, and the joy of flying in my dragon form.

I don't want to die.

The familiar stretching and growing takes over my body. The sting of the transformation is nothing compared to the pain in my heart. I hesitate, my dragon body tumbling toward the earth, and I consider not pushing out my wings. I've cheated death yet again.

Fly! my mother commands, her voice allowing no room for refusal.

I stretch my wings and fly.

For a moment, as the elation of my dragon self fills my heart, I forget everything and point my nose in the direction of the sky. My wings beat the wind into submission, and I soar toward the sun. But then it all comes back to me. Heaviness fills my heart. I turn and dive to where Carrick is waiting for me, a dark scowl on his face.

"Don't ever do that to me again. I thought you were dead."

I shrug and hold out a leg for him to climb.

"You're going to have to hold Liling," he says gently.

For a moment, I'm shocked. But he's right. He won't be able to hold onto me and keep her safe at the same time. I nod.

I gather her gently into my front paws, holding her as carefully as I can. Carrick climbs onto my back, and then I leap into the air, not looking back.

The flight back to our stronghold doesn't take long, especially when I'm flying as fast as I can. There are all sorts of supernaturals in our group. My father might know something that will help Liling.

Anything is possible.

But the dark hole inside me is spreading, and I know it's not true. There is going to come a point very soon where I have to give up on her. To admit it's over and done.

To admit that anything is *not* possible. Not anymore. My breath catches and smoke billows out my nostrils, hurting my eyes.

I land on the usual spot and give Liling to Carrick, gesturing with my nose that he should go ahead of me. I transform as fast as I can and throw on the first T-shirt and jeans I can find, then run down the hall after him. He hasn't gone far, despite his large steps. "Come on, Carrick. We have to see if anyone can help," I say, desperation in my voice. I pull on his arm, trying to get him to move faster.

Carrick shakes his head and looks down at me with large, sad eyes. "I don't know why you're acting like this, Mei. Liling is dead. She died back there, and we're taking her home to be buried. I'm truly sorry."

It feels like my heart is breaking all over again. I shake my head. "No. There must be something we can do."

"She's gone. And she wouldn't want you breaking apart like this."

Footsteps pounding down the hall interrupt our conversation. My father and Zane are racing toward us.

"What happened?" asks my father, sorrow etched into his face as he looks down at Liling, still in Carrick's arms.

"She was murdered by the pro-webber faction," says Carrick.

"More than just murdered," I say bitterly. "She took a bullet meant for me."

25

My hands are clenched tight. They have been for the last few days, and I don't know how to unclench them.

Liling's funeral was quick and economical. Zane did the honors, burning her body and then scattering her ashes over the mountains. It was beautiful and very, very final.

"Mei, come over here. Look at this," says my father. We're in the war room, and he's indicating one of the televisions.

I walk over, but it's like I'm walking through a twilight haze, everything is smoky and gray.

My father turns up the volume so I can hear what the overly made-up female presenter is saying. She's clearly excited about something.

"...rumors are spreading that the Earthbound's new version of the spell web will not only be stronger, removing up to 50 percent of the magic from the supernaturals, but it will also make them visible to humans. The lobbyists who have been concerned about supernaturals disappearing from our sight will be silenced if this proves true."

The man next to the presenter frowns. "There's still one big problem that nobody is mentioning." He pauses for dramatic effect. "They have to catch a dragon to do it."

The woman lets out a delicate snort and wafts her hand to one side. "The Earthbound have proven they're more than capable of capturing dragons. It's just a matter of time."

"I don't know. Those dragons are wily creatures. Look at that Mei Walker. Top of everyone's hit list, and she's still roaming our streets."

"Almost every person on the planet is searching for them. With this new revelation, the human population can rest easy about the supernatural problem."

"But will the supernatural population support this new spell web?" asks the male presenter.

The woman shrugs her shoulder delicately. "Who cares what the supernaturals want? They've been preying on humans for too long now. It's time to lock them away where they belong."

The sentiment is so common, and I've heard it so many times, I don't even blink. It's the news that Vincent's plans are out in the open that keeps me glued to the screen. "Have you heard from any of the groups who were pro-web because they thought they'd be protected?" I ask.

"All of them," says my father grimly. "Suddenly we're everyone's best friends."

"Even the USL?" I ask softly. Zane and Sergei *did* try to kill Seth; maybe he's convinced his group not to approach us.

"He was the first to contact me."

"What are we going to do?" The divide between humans and supernaturals seems wider suddenly. If they can take our power with no consequences, they'll choose that every time. Who wouldn't?

"What we're already doing. Meet with everyone who wants to meet with us. Plan some kind of coherent response to Vincent's actions."

"What are the Mountain supers saying?" Carrick left again straight after delivering Liling and me home, saying he had to get back to sort out the divisions raging among his people. "Have you heard from them?"

"Carrick says they're still divided. But the news of Vincent's deception is having an effect."

"What of Elder Rasmussen?" I ask carefully, trying to keep all emotion out of my voice.

"He's disappeared. Along with the man in black you described."

"Who was he?" My hands are clenched so tight, I can feel the half moons of my nails digging into the skin of my palm.

"The man who shot at you? We don't know. The Mountain supers are being tightlipped. I'm not even sure if he was from the mountain or not."

I shake my head. "He wasn't. But he did something to me. He has some kind of power we don't know about. I couldn't move, I couldn't even heal Liling." Suddenly I'm overwhelmed with memories of Liling in my arms, blood everywhere, her face looking up at me. Liling dying.

My father watches me closely, like he knows exactly what I'm thinking. "Even Si couldn't have saved Liling, Mei. She took that bullet right through her heart. I'm surprised she even managed to talk."

I told him that she spoke to me, but I couldn't bring myself to tell him what she said.

I don't know how to make her death mean something. I don't know how to grant her dying wish. It lies heavy over me, like a blanket made of expectation and sorrow.

I just nod, pretending I believe my father.

Zane comes to the door of the war room. "Are you ready, Damien?"

My father hesitates for a moment. "Mei...?"

"What?" I ask suspiciously.

"There's something I need to tell you."

My heart shudders, unable to deal with anything more. But I harden my resolve. Whatever it is, it can't be worse than what's already happened. "Spit it out," I say grimly.

"We're getting visits from delegations wanting to work with us. The people who've now realized how two-faced Vincent is."

"And?"

"The USL, Seth's group, is coming today. In about five minutes."

Before... this might have upset me more. But now I can't seem to get past the gray fog suffocating my mind.

I try to think of Seth, the last time I saw him, his flames rippling across the sky. The way he looked at me with a fierce anger in his flaming eyes. My chest starts to hurt, and the gray fog inside my head pulls back. Suddenly pain overwhelms me, and I can't breathe.

"Mei? Are you okay?" my father asks, his face concerned.

I want to scream, to yell, that no, I'm not okay. That nothing is okay. But then I remember Liling dying in my arms, blood pumping out of her chest, her whispered last words to me, and I know I can handle anything, if it will make her death mean something.

"Where are we meeting them?" I ask instead, my voice only slightly croaky.

He clears his throat. "I'm sorry, Mei, but we need them on our side."

"You're right. We need them if we're going to defeat Vincent. I'll be as quiet as a church mouse."

He hesitates again. "They don't want you in the meeting."

"What?" My brain is slower than usual, and I don't immediately understand what he's saying.

"They say you're disruptive and undisciplined," says Zane from across the room. "They don't want you there."

"But they want *you*?" I ask, anger in every syllable.

He shrugs. "They don't know me well enough to understand their mistake."

"They'll regret it as soon as they do," I snap. I'm not as upset with him as I was before Liling died, but it's still there, festering inside me.

He grins, unrepentant. "By then, it'll be too late."

I glance at my father. "Don't piss them off."

"Mei..." He hesitates, looking at me like he wants to say more.

I gesture at them to leave. "Go. I'm fine."

They leave the room together, and I try to feel okay about the meeting happening without me. I pace about the room, until I realize the only place I'm going to feel good is in the gym, working off some steam.

I change and head down, hesitating at the entrance. It almost feels like Liling could be on the other side of this door, waiting for me to spar with her. She'll joke with me in that quiet way of hers, and say that I'm not concentrating. That I'm making it easy on her.

For a moment, it feels real. I take a breath, open the door, and look around.

The only person in the gym is Sergei. I let out my breath in a rush, and clench my hands.

The Russian still hasn't changed back into a dragon, and he's calming down more each day. It's a lesson to me about the needs of a dragon—I'm not going to stay in one form or the other for too long.

"Hey," he says, not taking his eyes off the tiny punching bag he's currently hammering. He's not doing too badly for an amateur.

"Hey, Sergei. How's your training going?"

"Well enough."

"Mind if I join you?" I say, walking over to the practice mat on one side of the room. I don't need to spar. I can practice some *kata* moves. It's been too long. Si would be annoyed with me if he knew.

"Not at all."

An hour later and I'm sweaty, but satisfied with myself. For the last half hour, Sergei has been quietly watching my movements as I run through various *kata*.

"Would you teach me?" he asks as I pause to wipe my face with my towel.

"Teach you?" I repeat stupidly.

"To fight like that. I would like to fight like you."

I don't tell him I've been doing this since I was nine, with hours of practice every day from two grueling taskmasters. "Sure. I can do that."

He nods, a satisfied expression on his pale face.

At that moment, Zane pokes his head in through the door. "I'm giving them an escort out through the mountains. Letting a few of the more adventurous ones a ride on a dragon."

I make a face at him, still annoyed. "To make sure they don't circle around and attack?"

"So they get out okay," says Zane drily.

"Why are you telling me?"

"Just wanted to let you know they'll be gone soon and you don't have to hide anymore."

Indignation rises up through my chest. "I'm not hiding. Did they think I was hiding?"

Zane lets out a crack of laughter. "No, your father made it very clear he'd asked you to stay away. He somehow managed to imply that it was grudging without actually saying it."

"What did they say?"

"They said they'd be happy to work with us, and that Vincent had betrayed them by not telling them about his plans for the spell web."

"Nothing new, then."

"They had some intel about where he's keeping the machines and what kinds he's managed to rebuild."

"We already knew that from Sergei."

"It's always good to have intel confirmed by a second source."

I glance at Sergei, hoping he doesn't take offence. But he doesn't seem to be bothered. I can't tell if he's even listening.

"Was Seth with them?"

Zane nods. "He kept looking at the door, as if he was hoping someone might burst into the room and demand to be part of it."

"Did... did he look okay?" I don't what makes me ask the question. The gray fog is muddling my brain.

Zane shrugs. "He looked the same. Just with fewer flames."

It doesn't matter anyway. Seth doesn't remember me, at least not properly. And I'm on a mission. I have to make Liling's death mean something. Whatever the hell that means. "It doesn't matter," I mutter, mostly to myself.

He doesn't reply, just looks at me with compassion. "I'm going now. We'll talk when I get back."

I throw my towel after him as he closes the door, but it doesn't even get close to hitting him.

26

I 'm still in the gym when an alarm flares through the whole complex. I freeze, not sure what it's supposed to mean.

Since when do we even have an alarm system?

I look at Sergei, who looks like he wishes he could be anywhere else, and then head for the doors. I run through the corridor, meeting up with others who are clearly as confused as I am, and we head toward the main rooms.

On the monitors there's a strange battle taking place in the air.

Multiple tiny planes, like old fashioned drones no more than four or five feet long, are zipping in and around Zane's dragon form. The setting sun keeps striking the metal body of the craft at a particular angle as they zip around Zane, momentarily blinding the cameras each time.

"They're being controlled from somewhere else. It has to be somewhere close by," my father mutters to Roger, who nods in agreement.

The helicopter holding the majority of the USL contingent is hovering off to one side, and Seth is attempting to guard it with his body. Zane has four people clinging desperately to his back as he swipes at the planes.

He sends out a burst of flame and burns one of the airplanes, but another takes its place straight away.

There seem to be different weapons on each plane. One has bullets, another a flame shooter. A third sends out a wire and a small spark similar to a Taser.

"What's happening?" I ask my father. "How long have we had these cameras?" I glance overhead to where the alarm is still whining. "And the alarm?"

"We didn't know we had them," says Damien. He's staring at the screen in front of us. "It's on the perimeter of our mountain range. The cameras just started up in here at the same time as the alarm. Those little planes came out of nowhere and started shooting at them."

As we're watching, one of the people Zane is carrying jerks backward, then cries out and tumbles off his back. Zane tries to grab at him, but his movement is hampered by the dozens of small planes all around him. I close my eyes so I don't have to watch the man hit the rocks below.

"How did they find us?" All the possible scenarios fill my head. Can we really trust Seth?

"Must have followed the USL group in," says Roger, his silver hair flowing like an agitated waterfall.

My father glances at him, and then at me. Clearly he's not as convinced of that as Roger.

I stand there watching the screens for a moment longer, but I can't handle the stress of it. "I'm going out there," I say.

My father nods, and I'm not even sure he's heard me properly. But it's not a question. There's no one else who can fly like I can, or fight like I can. Zane looks like he needs all the help he can get.

I race out of the room and down the hall. Climbing the

stairs to the dragon landing, I pull off my clothes and leap into the air. Soon I'm racing through the sky, following my nose like a beacon. I hear the battle before I see it.

The damn planes even buzz like those remote control ones always do when I've seen them at seaside resorts or up on the cliffs overlooking the ocean. The only difference is that these ones shoot deadly flames and bullets.

I'm still a fair distance away when I see some kind of dart burst out of one plane and hit Zane on the leg. He howls, his pain disproportionate for what had actually happened. Dragon hides are thick.

Moments later, I understand why. Zane's transforming back into his human shape, right in midair. His passengers scream as they find themselves falling into nothing, the sound caught and carried to me by the strong mountain gusts. I roar and beat my wings, trying to get there before he and his passengers hit the rocks below.

As I watch, all the airplanes, including the ones that were taking potshots at Seth and the helicopter, dive toward Zane. They fly into a tight formation underneath him, creating an aerial platform. He seems woozy, and doesn't struggle as they buzz away, carrying him with them.

I'm almost at the first of the passengers, reaching out as far as I can to grab him out of the air. I hear a yell to the side as Seth manages to grab one of the other passengers.

I have the first passenger clutched—just barely—in one claw, and I dive down and grab the last passenger just as he's about to smash into rocks. My heart pounding, I soar back up into the sky. I push one of the men, some kind of chameleon shifter, onto my back, and he clings tight to the ridges. Above, Seth has the other man in his claws, but his burning flames are too hot. The man is yelling and struggling in Seth's grip.

Mei, he's going to fall!

I tip my wings and soar in Seth's direction, plucking the man delicately out of Seth's claws. Then I turn and head back to the stronghold, holding a man in each arm, and one on my back.

I don't check to see if Seth is following me and I don't let go of my passengers until we're back at the landing area. Then I change as fast as I can into my human form, and push them into the doors. They all look stunned. "Go! Run down that way. Find someone and let them know what happened." I'm naked, but I don't care.

Turning my back on them, I wave my arms at Seth, who is hovering over the tiny area, as if unsure whether to land. The helicopter is long gone, hopefully in a different direction to the little planes.

My father is running down the corridor toward me, his face more lined than I've ever seen it. "We can't let them have Zane. He's a powerful dragon. He'd be able to fire up the spell web on his own. They'd win." He yells the words at me like I don't already know this.

Glancing back up at Seth as he hovers over the landing place, I make the only decision I can. "I'll go rescue him."

27

We'll rescue him. Seth's voice is firm in my head.

I nod once, letting him know I heard. "Seth and I will go. Right now. They won't have time to do anything."

Dad's first instinct is to shake his head. "I can't risk Vincent getting all three of you," he says. "It's bad enough he's got Zane. We need a proper plan."

I don't argue with his assumption that it's Vincent who's behind the kidnapping. I'd bet my left wing that he's right. "He won't get any of us. I've been trained too well for that. Jeff and Si knew what they were doing. And Seth was SIG. We can do this. But we have to go *now*."

He looks from me to Seth and back again. He looks like he wants to argue, but all he says is, "Okay, fine."

"We'll be back soon," I say solemnly.

I change so fast, I don't even feel pain before I'm in the air, flying next to Seth and heading in the direction of those damn little planes.

I'm sorry, Seth's voice speaks softly into my head.

For what? I'm so focused on getting Zane back, I'm genuinely confused by Seth's words.

For treating you badly. For thinking you were the enemy.

For a long moment, I don't know what to say. Ever since I saw him on the television, back from the dead, that's all I've wanted to hear him say. Now... Liling is dead, Zane has been captured, and my brain is covered in a gray fog that's the only thing keeping me sane.

You didn't remember me, I say instead.

Seth's flames rise higher over his magnificent phoenix body as he flies next to me. *I remembered you from the moment I turned into a phoenix again. My memories came flooding back as I hovered over you. But I couldn't admit I was wrong so easily. I had to go back to them. They were my only family for so long.*

A lump forms in my throat. *You don't have to explain it to me.*

But I do. I promised you everything, and gave you nothing.

Tears choke me, but I burn them off with a short burst of flame. *Let's just concentrate on getting Zane back right now. We don't have time for this.*

I beat my wings, pushing myself higher into the sky, away from Seth. I catch his expressive fiery hazel eyes watching me several times as we fly, but he doesn't try to say anything more.

Before long, our greater wing span mean we've almost caught up to the planes. They're buzzing up ahead, their limp passenger still on the platform. *How are we going to do this?* I say to Seth. *What if they've got some more of those darts?*

We'll just have to stay out of range. Throw your dragon flames, burn and hurt everything that isn't Zane.

Are they remote controlled individually? Or is it just one person controlling them all? I'm trying to understand how we might defeat them. I hesitate. *Is it magic?*

They were zipping around us with too much intelligence not to be remote controlled by several people. And it didn't seem like magic was being used.

I nod, relieved he thinks that, too. Magic would have been harder to fight. As we get closer, I focus my attention on the closest planes. There are about half a dozen planes flying around the central ones that have formed the platform for Zane, who still looks mostly unconscious.

But not for long. I'm planning on burning every one of those damn-awful planes to the ground.

I swoop in, threading a long line of dragon flames toward the closest planes. They go up in smoke almost immediately, and nose dive toward the ground.

On the other side, Seth goes in closer and grabs one of the other planes with his hind claws, snapping it in half with a primitive screech.

Soon, the only ones that are left are those carrying Zane. Their buzzing seems to have intensified, and they've picked up speed. Someone has thought this through, and doesn't want to fail.

How do we get him? asks Seth.

We're going to have to go in and flame them, like I did the others. Hopefully we can avoid those little darts.

Seth seems unconvinced, but it's the only plan we have, so he follows me down when I head in their direction.

I send out a burst of dragon flame at the closest airplane, disintegrating it from the bottom up. I'm trying to avoid burning Zane, which is making it difficult. Seth grabs another of the planes and breaks it in half, his burning phoenix body glowing brightly as he does it.

There are only four more planes keeping Zane from

falling to his death. Seth grabs one and breaks it, and Zane topples to one side. I reach out and grab him off the planes, trying to keep away from whatever weapons they still have attached. Flames blaze out one side, and a hail of bullets batter my flank, but I lean sideways and they bounce harmlessly off my dragon scales.

Now that I have Zane safely in my arms, I send out a jet of dragon flame, taking great satisfaction as the three remaining planes burst into flame in front of us.

Clutching Zane to my chest, I look up to see Seth hovering protectively over us. A rush of triumph flows through me.

Shall we go?

Just as he's nodding his head in assent, another of the tiny planes zips in from behind him and streaks toward me. A tiny dart shoots out from the nose of the plane and lands in my neck.

I roar and flap my wings to give chase. But instead of the glorious feeling of flight, I feel myself changing. Sparks fly, and bones crack.

I'm human.

I'm still clinging to Zane as we plummet toward the earth.

28

My scream is loud and long as we free fall into nothing. It's not as much fun to fall when you don't have the option of transforming.

I twist around, trying to see Seth, but we're falling too fast. He's not going to be able to save us. I try changing back into my dragon form, but it's like I'm not even a dragon any more. Another scream of frustration erupts out of my mouth.

Who is doing this? *How* are they doing it?

The only good thing about this is that Zane is unconscious, so he's not going to feel it when he dies from being splattered against the rocks. We should have let the planes take him. At least he'd have lived another day. We could have figured out how to save him.

This isn't how Liling wanted me to make her death worthwhile.

I scrunch my eyes shut. A thousand thoughts fill my head. Images of the people I love. Things I've done. Things I regret.

Two pairs of sharp claws fasten around my middle,

piercing the skin on my stomach. Flames lick at my unprotected human skin, and I scream in pain, but manage to clutch Zane to my chest as we sweep through the sky instead of splattering to earth. My teeth clench together, and there's a roaring noise in my head, but we're alive, and that's enough.

Seth sweeps through the rest of his dive and manages to drop us onto a ledge close by. We land heavily, and the rough rocks scrape my skin, but I don't care.

We're alive.

I drag Zane away from the edge, his large frame barely fitting on the rock shelf. I look around, trying to find Seth in the twilight sky. A bright flame glows just over us, and I stare wide-eyed up at him. He saved us.

Taking a deep breath, I try to change into a dragon again. My magic fizzes and spits inside me, more of a reaction than I got last time, but still not working. Whatever was in those darts must be still in my system.

Peering up into the sky, I try to see if there any more of those planes around. I shiver in the mountain air. Vincent's getting smarter with his technology. It's terrifying to have all that destructive power aimed at us.

But dragons are like cockroaches. You can never quite kill us off completely.

I smile. It feels good to have outsmarted Vincent. Even if it was only just, I remind myself.

I try to change again, and this time I get a little further with the process, although I can't actually finish the transformation. It seems all I have to do is wait out the effectiveness of whatever was in the dart.

At least it wasn't meant to kill. Simply inhibit.

Seth is still above, flying in formation, like he's guarding us from whatever else might be out there. I feel safer knowing he's up there, which is crazy given that until now, he's been on the other side. What makes me so sure he's someone I can trust again?

Apparently I'm quite naive, because as I gaze up at him, I smile. He's majestic up there, his wings broad and long, his flames burning brightly in the reflection of the setting sun. I never stopped trusting him, even when he hated me and looked at me with rage in his one remaining hazel eye.

The smell of smoke wafts along the valley below us, and I wonder who else could possibly be nearby. The reason this stronghold was abandoned was because the only path leading into it was destroyed by a rock slide. Before we cleared the rocks, only creatures with wings or rotors could get in or out. We keep that entrance well hidden from outsiders.

A faint boom shudders through the mountains. I frown. What's happening? My intuition suddenly goes into over-drive. The urge to get back into my dragon form burns through me. Something is wrong.

I glance back over at Zane. He's starting to stir, and then his eyes open wide, staring straight at me.

"We have to get back to the stronghold," I say.

He nods and then winces in pain. "What happened?" he asks, his voice croaky.

"You almost got taken away by Vincent. Can you turn again?"

He shakes his head. "I'm too woozy. I can barely think straight."

I frown. "I got hit too, but it hasn't affected me as badly."

Zane puts one hand to his head. "I feel like I've been hit by one of those jumbo jets the humans are so fond of."

"I might have to leave you here for a bit. I need to get back." I try to change again. I'm still not able to do the final transition, and fall back against the rocks. "If I can ever change again."

The urgency to get back to the stronghold increases. I feel like insects are crawling over my skin, I'm so anxious. What could possibly be happening back there?

Zane fidgets too, and I stare at him, wondering if it's the same thing.

"Do you feel it?" I ask.

He glances up at me. "The need to get back? Like a rash I can't itch."

"What is it?"

He shakes his head. "Nothing good. We can't do anything about it until we can change."

"Seth is flying above us. He's protecting us."

"Can he carry us?"

I touch the cuts on my sides and stomach from his claws. The burns on my back sting every time I move. "Not really."

"Then we wait."

I stand up, looking around to see if I can find hand holds that will allow me to climb higher. I don't know if it would help, but it gives me something to do with my time. The urge to leap over the edge again is strong, but I manage to hold back, knowing that I might not be able to transform in the air like I did last time.

Overhead, Seth lets out a terrible screech and my body jerks in surprise. I squint up to where I saw him last and see a strange mass in the air. It's two creatures, twisting and turning through the sky, locked in a deadly embrace.

It's an aerial battle like no other.

One of the fighters is Seth, his burning body shimmering in the sun, his massive air and flame wings stretched out behind him. The second is a deep, devastating black beast, with a long, scaled tail dangling out behind.

Long, black, spidery wings beat above it, keeping it in the air.

Large metallic claws dig into Seth's sides, and Seth's front claws are locked into the creature's chest.

It's not a dragon, that much I know.

But I can't tell what kind of creature it might otherwise be. It seems to have the upper hand, whatever it is. I hold my breath as I watch, focusing on Seth, willing him to survive.

Zane stands and joins me at the edge. "What is it?" he asks.

I shake my head. "I've never seen anything like it. Another type of dragon?"

"Not one that I've ever seen."

We watch in silence, unable to intervene in the battle taking place over our heads. I clench my hands, my whole body tense.

The two aerial combatants swirl through the sky, desperately fighting for supremacy. They're weakening; if they're not careful, both of them will fall to their deaths. Seth screeches and launches an attack with his phoenix beak. He hits the scale-covered neck of the creature he's fighting, but it doesn't seem to affect it.

"I've never seen anything like it," says Zane softly. "In some angles, it looks like a pathway into nothingness. Like it's a black hole or something," he says.

I give him a startled look. "What do you know about black holes?" I ask.

"I've been watching science documentaries on television," he says defensively. "I have to learn to live in this century."

I guess he's right.

The fight is getting dirty now. Someone needs to gain the

upper hand, and fast. Seth uses his back claws to scratch at the black creature. His thick claws break through the tough scales and draw blood. He uses his wings to wrap the black supernatural in a web of fire, trying to burn him into submission. It's hard to know whether it's having any effect, the deep black of the creature hides any burn marks.

The black monster stretches forward with its head and snaps out at Seth. Instead of his body, it manages to get a few of Seth's feathers in its mouth. It pulls back in triumph, and Seth screeches as the feathers are pulled forcibly from his body.

The feathers light up inside the black lizard's mouth, burning bright, flames licking at the creatures face. It screeches, and spits them out of its mouth, shaking its head like it's in pain. One of the feathers drifts up and over the black supernatural, landing on the strange spidery wings on its back. Blue flames light up the creature's wing for a second, burning at the thin membrane. It screams, turning to flick out its long forked tongue, dampening down the flames and flicking the feather off its body at the same time.

The feathers drift downward, their burning fire replaced by a blue glow, and I will them to come to me. Phoenix feathers are dangerous in the wrong hands.

The feathers momentarily distract me, but a strange guttural cry from the black super draws my attention back to the battle overhead. Just as I glance up, it flicks its long tail around like a whip. The spiky ball at the base lands across Seth's back, and he arches his body in pain. It slams into his back again and again, until I can't watch any more. Seth's body seems misshapen, like the spiky ball has broken bones across his back. Seth must have released the black creature for a second, because it shudders and darts out of their deadly embrace.

Instead of finishing off the fight, the black lizard-shaped super flies off haphazardly into the darkening sky, one wing quivering and at a strange angle, and its long tail following behind like a streamer advertising a Halloween event.

Seth screeches into the air, his flames burning brightly.

And then he changes into his human shape, tumbling toward us, his body broken and bloodied.

29

I leap into the air in front of our ledge without thinking, pushing myself into the transformation.

For a second, nothing happens, and I remember I can't change. My heart hammers in my throat for two awful seconds as I plummet, and then the familiar pain travels over my body as I stretch into my dragon form.

My wings beat a powerful path directly to Seth. He's falling fast, but I can fly faster, and moments later I'm clutching his human body against my chest.

Zane has transformed into his dragon shape and is circling the air above me as I land carefully on the outcrop we just vacated. Zane's movements seem a little jerky, like he's still being affected by whatever it was in the dart, but at least he's flying.

I transform again quickly and place my human hands on Seth's chest. Closing my eyes, I take a deep breath, and then another, before using my dragon magic to heal the worst of his wounds.

The nastiest wound is his broken back. The spikes have

crushed a section of his vertebrae. I don't know if it's even possible to heal a body this broken.

But I have the extra magic of two souls floating around inside me now, and there's nothing blocking me from my magic this time. I feel the warmth from my mother's soul glowing inside me, and know she's with me. Tarsal doesn't surface, but it doesn't matter. I'm going to save Seth whatever it takes.

I hold my hand still and focus on pushing my magic into Seth. Very, very slowly I knit his bones back together, trying to remember everything Si taught me. I stem the blood flow and close the wounds. It's tedious work, and takes almost all my magic to do it.

I've never felt this empty of magic, except when it was stolen from me at the Mountain stronghold. I'm swaying as I sit beside him, willing him to be okay.

After a while, I realize he's awake, his single hazel eye fixed on my face.

"Thank you," he says.

I nod. Tears are flowing down my cheeks.

"Don't cry for me," whispers Seth. He tries to sit up, but he's still too weak.

I shake my head. I'm not just crying for Seth. I'm also crying for Liling, who I might have been able to save in the same way if my powers hadn't been blocked. After a few tries, Seth manages to sit up, and pulls me into his arms, holding me tight. I tense up, holding myself stiff. It feels wrong to be comforted when Liling's death hangs so heavily over me. But I'm so tired. After a few seconds of fighting it, I relax into his arms.

But the itching sensation returns, and I lift my head, looking in the direction of our stronghold. Overhead, Zane is still flying in formation, waiting for us.

"We have to go," I say, wiping a hand across my nose. "Do you think you can fly?"

Seth pulls away, standing up and offering me a hand. "I think so. Perhaps you should go first? Just in case?" He gives a half smile as I grab his hand and let him help me to my feet.

I take a breath and reach inside me, making sure I have enough magic. Just enough, I think.

I leap off the ledge, falling toward the ground, just like I did after Liling's death. My breath is sucked into my chest, and my heart stutters before its next beat. I hear Seth's gasp behind me. There's a zing of pain, a crack of bones and then I transform, sweeping up through the air on my golden wings, moving into formation next to Zane.

Can we go now? asks Zane, unimpressed.

Seth transforms into his phoenix shape, and he screeches as he takes off from the outcrop. He flies toward us, his battered body managing to stay in the air despite the best efforts of the black creature.

Are you okay? I ask.

He turns his head to look at me, his hazel eyes taking in everything. *I'm fine. I don't know what the hell that was, but it fought like the very devil.*

It looked like a devil too.

I nod to Zane. There's no time to waste. The urge to get back to the stronghold is as great as ever, and although nothing like this has ever happened to me before, I'm learning to trust my instincts.

Something bad is happening.

Seth nods. *I feel it too. The black creature came from that direction.*

The fear in my stomach sets a bruising pace back through the mountains. It's not long before we see smoke rising in the sky. Flames burst alongside it here and there. I push my body harder, desperate to get back.

We arrive to see the front entrance blown to pieces. There are dead bodies lying scattered about, all our people.

Who is doing this? Vincent?

Who else? replies Seth.

We fly over the area to the dragon landing spot and come in one at a time. I'm first; I've got my clothes on and am about to race off when Seth's voice stops me.

"Mei. Wait. We'll be stronger and safer together."

I glance back at him. "Hurry the hell up, then. My father is in here somewhere."

He grabs a shirt and trousers from the pile we keep ready, and we pause to wait for Zane. He still seems a little off, but he's better than he was. As he pulls on his clothes, he shakes his head, like he's trying to get rid of the cobwebs. "You okay?" I ask, frowning.

"I'm fine," he says in a rough voice.

We take off at a run and soon find our first fight. They're humans in uniforms I don't recognize. Three big men who look like they've seen a battle or two. They look me over for a second and then focus their attention on Seth and Zane behind me.

More fool them.

I take a running leap at the first man, slamming the side of my hand into his throat, and then kicking down into his groin.

It's hardly fair, but I'm not in the mood to play nice. They're attacking my home.

He doesn't go down, and makes like he's going to grab me. I move out of his way without missing a beat and slam a solid kick into his kidney. A second kick takes out his left leg under the knee, and then he's on the ground, groaning. I don't want him awake, crawling through the compound, so I slam a quick hand against the side of his neck and knock him out.

The other two are fighting with their opponents, although neither looks fully in control. I'm not in the mood to be nice, so I slam my fists into both ears of the man nearest me. He staggers back a second, and Zane throws a punch to his face that knocks him out cold.

Just as I turn to take out Seth's opponent, he kicks the man in the side and sends him reeling to the floor. Then he punches him in the jaw, knocking the man out as well. None of it's pretty, but it's definitely effective.

We run on. The war room is just around the corner ahead. A terrible smell hits my nose, and I slow down.

It's the stench of burning electrical equipment, but there's also an undertone of something else. Burning flesh.

I pull the others in to the wall just before the corner. Their faces are grim—they can smell just as well as me.

Poking my head around the corner quickly, I try to ascertain if any guards are patrolling.

I pull back behind the corner and close my eyes, wishing I could unsee what was there.

"No soldiers," I croak out, slowly sliding down the wall, until I'm sitting on the ground with my back against the wall. "But everyone's dead."

30

Z ane glances down at me and then moves over to the corner.

His face is impassive as he surveys the scene. He hasn't known these people long, but he's become part of the group. A tiny twitch appears beside his eye.

Seth follows, and he's equally grim. They both move forward, and I take a couple of breaths, knowing I have to follow them.

Except the first time I looked around the corner, I recognized Roger lying face down in a pool of blood, his long silver hair matted with dried gore and pieces of bone. I don't want to think about who else might be there.

It's too soon.

I'm not ready.

I'm breathing in gasps of air, trying to calm down, keep myself detached. I don't think I can stand back up, and there's a ringing in my ears that just won't go away.

But I have to find my father. He's got to be here somewhere. He's a wily bastard, he'll be fine. He just needs a bit of rescuing. And that's what I'm good at, right?

I take a deep breath, and push down all the emotions and feelings that want to surge to the surface. I lock them away inside me, until I can breathe calmly again.

Clenching my fingers tight against my palms, I push myself to standing.

Then I stride around the corner and down the corridor, catching up to Seth and Zane, who've stopped at the first body. By my count, there are twelve people lying in various positions along the hallway in front of the war room. They must have been protecting the information stored in the old computers.

Not very successfully, if the results are anything to go by.

I step over the body of Gregor, a super who's been with us from the beginning, and put my hand on the door of the war room.

"Wait. Mei, let me do it," says Zane.

His words make it clear what he's expecting to find behind that door.

"It's fine. Nothing I haven't seen before," I mutter, before turning the handle and walking in.

It's blessedly clear. No bodies.

I let out a breath.

But the monitors across our stronghold show fighting still going on in various spots. "We have to help them," I say.

The other two nod in agreement and turn to leave. "Wait. We need weapons," I say, walking over to an old computer that's been sitting in the corner of the war room the whole time. It's placed on an old cabinet and pushed into the corner, as if it's a machine that used to work, but doesn't any more.

I put a series of numbers into the keyboard, and a lock clicks in the cabinet and the door opens.

Inside are a series of small weapons that pack a huge

punch. My father's own little stash of protection. I try not to think about the fact that he didn't have a chance to use it when these people attacked.

I'm sure he's fine. He's a survivor, my father.

We each take knives, handguns and ammunition, and put them around our bodies in pockets, boots, underwear, and socks, as much as we can carry.

"Mei, just so we're clear. This is a direct attack on our home. This isn't a survivors kind of situation. We need to kill as many of them as we can," says Zane sternly.

I nod. For once, I agree with his bloodthirsty assessment of the situation.

Then we're off. We already know where our first stop is —the communal area where a small group are holed up behind some furniture. It won't be long before the soldiers break through their tenuous line.

When we burst into the room guns blazing, the soldiers don't know what's hit them. I'm an excellent shot, and so is Seth. The small unit of enemy soldiers is all dead within seconds. We race over and find five people huddled together, none of them my father.

"Thank you, Mei," whispers one of the women, tears in her eyes. I'm shocked to see Theresa reduced to a shaking mess.

"Where's Andy?" I ask.

She shakes her head. "He... didn't make it," she whispers.

I nod quickly. "We have to keep going. Stay here until we get back."

A couple stand up, determined to fight with us, but I shake my head. "We're faster and deadlier, just the three of us. If you want to do something, go to the war room and figure out if anything's been stolen."

I take off at a run, not even checking to see if Seth and Zane are behind me. It doesn't matter. I'd keep going on my own if I had to.

The next fighting zone is the sleeping quarters. People are trapped in the rooms at the end of the long, dead-end corridor, leaning out and shooting at enemy soldiers who've formed a barricade at the other end. We come up behind the soldiers, who are sitting ducks to our enemy fire.

We pause, waiting around the other side of a corner, taking a breath.

"On three," whispers Seth. "One—"

Impatiently, I step out into the corridor. My whole focus is on getting our people to safety, but I clear my throat, unable to shoot soldiers in the back without giving them warning we're here.

As soon as the first soldier turns and lifts his gun, I pull my trigger.

I'm faster than he is, and I'm shooting to kill. Si might have disapproved of guns, but he let Jeff teach me how to use them better than most people. The other four meet the same fate within seconds. I don't think Seth or Zane even got a shot off.

"Two, three," says Seth drily.

"I keep thinking to myself how glad I am that you're on my side," says Zane, looking down at the dead soldiers.

But I can't even crack a smile. I'm numb to their jokes. There's only fighting and saving my father in my head.

"It's me, Mei," I call down the corridor. "Everyone out of your rooms. You need to meet the others in the war room. Help anyone who needs medical attention."

People cautiously peer out around the doors, and then most come striding out as soon as they realize it's me. It turns out there are another seventeen survivors, but still no sign of my father.

"Let's go find the rest of the fighting," I say. There's no room for fear or anger.

I'm an avenging angel, come to save my people.

31

"Mei, slow down," says Seth, grabbing at my arm. "This is the main unit. I counted almost thirty soldiers in this area. You can't go rushing in with those numbers."

I shake off his hand and glare up at him, knowing he's right but resenting him for mentioning it. "Fine. What do you suggest?"

"We have surprise and our supernatural powers on our side. We need to use them."

I cross my arms, but don't speak. He sighs. "You'll need to confirm this, but the area they're fighting in seemed bigger on the screen? Is that right?"

I nod once. "It was the gymnasium."

"Then one of you needs to shift into dragon form. You'll be able to take out more of them with dragon fire. Then the other two can use that dragon fire as cover."

"So who transforms?" I ask, looking over at Zane.

He shrugs. "I'll do it. I'm not as good a shot as you, and I'm bigger in dragon form. Plus I'm scary, rather than all girly like you are."

"Pardon me? Did you just call me *girly*?" Indignation rises to the surface.

Zane shrugs. "Red and gold dragons aren't as intimidating as black dragons. It's a fact." He smirks at me, and I almost rise to the bait.

And then I remember what's happening, and my expression slips back to grim. "Come on, let's get this over with."

We sprint to the gymnasium, and I hear the noise of the fighting before I see it. The door has been blasted off the entrance, and there are soldiers crowded around the entranceway, shooting toward one side that's been boarded up.

This time I don't offer any warning. I pick off three soldiers who are about to shoot into the gymnasium. We stride up to the doorway and peer through.

There's an enormous pile of furniture, gym equipment, and even the mats that were on the floor, all protecting the people behind it. They're using their ammunition judiciously, shooting only when any of the soldiers makes a move toward them.

Unfortunately for them, the soldiers have created a ring of metal around the makeshift pile, and are using it to move ever closer to their victims. The soldiers don't notice that not all the shooting behind them has come from their own side, they're so focused on picking off people from behind the barricade.

There's just enough room for a dragon, and Zane roars as he slams his way into the room, breaking apart the doorway. The soldiers turn, and several of them just gape, too surprised to move. However, as soon as Zane starts shooting out dragon fire, burning their soft human skin to ashes, they run.

Seth and I enter behind Zane, shooting around his

shoulders and using his scales as protection. Time slows down and I concentrate on killing these men who've dared to enter our sanctuary and attack my friends.

One by one they fall, until there are only two or three soldiers left hiding among the metal barricade.

With a yell, one of the soldiers leaps out shooting, while the other two run for the door on the far side of the gymnasium. I calmly shoot the man in the chest and watch with dark eyes as Zane takes out the other two with one breath of dragon fire.

I stride toward the mangled structure. "It's me, Mei. Who's in there? Is everyone okay?"

Sergei pokes his head out, still in human form. His face is even paler than usual, and he's covered in blood. He doesn't say anything, just blinks owlishly at us.

I climb over the edge of the structure and discover another group of survivors, too many of them to count easily. There's a mix of supernatural forms, and everyone is covered in dust and blood, like there was some kind of explosion. Scanning the faces, I don't see my father. "Has anyone seen Damien?" I ask.

"Mei," says Zane softly. "He's over here."

I scramble over to where Zane is crouched beside a figure covered almost entirely in blood and gore. The eyes open, and I recognize my father's brown eyes looking out at me.

"Oh Jesus, Dad. What the hell happened?" I grab his hand and lean forward, trying to wipe the blood off his face with my other hand.

He gives a half smile. "They set off... detonations," he manages to wheeze out.

"Shh, Dad. Forget I asked." I put my hands over his chest and try to use my healing magic on him. But I've only just healed Seth, knitting his bones back together, one of the hardest things to get right. I don't have anything left but scraps of magic for my father. I glance around in panic.

"We need to get you to a hospital. Or a medic. Is Fiona around?" I look behind me, as if she's going to pop up out of the woodwork. The grim faces of those nearby tells me what I don't want to ask. Fiona's dead.

"They killed probably a third of our people with the bombs," says Damien, his voice sounding a bit clearer.

"How did they know where we were? How did they get in?"

He shakes his head. "We don't know."

One of the other men, Charlie, looks at Seth accusingly. "It was your group. It had to be. Someone in your group gave us up to Vincent." It's weird to see the hate on Charlie's usually smiling face.

Seth shakes his head. "It wasn't us. I know and trust everyone who was with us."

Charlie doesn't look satisfied, but he quiets down for the moment.

"It doesn't matter," says my father, his voice rasping. "We need to regroup. Figure out what Vincent's men wanted here."

"Were they Vincent's men? They had a different uniform," asks Seth.

"He... was here. He was looking for... someone." My father glances up at me.

"He was looking for me," I say grimly, interpreting what he's not saying.

"There was another man with him, a super," says Charlie. "He... he killed a few people." From his face, I don't think he killed them nicely.

"He had eyes like the devil... and was... wearing all black," says my father. "I think it was... your man in black."

"He was here?" I push back away from my father. This is all too much. It's too personal. The death of all these people is starting to feel like it's my fault. "Why would he be helping Vincent? Surely everyone knows by now what Vincent plans to do?"

"Vincent is smart," says my father slowly. "He will have promised him something."

I turn to Seth. "Do you know him? The man in black?"

He shakes his head. "Was he the creature I fought? That black flying lizard thing?"

I put one hand up to hold my throbbing forehead. "I don't know. I don't know anything anymore."

Zane pokes his head around the corner, his muscled chest clearly visible. "We need to gather everyone together in one place and debrief. Figure out what we're going to do. We're not safe here. They could come back at any time."

Around us, people start standing up, helping each other to walk or shuffle toward the exit.

"Where does it hurt, Dad?"

"On my side. My arm." He glances down. "My chest. Maybe my leg too? I'm not really sure."

"Are you going to be able to move?"

Seth stands up and brings back one of the planks that we've been using as a step up in the gym. "We can put him on this, use it as a stretcher. I don't think he's going to be able to move any other way."

"I wish Si was here," I mutter, looking down at my father's body. "I'm going to try a little bit of healing, Dad. I don't have much left in me at the moment. But I think I can do enough to get you to where everyone else is gathering." My chest hurts as I look down at him, bloodied and raw.

He nods. His skin is starting to look waxy, and my hands tremble as I place them over his body.

My magic splutters, and I have to drag it out from the corners of my soul. Eventually, the soft tendrils of healing magic start working their way from my fingers and into his body. I've barely begun when I feel my reserves dry up again. I feel dizzy and black dots appear in my vision. I used up too much of my magic on healing Seth and now I can't heal my father properly.

Blood everywhere. Dead eyes staring up at me. *Make my death worth something...*

I shudder and push the memories away. I have to stay focused. It's the only way to survive this.

I frown down at my father, trying to assess whether I've helped at all. His skin is a healthier color, and he's moving a little easier. "I'm sorry. I can't do any more," I whisper.

He smiles up at me like I've managed a miracle. "That was enough. I'm stronger now. I can keep going. That's all we need."

"I'll convince Si to come and heal you."

My father shakes his head. "He won't come. He's still angry with me."

"That doesn't matter, not when your life is at stake."

"Let's just take this one step at a time," says my father gently.

32

I t doesn't take long for everyone to assemble.

Out of more than three hundred people who were living in our stronghold, there are now less than forty. All those people wiped out in less than an hour. I try not to think about it. It's a ragged group that remains, and I keep glancing around, expecting to see Roger, Fiona, or Andy, or one of the many other people who died so unnecessarily.

My father is in the middle of the room, issuing orders and generally organizing the retreat from our home of the last few months. For someone like me who's used to moving around, it's been a special kind of place, one where I was able to relax and feel comfortable. Leaving it, especially like this, with so many deaths marking our departure, feels wrong. But we have no choice. Vincent knows where we are now, meaning we're vulnerable to another attack.

I rub my hands together. They're raw from the scrubbing I gave them before coming back up to the meeting area. I volunteered to be part of the clean-up crew who carried all the bodies to our outside landing area—it was the only place we could think of to put everyone together to allow us to burn all the bodies.

Most of the survivors came to the landing area and stood by as Zane and I burned the bodies using our flames. The ashes rose into the air around us, clinging to our scales, and the smell of burning flesh nearly made me gag even in my dragon form.

It was gruesome work, but I memorized every single one of those faces. Next time I meet Vincent, I'll remember them. No more feeling sorry for him or his people. No more arguing that perhaps he's right about some of the dragons.

Zane and Seth—on my father's orders as soon as he realized there was someone left to interrogate—went back to the original three soldiers we fought but didn't kill. I don't know what happened precisely, but only one of the three men survived the encounter, and that soldier is now lying in the infirmary, tied to the table.

"Mei!" My father's voice carries across the room, despite his less than ideal state. He's still covered in blood, but he seems to prefer it that way. He's been talking to Seth, and they're both looking at me strangely.

I walk quickly over, trying to determine if he needs more healing magic. I've managed to give him a couple more short bursts since the first one in the gymnasium. His color seems better and his voice is certainly stronger.

I'm also trying not to focus on Seth's familiar face and the way he's looking at me as if he doesn't hate me anymore.

"Mei, I need you to go with us to see this soldier. I want to ask him some questions."

"Aren't we leaving soon?"

"Exactly. So let's go." He stands up, wobbles slightly, and then strides off as if I didn't see a thing. Seth gestures for me to go next, and I follow my father, wishing I could just heal him right here and now and be done with it.

But knitting Seth's vertebrae together took it out of me. I desperately want to contact Si, but Vincent's soldiers destroyed all our communications equipment. We won't be able to get any outside help until we leave this place.

When we get to the locked room that Zane is guarding, the older dragon looks at me. "You sure you want to do this?"

I glance at my father, who shrugs. It's my decision. I nod grimly, the feeling of carrying Fiona's limp body to the mass gravesite still imprinted on my brain.

We all follow Zane inside the room. The soldier is lying on the metal table, his hands and feet firmly tied to the sides. Seth and my father take a position on the far side, and I stand with my arms crossed on the other. He struggles a little when he sees me, and his eyes widen. I don't know what I've done to instill such fear. He doesn't even glance at Zane, who is standing by his feet and is probably more dangerous than I will ever be.

My father limps to his side and smiles down at the man. "You recognize Mei?" he says softly. "You know how powerful she is?"

He starts struggling harder, as if he could actually get away from us.

"Mei could rip you apart, right where you're lying. She could burn you slowly, piece by delectable piece, until your taste buds watered for a taste of the meat you'd smell cooking."

My father's words float over the soldier, and the man goes paler and paler. Sweat drips down his face, and a couple of times he tries to pull himself out of the straps around his wrists.

He keeps giving me wild-eyed sideways glances, like he

believes everything my father is saying. It's not hard to get him talking; I don't even have to touch him.

"Vincent wants her. That's why he was here. He was very angry when he realized you weren't here."

"Who's the man in black?" I ask.

"I don't know." The soldier shakes his head vigorously. His green eyes are fully dilated, and his hair is slick with sweat.

I take a step forward, glaring down at the man.

He starts shaking. His boots make a strange noise as they shudder against the metal of the table. I don't break my gaze, but allow the flames to glow in my eyes.

"There are rumors," he says, the words tumbling out. "I don't know for sure."

"What are they saying?"

"That he's called a Minokawa. From some tiny island in Asia. His kind hate dragons."

"Why?" I ask.

"He tells stories about the things dragons used to do to humans and other supernaturals. Especially your kind." He glances at me significantly, as if I'm a different dragon to the rest.

"What do you mean? My kind of dragon?"

"He calls you the three-souled dragon."

I glance at Zane, who shrugs. "What does that mean?" I ask my father.

"You have the ring and Tarsal," says Damien. As ever when he talks about my mother's soul being inside me, his words are clipped. "I believe it refers to that."

I frown. "But that's nothing special, right? Tarsal probably had more than that inside him."

Zane shakes his head. "Tarsal was an outlaw. Normal

dragons didn't go around stealing the magic of other dragons unless they'd renounced our society."

"He talked about it like it was common."

"Maybe among the dragons he knew." Zane shrugged. "I only have my own magic."

I feel Tarsal's smoky magic and my mother's clear, bright magic woven into the fabric of my soul. I can't imagine being without either of them anymore. "Not even when a dragon died? Like Tarsal did?"

"A dragon's magic is considered sacred. We would never have allowed it." Zane looks at me solemnly.

My heart is beating fast, and I don't know where to look. It suddenly feels like Zane disapproves of me. "Is that how most dragons would see it?" I ask.

"I can only speak for my clan," says Zane softly.

I stare at his face, trying to figure out what he thinks of me now. I didn't know it was considered such a taboo concept. Tarsal talked about it like it was common, at least for the survivors of the dragon wars. I shake my head once to clear it and let out a shaky breath, trying to understand why I always end up doing things the wrong way.

"Why did the man in black join with Vincent? Isn't he a super?" I'm determined to get things back on track.

"Like I said, he hates dragons. Vincent promised him..." The soldier hesitates.

"What?" my father says sharply. He places one hand on the man's shoulder, his long, pale fingers splayed out over the man's ripped shirt.

"Vincent promised that he could have Mei when Vincent is finished with her," the soldier says in a rush.

"What the hell does he want with me?" The words are out before I can think.

The soldier shakes his head. "He's real focused on

getting you, that's all I know. The dude don't even care that you won't have your powers or your ability to turn into a dragon any more once Vincent is finished with you."

"What's Vincent going to do with me?" I know the answer, but I want to hear it from the soldier.

The man looks at me like I'm stupid. "Use your magic for the spell web."

"Does Vincent have any dragons yet?" I ask.

"He had one, but you helped that one escape. It weren't a good one though, wouldn't have worked, so he just used it as practice. Messed with its head a little."

I think of Sergei, pale and confused, and my anger at Vincent rises another notch.

The soldier continues talking, as if he can't shut up now that we've started him up. "Vincent was planning to have another one by the end of today. We was setting up a cell all of yesterday. He was gonna get Mei here, 'cause he's real keen to have you in particular, and then he had a plan for a second dragon in the mountains somewhere."

I glance at Zane. So Vincent might have one of us even now. "How did he know where we live?"

"That was the easy part." He glances at Seth. "That one and his friends led us right here."

33

"We didn't know they were following us," says Seth for the tenth time as he paces the hall outside where the soldier is being held.

My father looks at him suspiciously, but I'm pretty sure that's out of habit rather than a belief they did it on purpose. "When was the last time you saw Vincent?"

Seth flushes. "At the meeting of his main supporters that Mei interrupted. Right before we realized what he was planning to do."

"He could have put some kind of tracking device on you then, I suppose."

Seth looks down at his hands, like he thinks something could be hidden under his nails. "Could I still have something on me?"

Damien shakes his head. "I checked already. It must have burned off somehow."

"Or it might not have been Seth who had the tracking device," I say. "He was quite prominent within the group. I would have gone for someone less..."

"Showy?" asks Zane.

"I was going to say conspicuous," I say, glaring at Zane.

Seth shakes his head. "I should have known. We should have been more careful. All those people..." He trails off, his expression haunted.

I take a step toward him. "You couldn't have known. Vincent is smart. He would have played his part to perfection."

"It doesn't matter," says my father quietly. "As Roger used to say, it's all water under the bridge now. We must move quickly to leave this place and find a new sanctuary." For a fleeting moment, my father's face shows his raw grief at the loss of his friend, and then it's gone, replaced by his usual determined expression.

"Where will we go?" I ask.

"I'll apply to the Mountain supers again. They may have another stronghold we can use."

"They still hate me," I say.

"Not all of them," says my father, his expression grim. "And perhaps this latest tragedy will help sway the tide."

"Do you want to go talk to their leaders?" Zane asks my father.

"Thank you, Zane. I think we should." He glances at me. "Mei, you stay here. I need you to organize the survivors and their possessions. One bag per person, no more. They must be ready to leave in an hour." He looks to Zane. "We leave in five minutes."

"Yes, sir," says Zane.

"What if you're not back in an hour?" I ask anxiously.

"Leave without us."

Seth steps forward. "What about me, sir? Can I come with you to visit the Mountain supers?"

Damien shakes his head. "It's too confusing. You were on another side not so long ago. Stay here with Mei and keep our people moving. They're still in shock. It won't be an easy task to get them all ready to leave so quickly."

My father and Zane stride away, and I'm left standing next to Seth.

"How did we get stuck with all the work, while they go flying?" I ask.

Seth glances down at me, a tiny curl on one side of his mouth. "At least you haven't lost your sense of humor," he says. His hair—now much longer than the regulation agent cut he used to have—is all messed up around his face. It suits him.

I shrug. "If you can't laugh at yourself, who are you going to laugh at?"

"Other people?"

"They're never as silly as I am." I start walking toward the main common room, trying to ignore the pang of longing I feel when I look at him.

"You're okay with not going?" he says, catching up with me.

"To the Mountain super stronghold?" I shake my head, probably a little too hard. Suddenly there's blood everywhere. *Make my death mean something.* I swallow hard. "The last time I went there... that's when Liling..."

"I'm sorry for your loss," says Seth solemnly. But it sounds wooden, too formal.

I stop in the hall. "Do you remember Liling at all?"

He keeps walking for two more steps before stopping and turning back to me. His scar is marked out clearly down his face. "Liling wasn't on our side when I... died. I don't remember being kindly disposed toward her." He hesitates. "But I remember you." His expression becomes intense, like he's focusing only on me.

"What do you remember about me?" I ask softly. Despite everything, my heart is beating erratically in my chest.

He takes a step closer. "Your bravery. Your protective instincts. Your caring." His words are little more than a whisper.

"That's better than before," I say, my eyes hungrily taking in every line on his face. "At least you don't hate me any more."

"I never hated you, not really," he says. He looks away, then back at me. "I tried, because I wanted to blame you for everything. But you kept doing things that didn't make sense. Not acting the way the villain in my story was supposed to act."

"I'm glad I'm not your villain any more." I frown, thinking over my words. "That's the weirdest thing I've ever said to anyone."

He grins down at me, genuine amusement on his face. He even looks a little carefree, for the first time since he was reborn.

Part of me wants this moment to last forever. In those dark hours after he died, I would have given anything to be standing here with Seth again. My hand lifts a fraction of an inch, and I wish more than anything that I could touch him.

But then I catch the smell of something burning. A bloodied chest fills my memory, and I take a step away. It's not the right time. "We better get started packing," I say softly, my voice filled with regret.

He stares at me a moment longer, as if trying to memorize my face, and then nods once. "We have a lot to do," he agrees. Then he turns quickly and leads the way back down the corridor.

I let out the breath I'd been holding and follow him.

In the main hall, everyone is gathering and talking

loudly. Some have bags and others don't. "I'll go this way, you go the other. Meet in the middle," says Seth.

It takes a while, and some cajoling and arguing, but eventually we have the full contingent of people ready in the main common room.

"The hour is almost up, right?" I say to Seth as he pauses beside me.

He glances at his watch and nods. "They'll be back."

A feeling of dread has built inside me, and I don't know if it's real or just my fear of losing another person. "Do you... do you feel anything?" I ask.

"About what?"

"I think something might have gone wrong," I whisper. I'd known when they were attacking our stronghold. Perhaps what I'm feeling is another premonition.

Seth shakes his head. "You're just worried. Your father and Zane are fine. The Mountain supers wouldn't dare hurt either of them."

As the minutes tick by, the feeling in my gut gets worse and I start pacing. Seth wanders back over to me and gently grabs my arm. "You're making people agitated," he says, nodding toward the worried faces nearby.

It's been a tough day. I'm tired. That's the only way I can explain the tears that leak out of my eyes and run down my face. Seth gathers me into his arms and holds me tight against him. I lean into him, feeling his warmth and his solid chest. His heart beats under my cheek, and I breathe in his scent.

"It's going to be okay," he whispers. "Your father is a tough old bastard."

"Mei! Seth! There's something coming in on the cameras!" Ben, a skinny kid who was the son of one of the camera operators killed in Vincent's raid, comes running into the room.

"What were you doing in there?"

He didn't even bother to look sheepish. "I figured we'd need someone monitoring the screens. Come on. Hurry."

We race behind him into the war room. Most of the monitors are either broken or just dead, but he's managed to power up three in one corner. On one screen is a gray-colored creature with only one full wing, the other burned and broken. It has a misshapen back and seems to be sinking lower in the sky the closer it gets.

Mei, come help us. The voice in my head is weak, but I recognize it immediately. "That's Zane and my father," I say running out the door. Seth is right behind me.

My clothes are off my body, and I've leapt into the sky before my dragon body is fully formed. My wings unfurl even as I beat them down against the wind, praying that I'm going to get there in time.

What the hell happened to them? asks Seth, already flying beside me in his phoenix form. Having him there calms my fiercely pounding heart.

I don't know. He looked gray.

I think it was ash.

It feels like fireworks are bursting in my head. *Ash?*

Like from a fire? Or an explosion.

I can't think any more, so instead, I concentrate on flying to where we last saw them on the screen.

They've dipped lower than is comfortable, and I dive down as soon as I see Zane's battered body. On his back, I recognize the misshapen body of my father, lying uncon-scious. How Zane's keeping Damien on his back like that, I don't really understand.

How are we going to do this? asks Seth.

I don't know. We have to get them to the ground. I don't know if I can carry Zane in dragon form.

But you heal faster in dragon form, don't you?

I nod. It's a difficult call to make.

We swoop down, and Zane looks up, heaving out a huff of breath when he sees us. *About time.*

I'm going to take my father off your back. Then we'll all land just over there. I point at a small flat section of rock that's barely big enough for one dragon to land on, let alone two and my father.

But Zane's too exhausted to even raise an eyebrow, let alone an argument. I manage to pull my father's unconscious body off his back and hold him tightly against my chest, my wings beating overhead. Zane half falls, half lands on the strip of almost-flat rock.

He thumps to the ground, and his head bounces against a boulder. I land on a higher rock and push healing magic into my father's body. I'm stronger now than I was earlier, and after a moment, I feel him moan and move against me.

Seth hovers protectively in the air over our heads, so I turn my attention to Zane. He must have managed to get this far on pure willpower alone, because I don't know how the hell he flew with one wing almost completely destroyed. I put my paws on his scales and pulse some healing dragon magic into him as well.

After a moment his breathing calms, and he opens one eye in my direction.

Thanks, he says.

What happened? I ask.

Zane swallows hard, as if the memory is a bad one. *They let us come in, and then they attacked us. There was an explosion. I don't remember much else. Carrick was there. He led us to safety and then had to return to the fighting.* Zane closes his eyes and lets out a long breath. For a moment, he doesn't breathe in again, and I'm about to send another blast of healing magic into him when his chest rises again.

The Mountain supers are on Vincent's side.

It's over. Vincent has won.

34

W*here are we going to go if the Mountain supers won't help us?* I ask Seth in an agitated tone. I'm sitting on the outcrop, my father cradled in my arms. He's still unconscious, but he's moving and his skin color has freshened up.

We just have to lead them away from the stronghold we're in now. Perhaps we'll find a cave or something. Seth is perched nearby, his flames swirling in the late afternoon sun. He has a halo of light around his head.

You want a bunch of stressed-out survivors to make camp in a cave?

He shrugs one elegant feathered shoulder. *If it's the only option we have.*

We have to get back to the others.

Yes. Seth looks down at Zane. His body is battered and broken. *We'll need him to return to human form.*

I wince, knowing exactly how painful that's going to be for Zane. *I don't suppose...*

He's too heavy for both of us.

I nod, knowing he's right. Leaning forward, I touch

Zane's flank. *Zane, wake up. You have to change.* I push tendrils of healing magic into his body, trying to save some for my father as well. Zane's injuries aren't life threatening, or at least they're not as long as he doesn't fall into a rock-covered canyon here in the mountains.

He blinks open one eye. *No. Go away.*

You have to. It's not safe out here. We need to get you into human form so we can carry you.

I can carry myself, he says, trying to lift his body again. After a moment, he thumps back into the ground and groans.

We don't have time for you to go all stupid about it. Change now. The lives of everyone else waiting for us in the stronghold depend on it as well.

He glares up at me, but moments later the familiar tingling as another dragon changes nearby goes down my spine.

In his human form, he has horrific burns all down one side of his body and one arm is almost completely destroyed. It's hard to see how this is going to be better for him than his dragon form, but it will only be for the few minutes it will take us to fly home.

Seth picks him up, his flames licking about his body, but Zane doesn't say a word.

We fly back to the stronghold in silence, and as soon as I land, I put my father down and change. Once Seth has landed and placed Zane down carefully, and we're fully dressed again, I start to plan.

"Zane needs to change back into his dragon form. The gym is the only place big enough for him to do that."

Seth nods and then picks up Zane from where he's lying unconscious on the floor beside us. I gently grab my father, and we take off as fast as we can. "We'll leave my father and Zane till last, to give them the most time possible to heal."

Seth is huffing as he carries the much larger dragon. "We have to get as many people out of here as soon as we possibly can. We don't know what they're planning," he says.

"I'll get Ben and his older brother to lead one group to the south stairs, and they can go down there and take the landrovers," I say. "There should be enough to carry at least half the group."

Seth nods. "We can take a few down to the staging point in shuttle runs."

We pass several people along the way, and the knowledge of what's happened to my father and Zane gets around quickly. The fear and panic is almost visible. The stronghold feels unsafe and dangerous, whereas once it used to feel like salvation.

In the gym, I lay my father down on the mats and press my hands over his head and chest. I push more of my healing magic into his body, trying to remember not to overload him all at once. Keep it slow, keep it gentle. All I have are rudimentary skills. We need to find someone who knows what they're doing.

We need Si.

"Can you get Zane to turn?" asks Seth.

I nod. "Yes. I'll stay here with them for a while. Can you...?"

"I'll start the evacuation. I think I can manage it."

"Talk to Ben, the kid from the war room."

Seth nods and is gone before I can think too much about it. When the door opens again a few moments later, I'm expecting Seth back with another question, but it's Sergei.

"Did Vincent get them?" he asks with a quiver in his

voice. He's carrying a first aid kit and comes closer, clutching it against his chest.

I shake my head. "The mountain supers aren't as good an ally as my father was expecting. I think the association with me has soured them to the cause."

He shakes his head. "It's the association with the man in black." He holds out the bag. "I thought there might be something useful in here."

Taking the bag from him, I rifle through the bandages and safety pins until I find some burn cream. "Here, use this on Zane."

Sergei looks down at the cream and then at Zane. "You want me to...?"

"I need to look after my father."

He nods reluctantly and moves to where Zane is lying.

As he rubs the cream into the horrific burns, I gaze down at my father's unconscious form. "Do you know how to force the change in someone?" I ask Sergei.

Sergei hesitates and then nods. "It's not a pleasant experience on either side."

"Zane needs to be in his dragon form. We have no choice."

"I will do Zane. You do your father."

I glance up from staring at my father and frown at Sergei. "What?"

"I do Zane. You do your father."

"But my father can't shift. He's not a full super," I say, shaking my head. Jeff told me the situation a long time ago. The SIG don't like agents who are too strong, so they make sure their trainees are only a fraction supernatural.

"He might not be a full super, but he has enough in him. I can feel it."

35

"How come you can feel it and I can't?" All I can think is that Sergei has finally gone off the deep end.

Sergei hesitates, staring into my eyes for longer than is comfortable. "I spent a long time as a dragon. It... it allows me to be closer to the other form. I can sense it in others."

"What kind of super is he?"

Sergei shrugs. "I don't know. Something akin to a dragon, I would guess. There's enough inside him to make the shift, especially if you help him."

I look down at my father, his pain-ravaged face. I don't have sufficient healing magic to help him. If there's any chance at all that Sergei's right, then making him shift is going to help.

I nod. "Okay. What do I do?"

"Just push inside his head and search for his other side. It will be obvious once you're in there. Don't stay for too long, just pull it out from where it's hiding, force it to become the dominant side, and leave."

I grasp his hand tightly and close my eyes.

Sergei makes it sound easy, but I'm pretty sure it's not. The coppery smell of blood mixed with burnt skin is affecting my concentration and it takes a few moments to calm down enough to use my magic again. But as soon as I'm inside my father's head, I sense it. It's tightly woven under layers of protection, like he thinks someone might try to steal that side of him.

When I touch the protective layer it starts to glow an angry red, and a burst of pain radiates through my head.

Damien, I whisper inside his head. *I need you to help me. I know you're in here somewhere. Just let it go. Let your guard down, just this once.*

For a long time, nothing happens. *Come on, Dad. You can do this. Let me help.*

I focus my magic, and send tentacles of it around his mind, trying to find another way to pull his other side to the surface. But there's no other way. I let my magic touch the protective layer again, and another burst of pain hits my body. He has to be the one to undo the protection.

Let it go, Dad.

It happens so suddenly, I almost miss it. It's like he lets out a breath, and relaxes. Like he's decided to trust me. The layers of protection fall away, leaving the dormant supernatural magic open and vulnerable. I feel the shimmering fear inside my father, the panic at leaving himself so exposed. Even if it's to me, his daughter.

It's okay, Dad. I'm going to help you. I push some healing magic into his weakened body, gradually, gently, trying to make the transition to his super form easier.

Take some of my magic. It will help. Tarsal's voice sounds as if he's speaking from far away. Perhaps he is.

Drawing on Tarsal's magic, I slowly help my father separate his human form from his super form inside his body. It takes a while, and my father seems to be reluctant, despite the zing of electricity that keeps zapping across his body. Then with a loud whoosh of air, I'm forcibly pushed outside his head.

I shake my head, trying to get rid of the dizzy feeling. It's the growl that tells me something is different, and I open my eyes. My father's still lying unconscious next to me. But that's the only thing that hasn't changed.

My father's super form is slightly larger than his human size, but his shape and skin have changed, and he now looks like a giant version of the color-changing lizard that may or may not be his ancestor.

He's a chameleon like Si, so it's not anything I haven't seen before.

Except it is.

His chameleon skin is silver and white, instead of the more familiar browns and blacks that help the others hide in plain sight. It seems fragile and thin, unlike the hardened exterior Si always had. In his lizard form, my father couldn't hide anywhere except right next to Sergei in Northern Russia. I reach out and touch his flank. It's soft and warm, and he twitches in his sleep.

Beside us, Zane's enormous dragon body emerges out of his human form in a crack of bones and energy. His large black-scaled limbs lie limp next to Sergei, and I stir, needing to help him as well.

Zane saved my father by bringing him back here. Despite our arguments, he's loyal and strong, and that's important.

I stand up and move to Zane's enormous body, placing my hands on his side. I feel his breath, thin and reedy, and his heart beating slowly. I push my magic into him, weaving it softly into the tiny micro-organisms that make up a dragon's body. As always, it can't be too fast, it has to be just the right speed for it to be successful. I have to keep reminding myself, repeating the words under my breath so I don't rush it like I want to.

I let out a breath when I feel it pumping through his veins, healing him from the inside out.

Just at that moment, the door bursts open. Seth rushes into the room. "We've got a problem. The others are all gone, evacuated either to the south or the north entrance, but there are two helicopters inbound, both marked with Vincent's logo, with large machines tied underneath."

My heart lurches. "How far?" Our patients are still too weak to move.

"I saw them on the screens in the war room. So however far away those cameras are placed."

"We have to hurry." Even as I say the words, I glance over at Zane's huge unconscious dragon form and my father's much smaller shape.

How the hell are we going to get them out of here?

36

Zane stumbles behind me, his large steps catching on the rough stone floor. Seth and Sergei only just manage to catch him before he falls. He's back in human form, but the change was difficult, and I think it's set him back.

But we don't have time to check.

My father was able to stay in his chameleon form because he's significantly smaller than Zane, but he's stumbling along beside me in a dazed state. As well as changing their form, most chameleons can hide by shimmering and shifting through a range of colours similar to their natural ones. Si had been mostly browns and blacks, sometimes mottled, sometimes matted, and he could hide anywhere, including right in front of my face, and I wouldn't see him. Si could also add scales to all or just part of his human body, which helped him in a fight.

My father, meanwhile, couldn't hide in the middle of a corn field with his white and silver coloring. He doesn't seem to be able to change to anything other than bright white, dull white, off white, metallic silver and matte silver. It's like being next to a beacon that's shouting, "Come find me! I'm here!"

We're down in the lower caverns, heading for the exit that the others took on foot not so long ago. There's no other way to get Zane and my father out of here. Neither of them is in any fit state to fly.

"Can those machines find dragons?" asks Seth.

"Depends what kind of machines they are," I say grimly. I'm trying to keep my father moving forward, and I can't think about anything other than putting one foot in front of the other and getting us out of here. "Just keep going."

The walls shudder above us. I glance up, my mouth open to ask the question, but then I realize I don't want to know what it was. So I keep my mouth shut and push myself down the hall.

We're not far from the exit when I hear the sound of baying. Dogs?

"Can dogs smell dragons?" I hear Seth whispering to Sergei.

"Not in my time," replies the Russian dragon. "But then, dogs weren't generally used as pets back then."

"There's no knowing what he's got up his sleeve," I say. "We have to hurry."

Just then, my father glances around us, his lizard features blinking slowly. He's been stumbling along beside me, but he tenses and then stops. He doesn't make a sound, just looks at me out of his strange reptile eyes.

Then he leaps away from me, onto the wall, and scuttles up and along the ceiling. His lizard feet stick to the rocks easily, and he scurries away like he's been doing it all his life. He turns the corner of the corridor, still attached to the ceiling, and disappears.

"That was weird," says Sergei.

I glare at him before running after my father. "Dad!" I call out in a loud whisper. My words seem to echo along the tunnel and I wince. Up above, the baying of dogs gets louder.

You need to find him. He doesn't know how to be a chameleon. My mother's voice is reedy and distant, like she's speaking from far away. I haven't heard her inside my head for a while. But I feel her urgency inside me like a coiled spring.

Running to the end of the corridor, where it turns a corner, I peer around, trying to glimpse his silver shape. I can't see him. He's gone.

The others catch up, and I turn scared eyes to Seth. "I don't know where he's gone."

You need to find him. Don't leave him. My heart is pounding in my chest in response to my mother's urgent entreaties. I have to find him.

"He's a tough guy. He'll be fine," says Seth.

"We need to search for him. I'll go back up the corridor. You keep going this way."

I start to move past them, but Seth puts out one hand and grasps my arm tightly.

"We have to keep going, Mei. There's no time to search for him." Seth's eyes track up over the rocky tunnel's ceiling. "If he can hide from us that easily, he should be able to hide from them."

Something rumbles in the rocks above, sending dust down over our heads. The dogs' baying and yipping is louder and more excited, like they've found a trail.

Don't leave him... Her voice is thin and reedy now, like she can't keep to the surface of my mind any longer.

Despite the terrible sinking feeling in my stomach, I swallow hard and nod at Seth.

I'm sorry, I whisper to my mother.

We move on, our strides speeding up into a run without anyone having to say the words. I keep checking for a flicker of silver in the tunnel around us, but I don't see a thing.

We finally make it to the exit, a hidden door in the middle of the tunnel. If I didn't have Seth here with me to show us, I wouldn't have known where it was. He sees my look.

"I didn't know either until one of the other survivors showed me. They were prepared for everything."

I pull open the door and hold it for the others to climb onto the ladder below. Zane struggles to step down, so we all have to hold him and carefully get him through the door and down the metal ladder into the narrow tunnel below. It's dark and murky down here, and I feel spider webs brushing my face.

But at least it's safer.

I climb back up to close the door. Before I shut it for good, I take one last look around and call out softly to my father. The sound of dogs is getting louder. Their barks are stronger, but now I can hear the sound of claws scrabbling on rock as they run faster and faster toward us. I call out to my father again, hoping against hope that he's just been waiting for the right moment. "Now's the right moment, Dad."

He doesn't answer. I don't know where he's gone, or how to find him again.

I shut the door firmly behind me and climb down the metal ladder to the others.

"You okay?" asks Seth.

I nod sharply, but don't speak. I can't. It's finally hit me, the realization of what this all means.

Our people are lost.
Our leader is gone.
Our cause is over.

37

"We have to keep fighting!" Zane's voice echoes around the small cave we're hiding in. He's pacing up and down the narrow space, his large form struggling with the low ceiling.

"There's no point," I say grimly. It's been three days since we escaped from our stronghold, and my father is still missing. "It was my father who had all the connections. We have nothing now."

We managed to catch up to the other survivors, but many people chose to go their separate ways. There didn't seem much point in continuing on together when all our leaders are dead or gone. We're down to just fourteen people.

My father's disappearance is the last straw for me. This fight against Vincent has taken away too much. Lee, Jeff, Tarsal, Liling, and now my father. I glance over to where Seth is sitting with Sergei. Even Seth has been taken from me. He says he remembers everything, but the last few months' worth of experiences have changed him. The scar running across his face is just the physical expression of that. He's not the same person. Is he someone I can still love? Does he still love me?

I don't know the answer to those questions, and it's haunting me.

Vincent has successfully taken everything. Sergei was right, he *is* more powerful than we are.

"There's every point," argues Zane.

I don't know where this new burst of zealousness has come from. No one else but Zane is feeling it. He's been trying to whip us up into a frenzy for the last day, and it's not working.

"What's your plan, Zane?" asks Seth, his eyes hooded.

"We attack head on. He'd never expect it."

"What about the machines that suck away our supernatural abilities?" I say. "Or the darts that hit us in mid-air?"

For a second, Zane's eyes flicker. Then he recovers. "Then we do it in secret. We go in and attack, destroy the machines. And the darts."

"There aren't enough of us. And of those who are here, most of us are wounded or exhausted. We can't find Vincent's soldiers."

"Then we assassinate Vincent."

"How is that better than what he's doing?"

"This isn't the time to take the moral high ground! He's winning, and I don't like it."

"He's won," I say softly, my eyes filling with tears.

Zane sounds just enough like my father to make it difficult to listen to him. I stand up and move away, heading toward the tunnel that leads to the opening of the cave. It's cold and mossy in here, but it's better than being caught.

Standing next to the entrance, I gaze out at the early morning light as it moves through the mountains, dancing with the shadows.

"We have to make a plan," a voice says softly beside me.

I don't move a muscle. For some reason, I can tell where Seth is most of the time without even looking.

"To disband, to not get caught."

"Those are very defeatist plans," he says, a gentle rebuke in his words.

I turn to him with flashing eyes. "What other plans do you suggest? Perhaps we attack? So that everyone else gets killed? Or so I get killed? Or worse, captured? Then let Vincent put the spell web back up? How would that be? Is that what you've wanted all along?" Even as the words tumble out, I know they're unfair. I don't really mean them, but the rage and grief have been building up inside me for days. There have been too many deaths.

But Seth seems to know and understand what's happening. He looks at me with compassion and places one hand on my arm. His touch calms me, but doesn't stop the tears that are now running down my face.

"I can't do it any more, Seth," I whisper brokenly. "I miss Jeff. I miss Liling. I miss *Dad*. I miss them all."

Seth hesitates and then puts both arms around me, pulling my body against him. My head falls against his chest, and I feel his heart beating. My tears don't stop. I can't stop them, and the sobs are wrenched from my body as I try to figure out how I'm going to move on, yet again.

Seth makes soft noises, trying to comfort me, but there's nothing he can do to stop the tide.

"I'm sorry," I eventually get out. "I don't normally do that kind of thing."

"It's okay. You've been through a lot."

I make a face, trying to downplay my tears. "Thank you."

"It's the least I can do after everything I've done to you."

I shake my head vigorously. "You didn't remember. And

you were attacked. I'm not surprised you reacted the way you did."

Seth gazes down at me. "I promised you forever, to be at your side always, and then I deserted you. I attacked you. That's unforgivable."

"No, it's not. I forgive you."

Seth leans in, until our foreheads meet. "You shouldn't forgive me. I don't forgive me."

Slowly, I put my hands up to cup his cheek. His single eye searches my face, as if he's trying to see something. I don't know what he's looking for, but I smooth my thumb across his skin, lightly over his scar. "I would have reacted the same way. You were only trying to protect people from going through the same thing you did. I get that."

"I should have been protecting you." He lets out an anguished breath. "I don't deserve your forgiveness, Mei."

I give a crooked little smile. "I can protect myself," I say. "I'm a dragon."

Seth leans a little closer and touches his lips to mine, moving softly over the sensitive skin. I feel his rough stubble against my cheek, and his hands move up into my hair, holding me close. I shut my eyes, the heat of his body imprinted on me. I lean in, trying to get closer to him, to feel his skin against mine.

I feel like I'm burning up as our lips and tongues clash. I can't seem to get enough of him. It's like I've been lost in a desert, and he's the only water I've seen for days.

It's Seth who eventually pulls away, however reluctantly. I moan at the loss of the heat and try to pull him back into my arms.

"Mei, stop. It's moving too fast. You're grieving. I can't take advantage of you when you're like this."

And as easily as that, he reminds me about Liling and

my father and everything else that's hanging over me. The heat turns to dust, and I step back. My whole body, that moments before was burning up, now feels numb. I shake my head. "You're right. We shouldn't have done that."

"No, no. Mei, that's not what I mean." He cups his hands against my cheeks and frames my face. "I wish we could be by ourselves, to continue what we just started. But it's not the right time or place. You're grieving. We both have responsibilities. We have to finish this thing with Vincent."

The numbness starts to thaw. "I don't know what to do next," I whisper.

"We can work it out together," he says. "You're not alone. I'm here with you." He drops a soft kiss onto my lips, and the sizzle reaches my toes.

"Come on, let's go back inside and talk to the others. See if we can come up with a plan."

"You know what Zane will want to do. Go in with guns blazing."

Seth lets out a small laugh. "He's just one voice, Mei. And you have power too. People will listen to you. Never forget that."

We walk back toward the main cave, his warm hand clasped in mine. We're almost there, when I stop abruptly. "Seth, do you think my father is still alive?"

"I think that if anyone could possibly be still alive in that situation, it's your father," he replies. In the darkness of the tunnel, I can only see the flash of his eye as he looks down at me.

It's not the answer I was looking for, but it makes me smile. He's right, my father is one of the most resourceful bastards I know. He'll be fine.

A noise in the night sky behind us makes me turn back toward the entrance. Golden wings break the surface of the darkness. Someone is coming. My heart beats faster. Has Vincent found us again so quickly? Taking a few steps back to the entrance, I try to make out who it could be. Seth turns toward the noise as well, and his eyes burn with phoenix fire.

I feel the distinctive buzz of another dragon in the sky. One I've never seen before.

In a moment I've transformed, my blood-red and gold scales reflecting the pale moon. I spread my wings, trying to prevent myself from toppling off the narrow ledge that easily held myself and Seth in our human forms.

Who's there? I ask the dragon directly. My scales are standing on end like a cat preparing for a fight.

I am Elena. Her voice is silky smooth, strong and vibrant. *I bring Carrick to you. He asks you to trust us.*

I search through the night, and spot Carrick on her back. My scales settle down, and I fold back my wings. I transform again into my human form and look down morosely at my destroyed human clothes.

Seth disappears behind me and returns a moment later with a blanket. His hand lingers on my shoulder as he wraps it around me. We step back into the cave, and Elena lands, turning into her human form as soon as Carrick climbs from her back. She's tall and elegant, with long blonde hair and beautiful eyes. She's also completely naked and doesn't seem to care. It's only because Carrick hands her a long black dress that she pulls it over her head in a careless manner.

Carrick comes toward me, and I hug him tightly. He smells of basalt and comfort.

There's also blood on his shirt, and undertones of gunpowder.

I pull back. "What happened?" I ask.

He glances back at Elena. "There was a rebellion." He hesitates. "Led by me. I am now the Mountain King."

I can feel my mouth gaping, but I can't do anything about it, I'm so shocked at his news. "How the...? What...?"

"I will tell you the whole story sometime. But for now, we must hurry. Elena has a way to defeat Vincent."

38

"Elena is a Mountain dragon. She was a priestess before she was put to sleep deep in the mountains a long time ago," says Carrick.

"Not always a priestess," says Elena softly.

There's a tension in the air that I don't quite understand. Carrick glares at Elena. "She helped us win the rebellion."

"Not by choice."

I frown. "What is she talking about?"

"We were down in the bowels of the Mountain Stronghold and discovered Elena and two of her brethren." He touches a small amulet around his neck. "We found this with them. Turns out it can control a priestess who has taken the vow."

"She has to do whatever you say?"

Carrick shrugs. "Until I choose to set her free." He glares at Elena again. "Which will be a long time from now. She and her kind betrayed us all and helped the Earthbound set up the spell web three hundred years ago. She has much to atone for."

"What does that have to do with anything?" asks Zane impatiently.

"She was alive at the time of Vincent's machines and knows secrets that no other dragons were privy to."

"Such as?" I ask.

"Such as how the spell web is formed."

"How does that help us? We already know what Vincent needs. He hasn't exactly been shy about it," I say impatiently.

"Vincent has told you he needs the dragons, but there is a spell you need as well. Vincent found it in the old texts. I know it by heart." Elena's voice is soft, but it carries across the room.

"Again, how does that help us?" asks Zane. "Can we use it to stop him from creating another spell web?"

"No, there's no way to disrupt it, precisely."

"Then what's the point? Why are you acting like you've handed us a big secret?" Zane's tone is becoming impatient.

I hold my breath. Something has clicked in my head. "So you could recreate the spell web? Could we make one before he does? Maybe control it instead of him?"

Elena shakes her head. "We need some of the magic Vincent has running through his veins. It is Earthbound magic, and a spell web cannot be created without it."

My breath rushes out in disappointment.

"Then how the hell does that help us?" explodes Zane on the other side of me. I understand his frustration.

"There *is* a way to take control of the spell web from Vincent once he has created the spark that brings it to life. A dragon can wrest control from him with the right spell. We could take over."

"You could do that? We could—"

Elena interrupts my words. "I am oath-bound to never use these spells."

"Then, again, how the hell does this help us?"

Elena glances at Carrick. "I am prepared to break my lesser oath of secrecy."

"We have to hit them with everything we have!" Zane interrupts as he paces up and down the room again. "We can't mess around with spells that we don't even know will work."

"We don't have much to hit Vincent *with*," I reply. "And as soon as you or I come up against their machines, we're toast."

"Then we use stealth. Just a couple of us go in, we kill Vincent, and then leave."

I shake my head again. "We've done that before. He'll be expecting it. He'll have guards everywhere."

Carrick is standing as still as stone across from me. He was there with us when Tarsal died. He doesn't say a word, but the memories are dancing in his eyes.

Seth squeezes my hand. "How about I go in by myself, tell him I was wrong, and ask to join again?"

I hesitate, wondering if Vincent would really be that gullible. "I don't think he'd believe you. Not anymore," I say.

"What other options do we have then?" says Zane, the exasperation clear on his face.

Elena moves slightly, her hands clasped together in front of her body.

I sigh. "We can listen to what Elena and Carrick have to say."

"We don't know her. She could be lying," says Zane.

"I know Carrick. If he says this will work, it will."

"I'm from the same time as she is. I've never heard of dragon priestesses. There was no talk of them helping the

Earthbound." Zane stands right in front of Elena, his face pushed into hers.

Elena doesn't move. She's calm in the face of the anger radiating off Zane. "We were a secret group. Our practices... scared the other dragons."

"Why? What did you do?"

"Our magic is different to other dragon magic. In the right circumstances, we can see the future."

"You saw all this?" I wave my hand around the small cave.

Elena shakes her head. "We saw the destruction of the entire world by the dragons. Everything turned to fire and ash by our uncaring and destructive ways." Her eyes fill with tears. "We did the only thing we could to save the world."

"They killed everyone!" yells Zane, his eyes wild. "The Earthbound killed my entire clan. I woke to find everyone *gone*." His voice is raw with emotion.

Elena flinches at Zane's outburst, but doesn't speak.

I clear my throat. "What we need is to think outside the box." I'm trying to think like Jeff, the master strategist.

If you can't win by going through the front door, find a side door or window that's unlocked.

"What we *need to do* is go in there and kill that son of a bitch," Zane grinds out.

"We wouldn't get any further than the first machine, and that's probably set up at the entrance gate, waiting for us," I reply, trying to stay patient. I know what Zane's going through, I feel the same frustration that's driving him.

"We can't just sit here and watch him take over. Once the spell web is up, and under the control of the Earthbound, that's it. We're back to having that yoke around our necks." Zane pulls at the neck of his T-shirt as if he can feel something tightening as he speaks.

Sergei nods. "I don't want to go back under the spell web. I would rather die fighting."

I stand up and start pacing. "There must be some other way than having the lot of us die fighting him. We can't face him head-on. We all know what will happen." I glance at Seth. "And one firebird alone isn't going to be able to take on everyone else while we writhe on the ground. Because I promise you, that's what will happen." An image of Tarsal lying prone on the ground, pain across every line on his face, flashes through my mind. I'm not sure whether it's from my own memories or Tarsal's.

Elena waves one elegant hand. "You do not have a choice. I have looked into the future. If you do not work with me on this, you will all die and Vincent will win."

Her voice, which was so soothing at first, is starting to grate on my nerves.

39

"You don't know that," I start to say.

She just looks at me with her knowing eyes.

"Okay, so you can. But what makes you think that taking control of the spell web is the better option?" I've worked hard to master living without it. "It goes against everything we've been fighting for."

"It's the only option that doesn't foretell death and destruction for everyone on the planet." Elena's face is impassive, but her eyes burn with an intensity that I find hard to look at.

"We need to find out if he's captured a dragon," I say, glancing around at the others. "See how far along he is."

"The only way we're going to do that is by leaving the mountains and going back into civilization," says Seth.

I shrug. "We were going to have to do that anyway."

"What if he's found his two dragons, what then?" asks Zane.

I understand Zane's desperation. I feel it too. If we let Vincent win, that's it. We won't be able to change or destroy the spell web once it's taking half our powers. We need to attack him now, while we still have the magic to do it.

But should we trust Elena? Carrick is standing nearby, his large frame locked into a stiff pose. "Carrick, what do you think? Is she right?"

"She must speak the truth. That is the first command-ment I placed on her when I understood what I held in my hands."

My brain is thinking furiously. I try to look at the situation from every angle, like Jeff taught me. "What happens when Vincent dies?" I ask Elena. "Who's in charge of the spell web then?"

She frowns, not understanding my question. "What do you mean?"

"Is he creating a spell web that relies on Vincent being in charge? Or does it pass on to the next person?"

"It should pass on to the next person who leads the Earthbound. If it's done the way Vincent wants it done."

"Do they have some kind of connection to it? The leader of the Earthbound?"

"It's where Vincent gets his magic. He's only a very weak supernatural; most of his magic comes from the spell web. The only exceptional magic he has is his connection to the Earthbound heritage that's integral to the spell."

I shake my head. "So how would it work?"

"We need Vincent to perform the first half of the spell, stealing the magic of a dragon and using it to spark up the spell web. Then we can take over the spell web from there," says Elena. "We could steal it right out from under his nose."

"We'd have to get in there, wait for him to steal the magic of a dragon, and then somehow overcome him and his guards just before he uses the second dragon to power the spell web? Then do it ourselves so we're in control of the spell web?"

"That about sums it up."

"That's crazy." But even as I say it, the tendril of an idea seeps into my head.

"It's difficult. There's a difference."

"I could give myself up," I say, my hands trembling as I push them deeper into the pockets of my jeans. "I know the magic of the spell web."

Seth launches to his feet. "No. You know what he'd do with you."

"He'll take my dragon magic and then hand me over to the man in black, probably for some kind of torture." I raise an eyebrow at Seth.

"Exactly. Why are you acting as if this is a good idea?"

"Because all this is my fault. And because I have an affinity for the spell web. I always have." I felt the inside of the spell web last time, that was how I destroyed it. I glance at Elena and see the confirmation on her face. This is what I have to do. "And you guys are going to save me before anything bad happens."

"You'll lose your dragon magic. You won't be able to transform," whispers Seth.

I nod shakily. "Someone has to do it." I don't look at Zane or Sergei. I can't. I don't want to see the pity and fear I know will be in their eyes. One of us has to give up their magic for this plan to work. I'm prepared for it to be me.

Seth takes my hand. "The last time we confronted Vincent, Tarsal and I wound up dead, and the rest of you weren't much better. This is not a good idea."

"It's the only idea we have," I say. "It's better than storming the place."

Zane has stopped pacing and is staring at me like I'm

crazy. "How is this a better plan? You'll end up with no magic at all."

Taking a deep breath, I stand up. I look at everyone, one by one. "This whole situation is my fault. I got rid of the spell web in the first place. I started all the problems." I take a breath. "Liling would still be alive if it wasn't for me."

Make my death mean something.

This would mean something. Using my magic to get control of the spell web will save the world.

This is why she saved me.

Seth growls under his breath. "Enough with the pity party, Mei. This isn't your fault. Vincent is a power-hungry megalomaniac. If it hadn't been you, it would have been someone else up against him." Seth's words are rushed, and he's staring at me as if he can force me to change my mind through mind control.

Waving my hands at his words, I shake my head. "I'm not asking for your pity. I'm just explaining why I'm going to be the one to give myself up. Vincent wants me, and I'm the only dragon he's so desperate to have that he won't ask questions. He'll believe me when I say I want to talk to him."

"But what about the rest of us? How are we going to get in?" asks Zane.

"I don't think you can," I say softly. "It will be up to me to fix this."

"You need a second dragon to start the web," says Elena softly. "I must be there, and someone else must go too." She glances at Zane and Sergei.

"I'm coming too. I'll say I persuaded you to talk to him." Seth grabs my hand. "You're not going to talk me out of it."

"No. I don't want you to put yourself in danger." But my words aren't all that persuasive. Part of me wants him there.

"I'm not letting you go on your own," says Seth grimly.

I want to be strong enough to say no, to say that he's not allowed to be there with me. But it's taking everything I have to stand here and volunteer for this. I'm scared, and I don't *want* to do this alone. I need Seth there with me. I nod once, but can't bring myself to say the words.

Sergei quietly clears his throat from where he's sitting in one corner. He's been silent this whole time. All eyes turn to him. "You will be a shadow dragon."

"If he doesn't kill me first," I say shakily. No one laughs.

"You'll lose all your powers. Even the change to your dragon form will be out of your reach." Sergei is pronouncing each word carefully, like he's saying them more for himself than for me.

"I know," I whisper. "But I wasn't a dragon for most of my life. I wasn't taught to rely on my magic. It won't be so hard on me as it would be on another dragon." It's a lie, but I try not to let it show on my face. The thought of not being able to fly or to feel my dragon body ever again is tearing me apart.

But someone has to fix this mess we're in, and I'm the one who created it. Who better to give themselves up?

And it'll make Liling's death worthwhile.

"I'll do it," says Zane suddenly, his voice cracking in the middle. "I'm older. I've had a good life."

I shake my head sadly. "He won't believe you. He'll ask questions and try to understand why you're giving yourself up. He'll be wary."

"And he won't be wary when you show up to volunteer?"

"He hates me. He's obsessed with me. It's weird and creepy, but it's true."

"That's not enough. That's just hoping."

I bite on my lip, thinking. "Perhaps we can make it seem like I'm trying to sneak in? Then he won't realize."

"Then I could do it," says Zane.

I shake my head. "You don't have the experience of the spell web that I do. And it's me Vincent wants. Let him think he's getting what his heart desires, get him a little overexcited, so that when we strike, it's a double surprise."

Zane stares at me for a long moment. It's the most serious I've seen him. "When do we move?"

Moonlight is still filtering inside the cave. I glance at Carrick and then Elena, who shrugs delicately. "First thing tomorrow," I say decisively. "We'll fly out, check the news when we can, and then get to his compound by noon. This could all be over by tomorrow night." I offer up a small smile, trying to encourage the others.

All I get back are grim expressions.

40

"What do you mean, they've gone?" I say, incredulously.

I feel like I've been robbed. Betrayed yet again.

"Zane and Sergei have gone. They're not outside," Seth repeats. His expression is more relieved than outraged.

I start pacing. "Maybe they've gone to find water. Or something to eat." But I know what's happened. They've taken off. They're trying to do the right thing and not let me be the one to give myself up.

Beside me, Elena calmly packs her travel gear. Did she know this would happen? How much of the future can she actually see?

Seth shakes his head. "No, they've gone." He eyes up their sleeping bags. "Carrick thinks it's been a while."

Carrick is outside, scanning the skies. "How the hell did we sleep through them getting up?" I look suspiciously at Seth. "You didn't plan this with them, did you?"

He holds up his hands and shakes his head. "Nothing to do with me," he says.

"Come on then. We need to go." I throw my few posses-sions into my bag, including new clothes in case I have to change unexpectedly, yet again, and the remainder of our food and drink.

Seth doesn't move, and I glance up at him, frowning. "What's the matter?"

"Perhaps this is for the best, Mei," he says.

"What are you talking about?"

"Let the older dragons take care of it. They can try to make the plan work."

"How the hell are they going to make it work? I'm the one with the affinity for the spell web. Elena is the one who knows the spell. Did any of you think of that? Stealing the magic from Vincent isn't as simple as just being there."

Seth nods, as if expecting my answer. "Then let's go."

Looking around the room, I'm afraid I'm too late. They've got a good couple of hours on us, and Zane and Sergei are both powerful dragons when they're flying. I've spent some time healing Zane over the last couple of days. Now I'm annoyed that I bothered.

"Okay."

We're in the air flying within five minutes. Carrick rides on Elena's back, and Seth and I are in formation on either side of her. We're heading toward the desert where Vincent's compound is hidden.

My wings beat against the air currents, strong and powerful. In the distance, cars are moving like ants along the highways. My magic flows through me, part of me like nothing else I've ever experienced.

The thought of losing all that is tearing me apart inside.

But I won't let another dragon do it for me. I can't. My connection to the spell web has always been so much stronger than the other dragons, and Elena as much as confirmed it had to be me last night.

It would make Liling's death worthwhile. If I can save everyone, I'll fulfil my vow to her.

The more I think about it, the more I'm convinced I'm the only one who can steal the web away from Vincent.

An hour later, we're out of the mountains. When I see a large town ahead, I turn my head to Seth and Elena.

Let's stop here. See if we can find a news station.

Seth doesn't answer, but starts banking downward, heading to the edge of the town where we can see a wooded parkland. In this new environment without the spell web to hide us, it's harder to remain inconspicuous.

Pulling out my clothes, I'm half dressed before Seth lands next to me.

Elena lands with Carrick on her back. He's pale, and I remember how much he hates flying. "You two wait here. We'll find out what's happening, and then we'll be back."

Seth and I walk toward the main street, trying to look innocent. Neither of us has the markers that make us immediately recognizable as non-human, but sometimes more perceptive humans can see that we're not what we seem.

It would be annoying to have to fight our way out of here.

We find a small bar that's showing golf on a tiny television in the corner. There's no one else sitting at the bar, so we wander over.

"Two beers, please," says Seth, his tone casual.

The bartender smiles and nods at both of us. "You tourists?"

"Sure are," says Seth. "Can't get enough of this area. It's beautiful."

"It's been a little less scenic recently, what with all the

supernaturals infesting the area. But once we get rid of that lot, it'll go back to being the nice quiet little hamlet we all love."

I swallow back the words I want to say and just nod.

"Can we change the channel?" Seth nods to the television. "We haven't seen the news in a few days."

The bartender shrugs as if it's no skin off his nose and uses the remote to flick the channel over.

We sip our drinks and wait impatiently for the presenter to get through the previous hour's sports news and then the financial program. But eventually it's there.

The news anchor is almost bouncing up and down in his chair, he's so excited. "Breaking news: The Earthbound have announced the capture of two dragons. The necessary final step to restart the spell web has been completed," he says, his suave newscaster's voice suffused with glee. "Some groups are still against the move, but the President is firmly in support, saying it is the only way to keep US citizens safe from the supernatural threat." The presenter shuffles his papers for a moment. "Let's go live to our supernatural expert, Dr. Alicia Redding."

The screen flicks to a new image, this time with a dark-haired female reporter holding a microphone and a tall, slender woman with glasses and long blonde hair pulled back off her face. The reporter starts speaking. "It's been less than four months since the spell web came down and humans were exposed to the seedy supernatural underworld. Supernatural expert Dr Alicia Redding believes that the spell web is our only hope of freeing ourselves from this nightmare."

The woman clears her throat and stares at the reporter with an intense green-eyed gaze. "I didn't quite say that," she says softly. "I said that the present situation has tipped the balance of power in favor of the supernaturals. It means humans are much more fearful than they ever were. Allowing the Earthbound to reinstate the spell web is the only way to right that natural balance."

"What do you think about boosting the level of the spell web? And that we'll still be able to see the supernaturals?"

"Both seem like reasonable answers to a difficult situation," she murmurs.

"What do you say to the people who want to destroy the supernatural community entirely?"

"I don't believe that's a useful solution. There's much we can learn from the supernatural community. Technology that could be developed through studying their genes. We would lose the opportunity of a lifetime if we decided to destroy them completely."

Seth rolls his eyes in my direction. "Why do I get the impression she wouldn't mind if we were all locked up in a laboratory?"

I nod. "She's not exactly giving me good vibes."

"Do you really think they've got Zane and Sergei already?" asks Seth in a low undertone. "I mean, even if they do, I was expecting maybe a breaking news kind of story. But this is all set up. Thinking has gone into the programming. Like they've been planning this for a day or two."

On the television screen, the reporter has passed the feed back to the main anchor, a blonde woman with too much makeup. He's right, they seem like they're going off a well-rehearsed script.

"It occurs to me..." He hesitates.

"What?" I say impatiently. "Just spit it out."

"You rescued your father. You rescued Sergei. You're getting a bit predictable. What if he's setting a trap?"

I open my mouth to object, to tell him to stop being

ridiculous. But it makes a strange kind of sense. "He's setting me up," I say instead. A sense of rightness settles in my chest. Vincent has figured me out, and he's attempting a very clever ploy.

"I think so." Seth leans in and grabs my hand. "We need to think our plan through."

Except I'm not going to play games with Vincent, and I'm not afraid of him. "It just makes it even more imperative that I'm the one who puts this plan into action," I say firmly. I squeeze his hand in mine.

Seth shakes his head, his expression a little wild, his eyes glowing red. "That's the opposite of my point. He's waiting for you, Mei. He'll have everything set up to disable and destroy you. That means you shouldn't go at all." Seth's voice is rough with emotion.

Leaning into Seth's warm body, I put my arms around him, and close my eyes, wishing we could just disappear, find a small place just the two of us.

But that's not my life. "Just because he wants me, doesn't mean he's going to get me," I say softly.

"Doesn't it?" he replies, just as softly, into my ear.

41

Every time I've ever been here, bad things have happened.

We're flying toward the Earthbound compound, the lush greenery visible for miles around in the barren desert. The other times I had hope, something keeping me positive, even if it seemed remote.

This time, I know it's going to be bad. Even if we win, it'll be bad.

I can see it on Elena's face as she stares at me when she thinks I'm not looking. I'm going to have to give up my powers to make this work. At least I think I am. Who knows if our cock-a-mamie plan will actually work.

I knew the feel of the old spell web and could manipulate it to my will. I felt it intimately just before I destroyed it, too.

Elena has talked me through the spell, and she'll be there with me as it's working. Her dragon magic should be enough to finish creating the spell web. But does that mean we're going to be able to wrest control from Vincent?

I don't know.

But Vincent can't be left to take over the world. The humans think supernaturals are the scariest things in the world. But a man like Vincent, he's much scarier.

Where shall we land?

I don't think it matters. We're giving ourselves up.

I swoop through the sky and glance back at Seth. For the thousandth time, I wish he would go with the idea of hiding and then leaping out at the right moment.

But he's adamant he won't leave my side. Part of me is thrilled with the idea of his love burning brightly inside him.

But mostly I wish he would listen to reason. When my powers are gone, I'll need him even more. Both of us being destroyed won't help.

We swoop in, landing on the back lawn, and change into human form. Elena takes her dress from Carrick, and Seth and I change into the clothes we were carrying. The idea is to sneak into the building, get as far as we can, and then allow ourselves to get captured. The sun is scorching hot on the stone footpath, sending heat waves up into the air. Birds sing in the trees around us, and there aren't any guards visible.

"Where is everyone?" I ask Seth.

He scans the area, his face a grim mask. "I've got a bad feeling about this."

"I've had a bad feeling about this since we left the cave."

"Then let's leave this place and think of a new plan."

I shake my head firmly. "We can't keep running from Vincent. He's attacked us, killed people we love. We have no choice."

"There's always a choice."

"Not for me there isn't." I've been thrown into this world my entire life. Not for anything I've ever done, except being born.

I glance at Elena and see the truth in her eyes.

We enter the low building through a side door and sneak down the tiled hallway. My heart is beating like it's in a speed drumming competition. Lush potted plants grow out of pots set at regular intervals along the wide corridors. Memories flicker through my head. Carrick and Liling confronting me. Amos. *Vincent.* Seth dying. Being shot and then healed by Carrick.

Concentrate on the here and now. Anything else will get you killed. Tarsal's voice is stern, like he doesn't approve, but he's helping me anyway.

You're right, I don't approve. But seeing as you're here, you need to focus.

He's right. Firmly I bring my mind back to the present.

Carrick is leading the way through the compound's myriad hallways, Elena right behind him. He knows the way, he lived here, serving as Vincent's hired muscle for a long time. I know it's difficult for him to come back here as well.

Seth is behind me, his heat radiating out even in his human form. I wonder what Seth thinks of our mission? This is what he wanted, what his group were fighting for, to put the spell web back in place. I struggle to catch my breathe for a moment, as I really, seriously contemplate what we're about to do. How have we come to this? Are we really desperate enough that we're willing to let Vincent create the spell web again? Allowing the spell web to be put back in place is against everything my father believes in. Everything I've come to believe in.

Everything Liling believed in.

What would she say about it? Liling worked so hard alongside my father to create a world without the spell web. Will it really fulfil my vow to her if I become a shadow dragon and put the spell web back in place? The thought makes me stumble, and Seth grabs me before I fall.

"You okay?" he asks.

I nod, berating myself for not being able to follow Tarsal's advice. I need to concentrate.

Tarsal gives a low grumble that vibrates around my body. I guess he's agreeing.

The latest hallway becomes a wider corridor, and then we're at the huge wooden doors that mark the entrance to Vincent's even more massive chamber, the place where I first met him. I walk forward carefully and open one of the doors, peering inside. It's empty, the large dragon-fighting murals gazing creepily down on nothing.

"Where is everyone?" asks Seth, echoing my thoughts.

"Perhaps we have the wrong place?" asks Elena.

"He's here somewhere," says Carrick, his voice grim. "A leopard doesn't change its spots."

"We have to keep going down. They must be in the basement levels," I say.

"But where are all his guards? Why is no one here?" asks Seth.

"I don't know." I try not to think of all the terrible possibilities. "Let's search the basement. If they're not there, we regroup, try to figure out what we're going to do."

"He's here," says Carrick again. He walks past the archway and further into the great chamber, as if drawn by unseen forces. Elena follows, gazing around at the graphic images on the walls. Both say nothing.

I remain in the hallway, unable to move further into the

room. I don't need to see the paintings of dragons being murdered. It was bad enough when I didn't know what I was.

I turn to Seth, struggling to find some comfort in this place. Little flames dancing in his eyes are the only outward sign he's agitated by anything we're seeing. I grab his hand and pull him to me, planting a scorching kiss on his lips.

It's a stupid thing to do in enemy territory, but I do it anyway. Heat fills my body, my veins run with liquid fire and I struggle to get closer to him.

All too soon, we both pull back. "Time to go," I say softly.

"Time to go," he agrees, leaning his forehead on mine, holding me in his arms.

A noise by the door makes us step apart, and I look up just as Carrick and Elena return to the hallway.

"There's nothing in there that tells us where they might have gone," says Carrick, ignoring the fact he just caught us snuggling in the middle of a dangerous mission.

I shake my head to clear it. "Downstairs it is, then," I say.

Striding off in the direction Carrick indicates, I lead us toward the last place in the world I want to go. We find a set of stairs and begin our descent into the bowels of the Earthbound compound.

Every step we take seems to echo around us, making too much noise. We go lower and lower, until I stop. "This feels like the right floor. Carrick?"

But he shakes his head. "I didn't often come so far down. I'm not sure."

My fingers shaking, I turn the handle of the door to the level and peer out through the tiny crack. The hallway is empty, and I push the door wider.

In my head, by the time we got to this point, we would

have been in the hands of Vincent's men, so we wouldn't have had to guess our way to the right place.

"We're in the wrong place," I say to Seth. "They can't be here."

And then noise erupts around us.

42

I t's like there's been some kind of noise dampener over this part of the compound. Soundproofed rooms, or maybe a soundproofed wing.

A dragon roar echoes down the hallway, and the sound of running feet and shouting men can be heard clearly. But there's still no one visible.

"What the hell...?" says Seth. He looks as confused as I feel.

"That's Zane." I run along the empty corridor toward the noise. Seth, Carrick, and Elena follow close behind me.

At the end of the corridor, there's a T-junction, and I hesitate, but another dragon roar helps me figure out which way to go. I turn left and sprint down the corridor, the sound of our feet covered by the noise coming from the room at the end. The door has chains and deadbolts on it, clearly so no one can get in or out this way. There must be some kind of other entrance to the lower levels.

I pull on the chains, but they don't budge. Even my dragon strength can't move them.

"Step back," says Seth. His eyes are flaming, and he's

partially transformed into a phoenix. I pause a moment, enthralled by the flames coating his body.

"Move," he repeats, his voice lower and somehow reverberating around the hallway.

I step away.

Seth glides forward, flames lapping at everything around him, and touches the first set of chains. The metal melts at his touch like it's ice turning to water. The lock and the other chains fall to the ground in the same manner, hissing softly as they fall. The metal bubbles on the floor, burning a little into the concrete, before cooling off.

"Don't touch the metal when we go through the door," says Seth, his body returned to normal. His eyes still glow a reddish brown, instead of his usual hazel.

I nod, awed by what he can do.

A dragon's roar reminds me of why we're here, and I refocus onto the door itself. "Do we burst through, or go in quietly?"

"I don't think it matters either way. They're dealing with an angry dragon. They're not going to notice us," says Carrick.

A second dragon roar is added to the first. "Sergei," I whisper. The Russian dragon hadn't changed from his human form since we rescued him from Vincent, and he'd noticeably calmed down. He doesn't sound calm right now.

"Come on," I say, no longer hesitant. I'm eager to get in there and help the others.

I push open the door and walk into chaos. The room is enormous, much bigger than the room where the previous spell web was located.

There's a massive sloping entranceway that disappears from view, at the far end of the room. Light is streaming into the cavernous space from that end, so I'm guessing it must lead outside somehow.

Inside there are literally hundreds of guards in the light brown uniform of Vincent's men. Most of them are holding down chains and ropes that are tied over the back of Zane in dragon form, his black and gold scales shimmering in the lights that shine directly onto his body from the ceiling.

Sergei is further down the room, with fewer guards. He's putting up less of a fight, and his scales don't seem quite so brilliant in the lights. Looking around, I try to find Vincent.

At first, I can't see him, until Zane flicks his tail high in the air and slams it into about ten guards, knocking them backward and slamming them into the wall. None of them get back up.

On the other side of Zane, I finally see Vincent watching with amusement from behind a metal cage. Right next to him is the big machine I recognize from when Tarsal and I were stunned last time. Fear fights its way into my throat and a bitter metallic taste infests my mouth.

All he has to do is flick a switch and we're all useless. Why isn't he doing it?

"He needs you to be in dragon form for the spell," says Elena, like she can read my thoughts. I flick her a quick glance, wondering if she actually can.

"This isn't going as I planned. I thought we'd be his prisoners by now," I whisper back. "Do you think we should get closer to him?"

Zane roars again, this time breaking free of the chains holding him on one side. The guards on the other side scatter like ants, and Zane stands on his back legs and breathes fire around him.

"So much for letting Vincent use his power to recreate the spell web," I whisper.

"Planning to do it and actually doing it are two different things," replies Seth. He's looking at me with a meaningful expression.

"The difference is, I'm prepared to do it." I hesitate, then make a decision. "We need to get around to where Vincent's hiding. I need him to replace me with Zane, and he's not going to do that if he can't see me."

"Don't we need Mei's powers for the second part of the spell?" Seth looks at Elena, his eyebrows raised.

This is one part of the plan that I hadn't thought about. Will I need my dragon powers? Or will a shadow dragon be enough to control the web?

"I will be able to control the spell web, if you cannot do it," says Elena, her strange eyes focused on mine.

Carrick glowers in her direction, but he doesn't argue. Part of me is reluctant to trust her. She's only helping because Carrick has her under his control.

Zane lets out a pained roar, and when I turn, there's a spear sticking out his side. Vincent no longer looks as amused as he did earlier. "Okay, fine. Let's just get around there. Anything is better than Vincent being in control." I glance at Carrick. "You better know what you're doing with her."

"We have to try. We cannot let Vincent succeed. Elena has seen that future, and it is not... pretty." Carrick's expression is urgent, and his craggy face more grim than I've ever seen it. He's truly scared, and it's his fear that finally makes me move.

I sprint across the room, behind the guards, directly toward Vincent. He doesn't notice us until we're almost on him, and when he recognizes me, his face shows shock and then calculation. He smiles at me and then flicks a switch on the machine next to him.

Zane and Sergei scream, but I can't look behind me. I know how painful it is to be forcibly transformed from dragon back to human. As it is, I feel like I've been hit with a brick. Behind me, I hear Elena groan. I forgot to warn her about the effects of the machine on a dragon in human form.

"You need me to transform into a dragon, Vincent, for this to work. Your machine won't help you put the spell web back in place," I say, between clenched teeth. I have my fist clenched into my stomach, trying to keep myself upright.

"What makes you think I want you to be any part of my new spell web?" says Vincent. But he can't quite keep the expression in his eyes bland, and I can see he's desperate for it. He's just trying to play a game with me.

"Switch off the machine and let the others go. Then I'll be the first dragon."

Vincent shakes his head. "You're in no position to bargain. I have you all here, under my power."

"Let them go, or I will make this very, very difficult for you," I say. Beside me, I feel Seth changing into his phoenix form. "We might not win, but we have the power to make it very uncomfortable for you. You might even die. But if you let Zane and Sergei go, I will do it the peaceful way."

"What guarantee do I have that you will keep your word?"

"Unlike you, my word can be trusted."

"And who will I use for the second dragon?" He asks the question, but I see his gaze flick to Elena. He knows she's a dragon. The fact that she's currently bent over in pain gives it away.

"Who do you think?" I say. I can feel Tarsal's magic inside me, protecting me from some of the pain of the machine. It's definitely one of the times when it's a benefit to have two extra dragon souls inside me. My mother's ring is running hot on my finger, and I know she's helping too.

The others are all completely immobilized right now.

"You give yourselves instead of these two?" He waves his hand disparagingly at Zane and Sergei, lying naked on the concrete floor.

"We do. Now let them go."

Vincent says something in a low voice to the guard standing next to him. The man nods and leaves the small cage. In minutes, the guards are picking up Zane and Sergei and dragging them back up the ramp that leads outside.

"They need to take them outside of the compound," I say. "Out of reach of the machine."

"You'll forgive me if I don't feel like obeying your every order," says Vincent smoothly.

As he speaks, strong hands grip both my arms, dragging me away from Seth and the others. A gun is placed at my forehead.

"If any of you, including the firebird, try to rescue her, I will have her killed and simply use one of the other dragons. The only way for her to live at this point is to be used in my spell." Vincent smiles like the cat who got the cream, and he opens the door to the cage, clearly feeling confident now that the machine is in operation.

I lock eyes with Seth and shake my head slightly. This is all part of our plan. We want Vincent to think he's in control. Using me for the spell web is all part of our plan.

"Listen to your pretty little dragon," says Vincent. "She knows when she's beaten."

I only just manage to control the urge to kick him where it hurts.

43

I n moments, Seth and Carrick are being held by Vincent's guards.

It's clearly difficult for both of them to remain calm and not to fight back.

Even though I could get out of this situation in seconds —as Si always says, guns are the lazy way to win a fight—I let the guards woman-handle me over to a large set of chains. I just have to keep reminding myself that it's all part of the plan.

"You will change into your dragon form and my guards will put the chains on you immediately," says Vincent. He's so busy being smug, he doesn't notice we're not fighting back as we should be.

He walks back to the machine and flicks the switch. Immediately the pressure on my entire body eases. Elena sighs and faints. The two guards holding her arms are now supporting her entire weight.

I let off a low, sub-vocal growl, but don't say a word.

"If you want your friends to live through the day, you will do as I say," says Vincent. His self-satisfied expression is almost more than I can bear. The urge to break free of the pathetic restraints of his guards and punch him between his eyes is incredibly strong. All it would take—

I manage to inhale a deep shuddering breath and hold myself still.

Closing my eyes, I concentrate on turning into my dragon form. It's like slipping on a comfortable skin. It's strange to think that the first time I visited here, I didn't even know what I was. Vincent's tests to see if I was a dragon almost killed me, but he didn't care.

I don't think much has changed since.

When I open my eyes, I'm standing several meters taller than everyone else, my dragon form dwarfing them all. I open my mouth and show my teeth to Vincent, snarling in a purely instinctual manner at my enemy.

Cool metal touches my legs. They're putting the metal chains around my back legs. A guard comes toward me with smaller chains for my front paws. I growl at him. No way am I going to submit to everything being chained up.

"Remember your promise," says Vincent.

"She doesn't need the chains. She'll do as you wish," says Seth. He's standing next to the wall, flames in his eyes. Guards flank him on either side, guns pointed directly at his head.

"If only I could believe you," says Vincent. He nods at the guards to chain my hands.

Everything inside of me screams not to let him do it, but I have no choice. We can't let Vincent win, or it will mean the destruction of the world as we know it, for human and supernatural alike.

I slowly hold my front legs out for the guards to chain me up.

As soon as the chains are on, I feel magic sizzle along

them. Pain slides up my whole body and I roar into the air above me.

"What have you done to her?" asks Seth, struggling against his guards.

"Just a little protection. I don't entirely trust her motives in all this," says Vincent.

The pain subsides, and I glare down at Vincent.

"The next part of the procedure won't take long at all," says Vincent. He holds up a small square metal box, decorated with patterns carved into the surface. Some of them seem familiar; they're like the carvings on much of the stonework in the compound above us.

Vincent opens the box slowly and starts muttering under his breath. He's casting the Earthbound spell. I glance over at Elena, but she's still passed out on the ground.

He's still weaving the spell, using his connection to his Earthbound ancestors. I can feel the discordant buzz of the magic, increasing and increasing until I try to hold my paws over my sensitive ears. They're locked in place by the chains, keeping me immobile. Vincent's face is lit up from a glow inside the box, his expression euphoric.

I feel sick, my whole body shuddering in reaction.

Moments later I begin to feel the pull of the box. It's like my magic is being forced out of me through a tiny cord, directly to the box. At first, it's just pulling the loose ends out, the stray magic that doesn't hurt or seem to matter.

But then it starts moving faster and faster, the continuously moving thread of my magic disappearing swiftly into the metal box. The thread becomes the size of a rope, which becomes the size of a metal chain, which becomes...too big. It's taking too much. It's sucking my insides out of me, and I let out a thundering roar.

The agony is intense, and I can't think, can't breathe. Panic—intense, painful, horrific—is all I can focus on.

I've changed my mind.

I can't do this.

Having Vincent steal my dragon magic seemed like something I could do, a payback for the terrible act of living when Liling died.

But it's not. I can't do this.

My magic is a part of me, integral to my very soul. How could I think this would ever be something I could live with?

Through the panic, fear and pain, two voices rise up inside me.

They're singing, softly, gently. An old song. The dragon song, sung to young dragons as they turn for the first time. It eases their pain and stays their hunger until they can find the only thing that will sate their burning desire for sustenance.

I recognize the voices. My mother and Tarsal are doing what they can to help me through this. My brain is foggy and confused. But because of the song, the pain is numbed. I take a gasping breath.

I don't want to do this anymore.

Don't worry, Mei. We will go in your stead. Together we will be enough to start up a new spell web. My mother's voice is soft inside my head.

At first I'm confused, trying to sort through what she's saying. *What? No!*

Don't worry, this is for the best. The world needs you. Tarsal sounds like he's smiling, even though he doesn't have a body.

But you must change back into your human form right now. The spell is coming to a close, we will leave your body in a moment. We will push your magic back into you, once we get inside the spell web. Vincent must not know what has happened.

No! Wait, don't do this. We can figure something out.

There's no time, Mei. If you don't change now, our sacrifice will be for nothing. My mother's voice is stern. *Don't do that to us.*

Turn. Tarsal's voice is a growl.

Without questioning them further, I turn, falling to the ground, my naked body sprawled over the chains that moments before held my dragon legs immobile. My magic pulses back inside me in one tremendous burst that makes my whole body sizzle with agony. I groan as my magic crackles through me again.

There's a loud buzzing next to me, and I open one eye. The box is now the center of a large glowing ball of magic. Vincent has backed off, his face shining in the effects of the magic spell he's just created.

"It worked," he whispers.

I reach out with my mind, and the spell web feels achingly familiar. I don't know whether it's because my mother and Tarsal are inside it, or it's just that I loved the last one so much.

"Elena?" I croak out. The priestess better come to the party now. Next to her, Carrick's face is a mask, but there's a small twitch next to his eye. He's just as worried as I am.

Elena's still lying next to the guards on the floor, her whole body flaccid. She's unconscious.

Vincent follows my gaze and laughs. "Ah, yes. She was uncommonly affected by the machine. Some dragons are." He shakes his head. "It means we'll have to go back to plan A for the second part of the spell web." He waves a hand.

Moments later, two guards drag Zane, kicking and fighting, back down the ramp.

"You were supposed to let him go," I growl at him.

"I don't make deals with dragons," he replies coldly.

My gaze flicks again to Elena, the only one who knows the spells we need to finish what we started. Why didn't we think to have more than one person with the spells memorized?

"Wake up, Elena," I say urgently. But she's still out for the count. Behind me, Zane roars. If I don't do something, he's about to become dragon toast.

My guards are no longer looking at me, they're focused on the larger dragon who's struggling against their colleagues on the other side of the room. They think I'm no longer a threat—what they don't know is that even if I *had* lost all my magic, I was trained by someone who didn't believe in relying on it. I could kick their butts from here to Sunday in my human form if I wanted to. But I'm not relying solely on my ability to fight in human form. This time I have something more.

I close my eyes and touch the spell web. My dragon magic is still strong, even stronger than the last time I destroyed the spell web. My connection to this new spell web is also clearer than before. My mother and Tarsal are making it easier for me to fuse with its magic.

A lifetime of living interconnected with the last spell web is helping me find my way inside this one, to merge my magic with the power seeping out from it. I don't know the spell Elena was going to use, so I have to just go with my gut and hope for the best. My whole body shakes, and I don't know if this is the right thing to do.

What if I make it worse?

But I have to try. I can't let Vincent hurt Zane, or take control of this spell web.

I cover the spell web with my magic, stretching out

along its grid, trying to find its source. The full power of the grid isn't in place yet, it's not covering my body or the body of any of the supers around me. It must be the magic of the second dragon that puts the grid in place.

I keep scratching around, trying to find a way to take control of it out of Vincent's hands. I'm getting closer and closer to the center, the place where all the magic is held. The warmth turns to unbearable heat, but my dragon self basks in it, rather than being repelled.

This is exactly the kind of place my dragon loves, the heart of power, the heat of the core. There's a moment where everything holds still, and then it bursts free, flooding my whole body with a lava flow of energy like nothing else I've ever experienced.

"What's happening? What's she doing? Guards, knock her out." Vincent's voice sounds like it's coming from far away. It holds no sway here on this plane, and I ignore it. The scuffling and the shots fired don't concern me.

Even when I feel my external body being picked up and taken somewhere, it doesn't break my bond with the spell web.

"It's following her! She's taking the spell web!" Vincent's desperate voice sinks into oblivion behind me, and I smile.

Vincent didn't win after all, and that's what's important.

44

"Mei!" The voice is intrusive, it won't let me sleep. "Mei!"

I bat at the voice with my hand, trying to make it go away.

"Wake up. We can't carry you both."

I open one eye and see Seth peering down at me anxiously. Behind him, Carrick is holding Elena in his arms.

"Wha'...?" I mean to say more, but the words are like glue, sticking to my mouth.

"Vincent's men are just behind us. We've melted the lock, but it won't keep them long. We have to hurry. We need you awake... And preferably in fighting form." Seth's voice is grim, like he's holding it together with the barest thread.

I open my other eye and groan as the overhead light makes my eyes hurt. Magic is throbbing inside me, shoving at the confines of my human shape. Seth pulls me up, and I groggily struggle to stand. My body doesn't feel the same—it's bigger, more expansive—and I feel like I have to relearn how to balance and understand the space around me. As my eyes adjust to being open again, I realize it all looks different. I can see and understand more about everything around me. There's an added dimension to what I'm seeing, and for a moment it completely throws me. A wave of dizziness hits me like a storm, and I stumble. Seth holds me up, and his familiar warmth soothes me.

"Mei," says Carrick. "Can you walk? We need Seth to be able to fight. And you."

I let out a steadying breath and look over at Carrick. "Is she okay?" I ask, nodding to Elena.

"I don't know. She hasn't come around." His features are drawn and he's struggling to remain calm as well. His usually bland face seems filled with emotion—I can see what he's thinking by the muscle twitch under his eye and the tightening of his mouth. It's strange and overwhelming, and I don't know quite how to deal with it.

Except I have to.

I straighten my shoulders. "Where are Zane and Sergei?"

"Zane broke free of the guards once you... did what you did," says Seth. "They were all trying to subdue you. I didn't see Sergei, but Zane took off once he saw us escape. I think he was going to help Sergei."

Good. Zane might be an overly zealous pain in the butt, but he's my friend. I wouldn't want him hurt because of Vincent. And Sergei... well, he's not as crazy as he used to be.

Clenching my hands into determined fists, I step out of Seth's arms. I'm wobbly at first, but gain momentum and strength as I walk haltingly toward our escape route. Glancing back at the others, I nod. "Let's get out of here."

"I'll lead," says Seth. His eyes are flames, and his whole body looks ready to change any second.

He moves past me, grabbing my hand and squeezing it for a second before moving on. He doesn't have any weapons other than himself—but then none of us do.

"Be careful," I whisper, reminded forcibly of what happened last time we came up against Vincent. The memories start to crowd my thoughts, but I manage to push it all down and move off after Seth. Carrick's heavy footsteps follow behind.

We stride along the corridor and up a set of stairs. I don't recognize the area we're in, and I don't know how Seth's deciding where to go. Probably guessing. I'm feeling stronger and stronger, and soon my muscles are moving fluidly again. The spell web is intensifying inside me with every step I take. Magic thrums along my veins.

But we're still in enemy territory and Vincent is like a Las Vegas magician, with the number of tricks he's able to pull out of his sleeve. We're not out of danger yet. Even worse, Elena is still unconscious and Carrick's carrying her. We need to get her out of here and find someone who can help as soon as possible.

Without meeting any more of Vincent's men, if we can.

I smile to myself. Technically, I wouldn't mind meeting some of his men right now. I'm spoiling for a fight. It would feel good to beat a few of them to the ground after they handled me so roughly back there. But Carrick is tiring; I can feel it through the spell web. I don't think he'd survive a fight, especially if he was trying to guard Elena from harm—

I can feel him through the spell web.

I stumble and almost fall.

"You okay?" says Carrick gruffly from behind me. He stops to lean against the wall, he chest heaving, Elena a dead weight in his arms.

"Yeah, I'm good," I say, trying to hide my shock. When I push at it, the spell web starts blossoming out into the world around me, giving information about everything around us, almost like another sense. It's like what I used to be able to do with the old spell web—except on steroids.

I can feel the heartbeats of the guards who are about to open the ground floor door and start chasing us up the stairwell. I feel the moth that's fluttering around in the lights overhead, and the mouse that's running back into his hole ahead of us.

The flames licking at Seth's body are more obvious to me, and the exhaustion in every square inch of Carrick's body blares out a warning signal to me as clear as day. There's an overabundance of energy around me, almost too much for me to even know what to do with it. I experiment with giving Carrick some energy from the web. What do I need it all for?

"What the hell?" says Carrick. He's still leaning against the wall, his face flushed and his eyes blinking like he's been hit with some kind of noxious gas.

"What's the matter?" I ask, hoping I haven't poisoned him somehow.

He shakes his head and looks at me. "Stop that," he says. "I'm fine." His expression tells me he knows exactly what just happened.

"You're exhausted. Have you even stopped for a rest in the last few days?"

"I'm fine."

"No, you're not. But at least you're a bit better now," I say. I peer along the spell web to confirm what I'm saying, and sure enough, all his vital signs are stronger.

He glances down at Elena in his arms. "If you're going to work on anyone, work on her."

I glance down at Elena hanging limply in his arms. There's such a snarl-up of magic and confusion inside her I don't know where to start. Her problem isn't as simple as a little more energy. "I'll do it as we walk. We should keep moving." Turning, I keep going up the stairs, jogging to catch up with Seth.

Behind me, Carrick starts climbing again, his footsteps more certain.

As we go, I start trying to figure out what's wrong with Elena. She's a mystery, an enigma I don't understand. Is she even telling the truth? Why did she faint at the first touch of Vincent's machine? There's only one way to find out.

I move along the spell web and immediately find Elena.

There's a strange patch of the grid, with the lines swirling and mixing out of the normal patterns. It's like something is attacking her, or blocking her from the rest of the grid.

We're still moving up the stairwell. Seth is out in front, almost to the next level, and I have to concentrate on not stumbling as I untangle the grid around Elena. It's tiring work; I don't really know what I'm doing, it's all instinct. I'm scared of breaking any of the connections in the grid, so I'm moving really slowly. I'm not sure why, but I'm convinced breaking any of the connections would be bad for Elena.

I'm halfway through untangling a particularly nasty piece of the grid around her when an explosion shatters the air. Seth is blasted up the stairs, and I'm pushed backward into Carrick and Elena.

We all fly backward down the stairs, smashing into each other, wall, and the steps. Pain erupts in various points around my body. Time slows, and it seems like forever before we land in a crumpled pile on the landing of the level we just passed.

The world spins around me, but I manage to look up.

At the top of the stairs stands Vincent, hands on his hips and his signature smug smile on his face.

45

I close my eyes again, figuring it's best to make Vincent think I'm out for the count. I reach along the spell web and make sure Seth, Carrick and Elena are okay.

Elena's energy is weak, but she's alive. Carrick is stronger, and his breathing makes me think he's only pretending to be unconscious as well. In the distance, I can feel Seth, still breathing although I think he might actually be unconscious.

My connection to the spell web has been muted somehow—Vincent has managed to find a way to affect my bond. I don't know how much magic I have at my disposal, or what I can even do against him.

My hand is hidden underneath me. I move it, trying to find some body part of Carrick's below me. I touch a muscled arm—Carrick's. I put pressure on his arm and feel it flex back at me. He knows I'm awake as well.

I hear Vincent's steps coming down the stairs. He's slow and methodical, like he doesn't have a care in the world. Perhaps he doesn't. Maybe he thinks he's won again.

The hell he has.

My mother and Tarsal gave up their souls to create the spell web, with the intention that I should be the one to control it. I'm not going to let Vincent steal it from me again.

My eyes flick open, and I roll off Carrick. I'm standing with my legs wide and my arms out in a guard position by the time Vincent places his feet onto the last step. Beside me, Carrick moves slowly, laying Elena's limp body behind us. He places himself just behind me. The feeling of strong stone at my back calms me and helps me center myself.

I glance quickly up to where Seth is lying on the level above. It's the fire I'm worried about.

"Here we are again, Mei. You and me, fighting in my stronghold." Vincent's voice is smooth as silk, like he hasn't just tried to kill us through an explosion.

"Get out of our way, Vincent. Just let us leave."

"I'm afraid I can't do that, Mei. You have something of mine." His eyes harden to steel, and if looks could kill, I'd be dead.

"What's that?"

"The spell web. You've attached it to you somehow. I want it back." There's a strange smell wafting from him, sour and dirty. He's desperate to get what I've taken from him. It makes him both more and less dangerous than I was imagining.

"It's too late," I say, the power pulsing around me. "It's done. I *am* the spell web. You can't separate me from it."

"Mei," says Carrick in a warning voice. "They're forming upstairs."

I look up to where he's indicating. Guards are filing out through the hole that the explosion made into the wall. Smoke rises around the gap, and they look like they're emerging out of a spaceship.

"Yes, that's right, Mei. I'm not alone here. You've come to

my sanctuary, *stolen* from me, and now you expect me to let you go like I don't have a problem? I don't think so." Vincent shakes his head sadly, like he's a disappointed grandfather.

He snaps his fingers, and two of the guards lift Seth's body, sagging in their arms. "Do you want me to kill him again? I did it once. I can do it again." His smile becomes victorious and vindictive. All trace of the elderly grandfather is wiped from his face.

I clench one fist tightly, forcing my instinctive rage to settle back down inside me. The last thing I need at this point is to lose control. I need to assess the situation dispassionately like Jeff always taught me, and look for holes in Vincent's plan. One thing I know for sure: he's not going to kill Seth again.

I reach out along the spell web. The connection I had earlier isn't as strong, but I can still access more of it than I ever could before. Perhaps I can use it to get at Vincent.

I open my whole body up to the power of the spell web, allowing it to flow into me, as well as my essence flowing *out* into it. I close my eyes as the energy snakes along my veins, coursing through my muscles and out of my skin. There's no difference between my body and the spell web—we're one and the same.

Everything around me starts to glow; the walls, the ceiling, and the stairs below, even Vincent's face. It's coming from me.

I open my eyes, but I don't see through them anymore. I'm seeing everything through many locations. It's overwhelming but powerful at the same time. Vincent has a strong spell web covering, and I pull it tighter around him. His smug expression falters.

"Let me go," says Vincent, his voice rough.

Upstairs, the guards have clustered around Seth, and I

use the spell web to thrust magic at them, pushing them back against the wall. Only the two guards holding Seth remain—I don't want them to drop him on the ground.

"No," I say in a voice that doesn't sound like my own. "Not yet. You're going to walk with us to the exit and see us out. You're going to tell everyone we meet that you're seeing us out. Or I will crush your windpipe with one flick of my wrist." I tighten my hold just there, so he can be sure I will do what I'm saying.

Vincent's eyes widen, and one of his hands automatically comes up to his throat. He scratches at nothing, his expression afraid. "You won't get away with this. I'll come after you again and again," he says, his voice scratchy.

"Move," I say, tightening my hold on his throat.

He turns and stumbles up the stairs we just fell down.

I make sure Carrick is okay behind me before moving. He's picked up Elena again and motions with his head that I should follow after Vincent. I take the stairs two at a time, wanting to check on Seth. He's starting to stir, his eyes fluttering. I push energy at him, needing him to have enough strength to walk on his own two feet. Then I glare at the guards until they put him carefully down on the ground.

His eyes open, and he stares up at me, flames in his eyes. "I feel you inside me," he whispers.

"I know. We can talk about it later," I say. "I need you to stand up now and walk."

He nods and struggles to his feet.

I put his arm around my shoulder, and we walk together, following Vincent.

He continues climbing the staircase ahead of us for another two sets of stairs. Then he turns to the door and waits for us.

Using the spell web to make sure the door is clear, I nod

at him, telling him to keep going. When he hesitates, my instincts kick into overdrive. Something's up. But everything seems fine through the spell web, and I can't sense anyone on the other side of the door. The only other option is that whatever machine he's using to mute my connection to the spell web must be keeping some of my senses numb as well. All I know is that my instincts are screaming something's wrong.

"Wait," I say. "Stop there for a moment." I'm a few steps down on the staircase behind him.

Vincent turns toward me, his face a twisted mixture of hate and smugness. He's clearly got something up his sleeve; I just don't know what it is.

I use the spell web to search him, to try and find an answer to my unease. What's happening? I just don't know. "He's up to something," I say to Carrick as we all arrive up on the same landing Vincent is waiting on.

"I say we get rid of him," he replies. He shifts Elena around in his arms—she's clearly heavy.

"He's our hostage to ensure we get out of here." I gesture toward the sky somewhere above our heads.

"He's more like a venomous viper waiting to take us out at any opportunity," replies Carrick, anger throbbing through his voice.

Next to me, Seth is silent, watching Vincent with a calm expression. "Let him try his worst. We've survived this far."

I look at Seth with raised eyebrows.

"Mostly," he amends. "Let's just get out of here as fast as we can."

Turning back to Vincent, I scowl. "Open the door," I say. All my senses are screaming, and I'm expecting a hundred guards to leap out at us on the other side.

Or perhaps another explosion—hence forcing Vincent to open the door this time.

He opens it slowly. On the other side there's a commotion, and at first I don't understand what I'm seeing.

A large pure white and silver chameleon, is fighting viciously with two guards.

One holds a thick rod and pushes it against the thick scales of the lizard, sending a jolt of electricity into its skin. It slides back to the ground again, lying slack in between the two men.

One guard holds a handgun to the head of the lizard and looks up at me.

It takes me a moment, but with a jolt I recognize who it is.

My father.

46

"I see you know who that is, Mei," says Vincent smoothly.

"Where? How?"

"We found him at the stronghold. At first I didn't know who we'd captured and almost had him killed. But something about his eyes..." Vincent trails off and turns to look my father.

"Don't you dare hurt him," I say. Everything inside me wants to leap on Vincent and gouge out his eyes. I only just manage to hold myself still.

Vincent shrugs. "That all depends on you, Mei. Give me what I want, and your father and all your friends go free. Hold back, and I will be forced to take action."

I push out along the spell web, skipping lightly over Vincent and on, until I can feel my father. He's trapped inside the lizard, unable to turn back into his human form.

I can feel his skittish thoughts, his inability to think clearly as a chameleon. I push a little magic back into him, and then calmly show him what to do to change back. I need him lucid, and a skittish chameleon isn't going to help me. At least not right now.

Focusing my attention back on Vincent, I stare into his eyes. I want to distract him for a moment, to let my father change. But I'm also trying to understand him, to figure out why he hates my kind so much. Why he hates *me* so much. It doesn't make sense to me, this personal vendetta.

"What made you like this?" I ask him suddenly. "Why do you hate me so much?"

"There is no hate. I'm simply protecting the world from dragons."

"But you're focused on me. What did I ever do to you?"

"You were born. You're a dragon! A vile, disgusting race bent on destruction and slaughter of innocents."

A strange certainty flows into me. "Who did they kill? Who did you know?"

Vincent shakes his head. "This isn't personal. This is for the good of all."

"Someone you know was killed by a dragon. And as you've been chasing me since my birth, it was probably my mother." It all becomes a little clearer now. Why he was so focused on me for all those years. Why he enjoyed the tests he put me through.

Behind him, my father is beginning the change back into his human form. I smother him in energy from the spell web, trying to make it as easy as possible. I don't want him screaming and alerting Vincent to what's happening.

"She was the worst of them," he says in a flat voice. "She felt no guilt or remorse. She killed indiscriminately."

"Who died?"

"My wife," whispered Vincent. "Amos's mother. She was on an expedition in China, searching for dragon ruins. They came across her in an old waterfall cave. She killed every last one of them, except one man to tell the tale." He laughs bitterly. "Always one to tell the tale."

My father is lying naked and gasping for breath behind Vincent. The guards have stopped paying attention to him; they're fixated on Vincent.

"I'm sorry for your loss," I say quietly.

"They attacked her," wheezes my father from the floor. "She said they attacked while she was deep in hibernation, hacking at her body with their picks and shovels. The only thing she could do to save herself was to send fire down the tunnel they'd dug." He coughs, holding his arms across his chest. "The man who survived was the only one who didn't go into the cave. He didn't survive through any planning on her part. She was just trying to save herself."

Vincent shakes his head wildly. "Lies. She killed my beautiful wife, and now you're going to pay for it." He lunges forward, his hands out in front as if to grab me.

I duck and step easily to one side, grabbing his arm before he can lumber into Elena and Carrick just behind me. I hear Carrick take a step back, and Seth moves up the stairs on the other side.

I force Vincent's arm up his back and move in close behind him. "I can take you out physically, and I can do it through the spell web. The choice is yours."

"Guards!"

There's a scuffle through the door, and I swing Vincent and myself around, mostly to have Vincent between me and any gunshots. But the two guards are lying on the floor motionless. My father stands in the doorway, naked as the day he was born, holding the Taser stick they'd used to keep him down in his lizard form.

"You won't get away with this," says Vincent between clenched teeth. "I have guards at every corner. The whole place is surrounded."

I hold him closely and wonder why I thought he was so all-powerful. His slight body is tall, but his muscles are weak. I'm stronger than him in every way.

Especially now I have the spell web coursing through my body, even the lesser version that's managing to seep through his contraptions. "Where's the machine that's blocking the spell web?" I ask.

"I don't know what you're talking about," says Vincent.

I pull his arm up his back, almost to breaking point. He grunts in pain. "It's on the floor where the explosion was."

Seth steps down from where he was standing. "I'll go destroy it," he says. He takes off at a run, his long legs getting him quickly back down to where we were.

"What's stopping him from making another one?" asks Carrick. "And another?"

I sigh, knowing he's right. "Do we destroy this whole place?" I'm not sure I want that either. It seems such a waste. But to leave it so that Vincent can use the information against us again and again seems...

"No!" Vincent's voice is panicked, and he struggles against me for a moment. "Don't destroy our compound. I'll do anything you ask. But you must not destroy our home."

I look over his shoulder at my father. "What do you think?"

He looks up from stealing the trousers of the guard nearest him and hesitates, considering his answer. "I say we destroy it."

"Wait." The voice is soft, half formed. Elena.

She's still curled up against Carrick, his strong arms

holding her to his chest. But her eyes are open again for the first time since Vincent turned on his dragon machine.

"You have something to add?"

"Don't destroy this place. It holds information, research, even stories from the ancient days. My people..." She hesitates and glances up at Carrick. "The Priestesses would be happy to take this place over and guard it from those who would abuse the information inside."

I shake my head. That doesn't seem like a good idea either.

"What do we do with Vincent?" I ask. He struggles against my hold on him, and I pull his arm up his back. The socket grinds and it's close to breaking point. He groans in pain. I try to feel upset or sad, but it's just not in me.

"We take him to the Mountain super stronghold. My people will take care of him," says Carrick.

I blink, remembering that he's now the Mountain King. Nodding slowly, I give a small half smile at Carrick. "Now that you're in charge and all," I say.

He bows his head mockingly at me.

And then a surge of power hits me so hard, I gasp. It roams my body and burns me up, trying to take over everything.

Seth has destroyed the machine, and the spell web is back inside me, like a freight train of magic determined to find every crack and crevice in my body and fill it to the brim with ancient magic.

I let go of Vincent and stagger back, grabbing hold of the wall behind me. I only just manage to keep my balance. Part of me wants to scream in agony. The rest is shouting with ecstacy at the power streaming through me.

Vincent directly in front of me, holding a knife he's

pulled from somewhere on his person. He lifts it high, even as I'm leaning against the wall struggling to control the wave of power.

I can barely lift my head, let alone stop the downward motion of his hand, clenched around the knife.

47

Time slows, and I watch almost curiously as the knife descends toward me.

I'm confused, wondering how it could have come to this. I have all the power of the spell web flowing through my veins, but I can't even save myself.

I can't control the magic; there's so much inside me that it's short-circuited everything. I can't move, and I can't attack via the web. I'm just waiting here, watching as the man I've been afraid of for so long finally gets his heart's desire. A crushing desperation fills my senses, but it doesn't change the fact I still I can't move. At least not yet, not in time to save myself.

I can't believe it's going to end this way.

Then a thick muscled arm steals around Vincent's neck, and yanks him backward in a powerful movement, taking the knife out of range. A second arm joins the first and I hear a loud crunch, as Vincent's neck is broken.

Vincent's limp body slumps to the ground, and Carrick appears behind him, his face grim. "I've been waiting a long time to do that," he says, his tone expressionless.

All the breath goes out of me at once, and for a moment I can only lie limply against the wall. Then Carrick puts his hand out to me. I grasp his firmly, and he pulls me to standing.

"Thank you," I whisper as I put my arms around his middle, leaning into his broad chest.

"You saved me once," he rumbles. "It's only fair to return the favor."

I let myself remain against his chest for a moment, taking strength from his solid form. Then I pull back.

"Let's get out of here," I say, my voice sounding distant and cold. I'm trying to sound normal, but I can tell from the expression on Carrick's and my father's faces that I'm not succeeding. Seth comes bounding up the stairs a moment later, and I nod to him.

"Your eyes are different." He glances down at the floor and does a double take when he sees Vincent. "What happened?"

"We have to leave now," I say, ignoring his words. "Seth, you lead. Do we go through the doorway?"

He hesitates and then nods. "I think we should." He puts his hand out in a gesture for my father to move forward, and then we all follow him down the hallway, with Carrick helping Elena stumble along at the rear.

It's an area I recognize and I know we're on the right level. We walk slowly, each of us trying to regain our strength. Despite what Vincent told us about guards on every corner, we don't meet any, and it's not long before we arrive at a set of doors leading outside the building.

We emerge onto the grassy lawns, and the feeling of the sun on my body is like I'm floating in a giant tub of sunshine, after being away in the dark so long. Zane and

Sergei are flying overhead, periodically shooting fire down at the small group of guards on the lawn.

My father strides in front. "Vincent is dead," he calls out to the guards. "The spell web is back in place. There is nothing here for you now."

The guards hesitate for a moment, unsure.

A large wave of dragon fire from Zane and Sergei decides for them. As a group, the guards jog toward a side entrance of the compound, leaving their weapons on the lawn.

Carrick looks around. "How are we going to take charge here?" he asks.

I shrug. "Don't they say that possession is nine tenths of the law?"

"We can't just start living here," he says, frowning.

My father turns to him. "Why not? You just need to provide some guards for the dragon," he glances at Elena. "As both protection and insurance, of course."

I manage to suppress a grin. My father isn't exactly being subtle. He doesn't even know who Elena is, but he can tell something's not right.

"What about the humans? Other people wanting to take back control?" Carrick glances at Elena. "I don't want to have to keep defending this place."

"The humans will have forgotten about the supers before much longer," I say softly.

"I thought—" Carrick's brow is furrowed.

"I'm in control of the spell web. I can decide how much or how little to take, and I can control the side effects, including whether the humans can see us or not. I choose not." My words are soft, but the power of the spell web hums around me as I speak.

I glance over at Elena. Her spell web grid is still very

weak, so I gently push some energy into her body. She stiffens and looks at me.

"You will remain here. Carrick will claim this place in the name of the Mountain supers, and he will protect it and you. If I ever hear so much as a whisper that you're doing anything underhanded, or using the knowledge in this place for evil, I will come back and destroy it."

Elena nods solemnly, unperturbed by my threat. "I will guard it with my life."

Carrick steps forward. "Where are you going, Mei?" he asks, his expression anxious. "You could come back to the Mountain stronghold with me."

I let out a short laugh. "You might be Mountain king now, but the rest of your people still mostly hate me, Carrick." I look at Seth, trying to understand what he's thinking and feeling, and then look back to Carrick. "I need to find somewhere to hide for a while where people won't be trying to kill me all the time. I have to figure this out." I gesture down at my body, which has started to glow again.

My father steps forward and shakes his head. "Not on your own, Mei. I won't let you do that. We'll figure something out."

Seth clears his throat. "Forgive me, sir, but she won't be on her own. I'll be with her."

Warmth spreads across my body and it's nothing to do with the spell web. I reach out for Seth's hand, and he places it in mine. "I promise we'll stay in touch, Dad."

"You're the bloody spell web. You better stay in touch," my father replies.

I hope you enjoyed reading the latest installment of Mei's adventures.

What's going to happen to Mei now she has the spell web inside her?

Where will Mei and Seth go?

And have the humans really forgotten all about the supers?

The next adventure is the most dangerous yet.

This time, Mei's the *Cursed Dragon*.

Read on for an exclusive excerpt from Cursed Dragon, book four in the Dragon Rising series.

EXCERPT FROM CURSED DRAGON

Seth surges forward, punching and then kicking at Si. Both attempts go wide, and Seth stumbles past his opponent, his breath heaving.

He's leaning over, struggling for breath when Si slams his arm down across Seth's back, making the younger man grunt in pain.

Si slams a front kick into Seth's butt, and Seth is launched toward the ground, only just getting his hands up in time to save himself from slamming his face into the dirt. He stays down a moment too long. Si goes over to him and holds out one arm.

I wince. It's an old trick of Si's.

Seth holds out one weary arm and grasps Si's proffered hand. As soon as they've clasped hands tightly, Si pulls an unsuspecting Seth to his feet, then slams his other fist into Seth's kidneys. Then he raises his knee and, in one quick move, slams it into Seth's groin.

Seth howls in pain and bends over, holding himself. His face and neck have gone a reddish purple.

"Never trust your opponent," says Si. "Even when it

seems like they're helping you. Your enemies will never help you."

Seth looks up at Si, and the flames in his one visible eye have taken over. Anger radiates from every pore, and flames are developing over his skin. His phoenix magic is spilling out into the ring. Seth snarls.

Si narrows his eyes, and his body is immediately covered in the thick scales that protect him from dragon fire—and presumably phoenix fire. It's a trick that only the most powerful and experienced Chameleon shifters can manage —staying human and using only one part of their Chameleon self as protection.

"Don't get angry in a fight. It's the fastest way to lose," says Si, never taking his eyes from Seth.

Seth pulls himself to standing. The flames over his body are burning brighter now. My dragon magic quivers in response. I can't help it. As much as I know that it's better to be cool and calm in a fight, there's something in me that really appreciates Seth when he's like this.

He's magnificent when he's angry.

Seth takes a step closer to Si, and suddenly his wings appear behind him, made of nothing more than fire and air. He's close to turning, and he's angry as hell.

"Turning isn't the way to win this fight," says Si. "Just like Mei, you can't rely on your magic. You need to use your head. To think your way through a fight. It's the only way to win."

Seth narrows his eye and seems to consider it for a moment. His wings disappear, and he loosens his stance. Si launches himself forward, slamming his hand at Seth's face. Seth moves out of the way—just—and takes the brunt of the force on his arm. He turns quickly and tries to get a hit onto Si's side, missing by a mile.

The older Chameleon is still the better fighter. Si moves impossibly fast, his feet blurred, and suddenly Seth is face-down on the ground, his back crunched down under Si's knee, one arm bent painfully back and in the air.

I can feel Seth's rage from where I'm sitting cross-legged at the edge of the dirt. The spell web is swirling agitatedly around me, like it wants to get out. My dragon magic is humming in satisfaction, somehow enjoying the spectacle. I'm not sure if it's the violence, or simply how close Seth is to changing that pleases that part of me so much.

Seth growls, and his phoenix wings appear again. They burn right through Si, who snarls and steps back, flicking his hands as if trying to stave off a burn. Seth surges up, and this time he's so close to changing, his entire body is covered in flames; his wings are behind him, and his good eye is full of fire mixed with the sharp tawny shade of his other self.

With a shake of his head, and a radiant flash of sparks that hit the dirt and spring away, Seth turns.

His phoenix form emerges out of his human self with a fluidity and grace that takes my breath away. Magic dances inside me in response to his awesome display. The air becomes burning hot, and sparks fill the space between Seth and Si.

The Chameleon takes a step backward, holding up his hands in surrender. "That's enough, Seth. We're done here today. You need to learn control, or you'll never win."

Seth screeches, and I hear the thought as clearly as if he spoke it: *Am I not winning this fight right now?*

"You might win a fight, maybe even a battle, but you will never win the war." Si just holds his stance, and watches Seth, too experienced to turn his back on the younger man.

Seth screeches again and takes a mighty step forward, until he's right up in Si's face. His wings are swept wide, and one of his enormous talons is raised as if to attack Si. Suddenly, I'm not sure how in control of himself Seth is. His expression seems wild, untamable, and fear surges to the surface. Would he hurt Si?

Standing, I race over. "Seth. Look at me. Stand down. It's over. Your fight is over." My spell web magic swirls around us, and I finally let it free, trying to dampen down Seth's rage to manageable levels. Seth's head turns to me, his tawny eye at first battling with the magic from the spell web. He moves, and for a moment, it seems like he might attack me instead. Instead he looms over my human form, fiery and fierce, willing me to back off and let him finish what he started.

Except I can't.

I have to help him control himself. I curl my hands into tight fists, plant my feet into the ground, and glare up at him. "The fight is over," I repeat to him. Our magic goes head to head, dust swirling around us as Seth's phoenix self rages at me.

Suddenly, a sharp pain, like a thousand giant needles, stabs its way down through my body, from head to foot. My whole body goes taut with the unexpected agony of it. The pain is everywhere inside me, sharp and stinging. I stare at Seth, shocked that he's attacking me like this.

But it's different to his burning magic. The pain isn't from the heat of his phoenix soul. It's agonizing—tiny pinpricks of pain covering my entire body, like fire ants who're each attacking individually. And they've brought some glass shards to scrape around over me. And maybe there's a bear or two sharpening their claws down my body.

This is something or someone I don't recognize attacking me from the inside out.

Bright light burns my eyes, and all the noise in the area

has been turned up, making my ear drums burst with pain. I can't hold in my scream. My legs turn to jello under me, and I collapse.

Si reaches me before I hit the ground. Moments later, Seth kneels on my other side, his now-human face creased with worry.

"What's happening? What's wrong, Mei?" Seth looks around us, as if he's searching for a sniper. It's probably what it looked like.

"Attacking...me," I manage. The pain is still rampaging through my body. I'm gasping in breaths like I'm out of air. I can't smell anything strange or see anyone around us who might be attacking me. "Someone's... using... magic against... me," I gasp out.

End of excerpt...

To find out what happens next, check out *Cursed Dragon* on your favorite retailer.

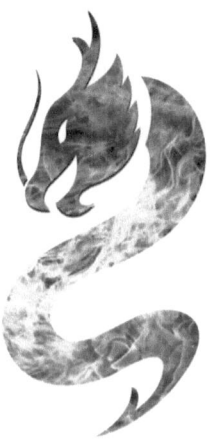

Hi! My name's Trudi Jaye and I've got a secret.

A secret society, that is.

Especially designed for people like you who love reading my books, the Trudi Jaye Secret Society is a place filled with magic and laughter, and most of all... free stories.

Everyone who joins the society is given access to an ancient tome full of the stories, novellas, bonus epilogues, and deleted scenes from all the different Trudi Jaye series.

Called **The Shadow Archives,** you can access it by clicking the link below, and joining the secret society...

Join Trudi Jaye's Secret Society... if you dare!

www.trudijayewrites.com/shadow-archives

Books by Trudi Jaye

Dragon Rising Series
Lost Dragon (Prequel Novella available via the Trudi Jaye
Secret Society)
Hidden Dragon
Searching Dragon
Fighting Dragon
Cursed Dragon
Warrior Dragon (coming soon)

Demon Hunter in Hiding Series
Dreams & Demons (Prequel Novella available via the Trudi
Jaye Secret Society)
Secrets & Demons
Agents & Demons
Magic & Demons
Dragons & Demons
Spells & Demons

Elemental Witch Series (With Tania Hutley)
The Trouble with Magic
The Problem with Witches
The Danger with Demons

Firecaller Series
Salt (Prequel Novella available via the Trudi Jaye Secret
Society)
Subtle Knife (Prequel Novella available via the Trudi Jaye
Secret Society)
Fire Mage
Royal Mage (coming soon)

Dark Carnival Series
The First Ever Wish (Prequel Novella available via the Trudi Jaye Secret Society)
If Magic Were Wishes
The Gift
Magic for Lost Souls (available via the Trudi Jaye Secret Society)
High Flyer
Hidden Magic
The Shadow Prophecy

Hi! I'm Trudi Jaye and I'm the author of this book.

I'm from New Zealand, where I currently live on a beautiful rural property surrounded by horses and cows (not mine!) with my lovely husband and my cheeky tween daughter.

I've been writing since I was a kid, and for ten years I worked as a magazine writer and editor, on topics ranging from hardware and electronics to holidays, recipes and university-level research projects.

Now I write novels full time.

I enjoy yoga, although I'm not very bendy, and karate, although I don't like the idea of hitting anyone.

www.ingramcontent.com/pod-product-compliance
Lightning Source LLC
Chambersburg PA
CBHW032243010726
47494CB00002B/603

* 9 7 8 1 0 6 7 0 0 4 2 5 5 *